MYST
PAT

Patti, Paul.

Silhouettes

$16.95

	DATE	DEC 1 6 2003
MAR -9 '99	MAY - 6 2002	
AUG 1 6 '99	AUG - 2 2002	
SEP 7 '99		
NOV 2 2 '99	SEP 5 - 2002	
APR 22 '00	OCT 2 7 2002	
SEP 29 '00	NOV 1 2 2002	
APR 16 '01	APR - 3 2003	
AUG 23 '01		
SEP 2 6 '01	JUN - 7 2003	
NOV 2 4 '02		

· DO NOT PUT MONEY IN POCKET

© THE BAKER & TAYLOR CO.

SILHOUETTES

SILHOUETTES

An Andy and Gabrielle Amato Mystery

Paul Patti

St. Martin's Press   New York

SILHOUETTES. Copyright © 1990 by Paul Patti. All rights reserved. Printed in the United States of America. No part of this book may be used or reproduced in any manner whatsoever without written permission except in the case of brief quotations embodied in critical articles or reviews. For information, address St. Martin's Press, 175 Fifth Avenue, New York, N.Y. 10010.

Design by Judith A. Stagnitto

Library of Congress Cataloging-in-Publication Data

Patti, Paul.
      Silhouettes / by Paul Patti.
           p. cm.
      "A Thomas Dunne book."
      ISBN 0-312-04684-7
      I. Title.
PS3566.A8248S5 1990
813'.54—dc20   90-37237
                              CIP

First Edition
10 9 8 7 6 5 4 3 2 1

*For my father and for my son, both of whom
have taught me so much*

Prologue

He opened the door of the expensive car, releasing the stale air, and noticed that the darkness and silence made for another perfect night to kill someone.

It isn't work if you enjoy it, he said to himself.

The air outside was noiseless, with only a calm sea breeze blowing past him. Inhaling deeply, he could immediately smell the salty, rich aroma of Palm Beach ocean. He patted down his expensive black suit, and giving the gun in his jacket pocket a reassuring tap, he sauntered across the promenade, heading toward the mansion.

He stopped at the side of a high, manicured hedge behind which was a fenced tennis court. He listened for sounds of approaching cars; there continued to be no noise at all, except for the now-subliminal breaking of waves on the beach not a half block to the east. He walked on casually to the gate, looking like nothing more than a businessman returning to his splendid home after a lecherous night in the underbelly of South Florida.

The gate bore a monogrammed *GL,* and underneath that

1

a confirming *1712* in wrought iron. He stared but did not become curious. He knew that police protection on the island was tight, and he had practiced to fit in perfectly with his surroundings and give an engaging and believable performance on a chance meeting with a Palm Beach town cop. He looked up and down the street once more, listening, and decided it was time to move.

Time to kill.

He started the timer on his Rolex diving watch. He wanted to take no more than ten minutes.

The infrared trip light was easy to avoid. He scaled the concrete and limestone wall and inched his way along the hedges until he was clear. He had picked a moonless night, and with his dark suit he was difficult to see from either the mansion or the roadway.

He cleared the main garden, a large fountain, another row of hedges with another perfectly manicured *GL* on top, and walked casually between the columns to the portico and front door.

He moved to the panel and quickly removed the key they had given him from his jacket pocket. He turned off the interior alarm; the key fit and turned perfectly. He replaced the key in his jacket pocket and fitted his thin black leather driving gloves snugly over his large hands.

He was off again, this time almost at a trot, moving around to the rear to make it look like a crude break-in. He knew that he couldn't be detected from the street, or now even from inside the house. His prey was trapped. The house was now nothing more than an expensive cage. He knew he would succeed.

He wove his way through hedges and statuary, going down expensive marble stairs and then up again until he stopped in front of the corner patio doors. He removed a small black metal flashlight from his jacket and twisted its top to cast a thin but bright beam into the interior of the estate.

The alarm panel inside also showed as deactivated. He swept the light to each side, then inspected the frame of the large glass doors. Pin locks up top, no locking device.

Just like they said.

He had the glass cutter and suction cup in hand and began to etch a softball-sized circle at the top right of the door. Six or so passes and he heard the familiar crinkle as the glass gave way. He gripped the suction cup and pulled carefully. The glass round separated and came cleanly toward him. He reached in and pulled out the pin lock, ignoring the already disarmed sensors.

He stood back and aimed the thin beam inside. All was still. He listened. Nothing more than ocean. He looked at his watch; two minutes.

Right on schedule.

He moved quickly to the standard patio lock on the edge of the door and repeated the performance with the glass cutter. He placed both pieces of glass quietly on the ground. Reaching through the door, he snapped the lock open. A moment later he was inside.

He tried hard to ignore the extravagant furniture, bric-a-brac, and artwork as he quietly made his way to the stairs.

Look at that fucking clock! Three grand. Easy.

He chuckled as the flashlight beam moved away from the clock to the wall and then to the foot of the stairs. He said to himself that the twenty grand he was being paid for the hit probably wouldn't buy wallpaper for even one room of this palace.

He smelled the new stairwell carpeting and admired its rich, blue sculpting, but he looked up, knowing it was critical now to concentrate only on his work. He stopped for a minute and listened. It was quiet, both inside and out.

At the top of the stairs he removed the small .22 auto, then the silencer, fitting them together like long-separated lovers. He stood looking at the open door to the master bedroom. The old man had gotten careless—there was no final locked door at the bedroom, which would have been a very difficult barrier to surmount. The old man had felt secure while in hiding, he knew. He had become fat and lazy.

Careless fuck.

It was time. He strode quickly to the open door. He could see the man in the expensive bed on the far wall. The silk coverings were thrown off and a single sheet covered the aging mafioso as he lay on his back, hairy nostrils tilted up at the ceiling.

He listened for the regular breathing of a sleeping man. Once he was sure his quarry was out, that he was not being set up for an ambush, he entered the bedroom quickly and awakened the man by thumping him hard on his chest. The mobster opened his eyes wide. He didn't look horrified, only surprised, as he stared up in disbelief at his attacker.

"Hey, Chuckie! This is for you from your friends!" The intruder lowered the silencer to the man's head, then moved it toward his mouth.

"Suck on it, Chuckie! That's what the boys want, they want you to suck on this!" The old man shook his head, eyes still open wide and staring up.

"You wanna chance to live? You gotta chance, but you gotta suck on this, understand?"

There was silence as their eyes met. Then the old man opened his mouth.

The intruder slipped the silencer quickly inside. The old man clamped his teeth hard, biting the silencer, gagging and thrashing his head, then trying to push him off, determined that his last fight would be a worthy one.

The intruder pulled the trigger, sending a hollowpoint bullet crashing through the top of the old man's mouth and zigzagging around his cerebellum, through the spinal cord, ending finally in the hypothalamus.

No more witness stands for you, you fuck.

He stepped back from the body as it began to heave, and

the head flew up and then hard again back against the pillow. Blood spurted out the mouth. To ensure his twenty grand, to make sure there were no mistakes, he placed the silencer on the dead mobster's heart and pulled the trigger again. There was no movement, no reaction as the bullet tore through dead flesh and the already slowing heart.

He shined the light up and down his suit, making sure no blood had spurted on him. Then he turned off the pinkie light and backed out of the bedroom. One last look at Chuckie showed only an aging Sicilian with hairy nostrils, eyes open wide and staring, blood all over his mouth and chest. The expensive silk bedsheets were ruined, he knew. *Big deal.* Whoever owned this house could afford it. He closed and locked the bedroom door, *like Chuckie shoulda done,* then hurried down the hallway and vaulted down the stairs.

He knew he shouldn't but he had to. He grabbed the small, antique oak mantel clock on his way out, securing it in his armpit. He considered other items, things that would easily bring him a second twenty grand on the streets of New York, but he shook off the temptation and bounded out the open sliding door.

Don't get greedy. An important Mafia rule.

He walked quickly, head up and ears open. The smell of the pristine garden enveloped him. He snickered at another *GL* he hadn't noticed on the way in, this one in a corner, atop a hedge, surrounded by roses. He heard only the heightened beat of the waves washing against the shore, telling him the tide was coming in and it was time to go. He looked at his watch. Eight minutes. *Perfect.*

The gloves came off with ease. They were absolutely smooth leather. There was no need to wipe up after his glove prints, since there was decidedly nothing the crime scene people could possibly lift. He tore the silencer off the gun and pocketed both behind the gloves.

Glove prints! Fuckin' cops, what else the cocksuckers gonna think of?

He moved the small clock to his back waistband as he climbed the wall. Once on top he flattened himself, alert for any human movements, ears open for the distinct, individual sound of a slow-moving patrol car. He was clear. He swung around and lowered himself to the sidewalk, scraping his expensive shoes against the wall. He stood straight up, brushing himself off for just a second, then strolled at a particularly slow pace the half block to his car, alert for people or vehicles.

He stopped the timer on his watch. Ten minutes in the huge mansion. Not bad. Not a record, but he was happy with it.

The trunk lid sprang open with a whooshing sound as he turned the key. He stowed away the gloves, gun, silencer, alarm key, glass cutter, suction cup, and finally, after glancing quickly around, the small but exquisite, heavily jeweled clock.

He was clear; now nothing more than a New York businessman with plenty of ID, wearing an expensive suit and driving a luxury car in ritzy Palm Beach.

So what's the problem, Officer?

He tapped in the five-digit code to the driver's door, and the door clicked and sprang open. He lowered himself into the leather seat, inserted the ignition key, and thought only of the twenty grand, the clock, and the leisurely two-day drive back north. He reached out to shut the door.

The arm reached in before he was aware of it, pushing him to the right. He glanced quickly, seeing only a partial silhouette through the tinted window. The hand was brawny, pushing his body over, then grasping his face and snapping his head to the right with one powerful motion.

He was facing the sidewalk, knowing what was about to happen, recognizing that he was trapped and helpless.

I'm dead.
The frame of the large .357 came inside and settled on his left ear. The bullet exploded, slamming him against the dashboard, his head dragging his limp body along, coming to rest on its back, half on the seat, half on the passenger floor.

The man stood and watched as the mechanism quietly sucked the door completely shut, leaving no opening, creating a tomblike silence, completely shutting out the salty ocean air.

1

Seabreeze

Andy Amato leaned back in his hard metal chair and blamed his boredom on the doldrums, figuring that if he had more to do or some exciting cases he wouldn't be feeling so blue.

His friends often told him that any cut in the fast-paced action he was used to would send him into a deep depression. He had never listened to his friends before, and wasn't inclined to start listening to them now. He smiled, thought of a perverse joke, and refused to be gloomy.

He had arrived at the West Palm Beach detective bureau almost a half hour before his official starting time of 8:00 A.M. He puttered around, made coffee, ate a Boston creme, checked Tuesday's editions of the *Palm Beach Post* and the *Miami Herald* for crime stories, then kicked his feet up on his desk, paper in one hand, coffee in the other.

There had been a large jewel robbery at the Town Center Mall in Boca. Four masked gunmen, automatic weapons. The store lost easily over a million in diamonds and gold, the article said. In Riviera Beach two drug dealers were shot

8

"for apparently no reason" while standing on a street corner. In Pompano a body was found in the trunk of a BMW, in the parking lot of a private airport. Pompano police suspected it was drug related. In North Miami, there was another street-gang killing. And two Miami cops were indicted by the Dade grand jury for beating up a car thief who threatened the family of one of the officers.

Just another South Florida day, Andy thought.

He almost dripped some doughnut creme onto his new Stafford shirt, the one he'd bought from Baron's in the mall especially to wear with his expensive new suit. He leaned forward just in time and the yellow goo dropped onto his desk blotter.

He glanced out the window at Datura Street, watched the pedestrians squint in the July sunlight, and for only a moment caught himself daydreaming that he was back in Miami.

Back in Miami. Shit. I'll stay here.

Gabe walked by, coming from the administration area, carrying her files for the day. Andy already knew what she was working on—three drug killings on Rosemary Street, all a month old, and a convenience store robbery-homicide from out near the Palm Beach Mall. Three active cases. *Big deal.* He had seven.

"Get your tail in gear, Teddy," Gabe said in her imitation Spanish accent. "Cap-i-tan Jake is co-ming down the hall-a-way." She turned another corner and headed to her desk.

She was the only one who called Andy by his nickname of Teddy, the only person he'd allow to. He liked to be called Andy, but even "Amato" was okay. But Lieutenant Andy T. (Theodore) Amato didn't like "Teddy." From his wife he figured he had to take it.

"Thanks. You get busy, too. Let's not have another boring day like yesterday," he called after her, watching the sway of her hips in her tight skirt.

9

He heard his commander approaching, so he swung his feet off the desk and opened the topmost file of his stack.

Captain Bobby Jacobson was a West Palm PD veteran even back in the days when West Palm Beach was considered nothing but a small, distant suburb of Miami and Ft. Lauderdale. He had watched the city and county take on their own identity in the late sixties when the interstate was finally put through, and had seen the city grow to the "concrete metropolis" he called it today.

Andy had known his boss only a year. And he liked him. Jacobson was reasonable, even congenial on occasion, and Andy liked his perseverance and style.

Barney Miller, Amato had thought when he first laid eyes on his new captain. *Fuckin' Captain Barney,* he'd said under his breath and had laughed right after first shaking hands and looking at the guy's face, mustache, and neatly combed salt and pepper hair.

Jacobson walked in with his still-present Marine Corps strut, even twenty-five years out of the service. He nodded at Andy and the other detectives, shifted his folded-up copy of the *Wall Street Journal* and a Styrofoam cup of coffee to his left hand, then fished out his keys and opened his office door.

"Get to work, Andy. You look bored. Don't look bored on city time, look bored on your lunch break." Jacobson flung open the wood and glass door and settled in behind his plain brown desk.

Andy walked up to the office door with a smile. "Fine. I won't look bored. I've only got seven cases, all snoozers. The dirtbags'll be in jail by Friday. I'm just tryin' to figure out a real mean, classy way to put the arm on them."

"Good. So everything you got now will be clear by the end of the week?"

"Clear. One hundred percent. I promise."

"And Gabe? What does she have that's still active?"

10

"She's got a few still open, but she'll clear those also, or she'll have warrants issued. Either way, we're not leaving you high and dry." They smiled at each other.

Andy thought of his upcoming one-year anniversary with West Palm PD and his and Gabe's much-deserved two-week vacation in Key West. He smiled as he saw them sipping Rumrunners at sundown on the southern Mallory dock. He could almost smell the rum.

He walked into Jacobson's open office door, carrying his large coffee mug. "Hey, Cap'n, I tell you the one about the waitress who runs up to the cop sitting in a restaurant?" Jacobson unthinkingly shook his head as he gulped coffee. "Well, she runs up to him all excited and says, 'Officer, there's a dead naked man out in the alley, and I think he's a cop!' So the officer says, 'If he's naked, how do you know he's a cop?' So she gives the officer an incredulous look and says, 'Because he's got a big hard-on and coffee runnin' out his ears!' "

Andy laughed out loud; Jacobson smiled and sipped again from his coffee mug. The captain's phone rang and Andy looked up at the wall clock—8:00 A.M. He walked back to his desk, laughing along with the other detectives who had overheard the punch line.

He buried his head in the case file he was working on. He read it completely through, then planned out who was left to talk to. He needed to make one more trip to the medical examiner's office. He had to go to the crime lab for toxicology and ballistics results. He had to stop by the sheriff's office for copies of reports. He had to go to the county jail to make another stab at having the dirtbag confess after being confronted with overwhelming evidence.

The fuck will cry and want his lawyer. Andy hated lawyers.

Gabe came by again, another detective with her. She smiled at Andy and he smiled back. He admired her tall, sleek frame, her straight, dark hair and thick eyebrows.

11

When she smiled her lips separated wide to show all her perfectly white teeth. He gave her a quick wink as she and the other detective continued on to the public waiting area.

He spent a few more minutes on his homicide folder. Then out of the corner of his eye he saw Jacobson stand up, say some parting words into the phone, and gently place the receiver back on the cradle.

"Amato! Get in here, bring your pad."

Andy sipped the last of his coffee and quickly rose, taking an old, worn, doodled yellow pad along with him.

"Get the door," Jacobson said. He pointed to the chair and Andy sat down, praying that it wasn't any kind of bad news.

"That was a call from the island, from the detective captain of Palm Beach PD. They're working a strange one over there. Two bodies. One in a mansion near the ocean, the other in a car nearby. They're requesting our assistance. Specifically, *your* assistance. I guess you've already made a name for yourself. They think it's organized-crime related, your specialty."

Andy didn't think of the compliment, all he could think of was blowing his Key West vacation. He could still taste the Rumrunner.

"Captain, I don't think I should be takin' any more cases right now. After Friday we go on vacation."

"I know. This is advisory only—they're just looking for some homicide expertise to unravel an apparent pile of shit over there. Spend some time with them, hold their hands, that's all—then it's all theirs."

"I've got my own cases to finish up. I may be late on those, you understand."

"Fine. I'll reassign them if I have to. These are our next-door neighbors, Andy; from the sound of it they got a real stinker of a problem over there. We can't really turn them down, we may need *them* one day. Get over there and see if you can help 'em figure it out."

12

"Gabe. I'll bring Gabe with me."

"Just you. No need to get us more involved than we have to."

"Respectfully, Captain, but that was the deal when me and Gabe came aboard here. We worked together in Miami, we're a great homicide team for the big cases. That was the deal when we got our transfers up here."

Jacobson looked irritated. "I realize that, but I don't like it. I've never liked it. I don't even like you two working in the same office together. I don't know how you can stand it, how you can make it work."

"There's lots of married couples in departments, lots of them working together. There aren't any problems, we've learned how to handle the hassles as they come up. Look, Captain, we've been through all this before. We're a great team, you know that, you've seen our stats from Miami, you've seen what we've done here. I can't work a big case without Gabe. She's good. She's *real* good, especially with small details. You know, it's like yin without yang, ping without pong, pancakes without syrup—"

"Okay, okay. Fine. Take her with you. But a few hours is all I want you two spending over there. They don't call it Fantasy Island for nothing. Things can get crazy, all mired up with the millionaires and billionaires and all that shit. I've worked with them over there before, it can be a real bitch. Politics, big shots, lots of money. Get in, give 'em some advice, and get out."

"Right. No problem. No way I'm getting involved in a complicated homicide, not with a vacation coming up."

Jacobson handed him a sheet of paper. "Seventeen-twelve Seabreeze, just off the ocean. There's a Palm Beach detective lieutenant there waiting for you."

Andy took the scrap of paper and put it between the sheets of his doodle pad. "We'll make it short and sweet, be outta there in no time."

Jacobson nodded his head and unceremoniously waved him out.

Gabe was over by her desk, typing up an arrest warrant.

"Put everything on hold, we're going somewhere," Andy said to her.

"Going where? Teddy, we—"

"Don't worry. We're not working it. It's over in Palm Beach, by the ocean. For some reason they're requesting my assistance, our assistance. Just advising. Get in, get out, nothing to it."

"That'll take the rest of the day! What about our cases? How're we gonna be able to leave for vacation Friday?"

"It'll all be taken care of. This is right from Captain Jacobson, no sense arguing." He looked at the curves of her ample breasts as they pushed out her flowered cotton blouse. God, he loved her body, even after almost three years of marriage.

She shrugged and turned off the typewriter, looking resigned to going with him. "Fine. Let's get going. You drive. And remember, in and out, right?"

"Right," he replied, smiling at her, recognizing the gaze that told him she didn't quite believe him.

He pushed the Saab 9000S Turbo to over sixty as he rounded the scenic curves of Flagler Drive, heading north toward the central Palm Beach bridge. Gabe had stopped talking to him, clearly annoyed at something—either his fast driving or their getting involved in a homicide case so close to vacation. He wasn't sure which.

So he just glanced at her and thought again what a lucky guy he was. Her body, her bony face with its clear features, her long and beautiful hands. Gabe—Gabrielle—was half French and half Greek, with beautiful Mediterranean features that could soften your resolve in even the most winnable of arguments. He considered himself a typical

14

third-generation Sicilian-Italian: medium height, heavyset, olive skin, black wavy hair, bushy mustache. Divorced from his first wife, with a son, Andy Jr., his pride and joy. He thought of himself as handsome and attractive to women. At thirty-six, he had turned down a few offers. He knew Gabe had, too.

They married after the third year they were assigned together in Miami PD homicide. Surprisingly, the department still let them work together, not wanting to split up a firecracker-hot homicide team responsible for a third of the division's arrests. They continued on another year, solving cases through Gabe's keen eye for detail and thorough knowledge of forensics and Andy's tough-guy image, sixth sense about danger, and flair for catching bad guys on the run. They worked their way up to be Miami PD's Detectives of the Year just before they quit.

Gabe wanted kids, so they started trying. Then she convinced him to get out of Miami and Dade County. West Palm PD, sixty miles north, was looking for minorities and Gabe qualified. The department readily agreed to accept them both, recognizing a seasoned homicide team when they saw one, and allowed them to keep their rank, transferred their pensions, and gave them a commitment that they could still work homicide together. Gabe was eager, but Andy was hesitant. He had fifteen years invested with the Miami PD, and he wasn't sure about such a dramatic move. But, finally, he accepted the transfer out of the steamy Miami underworld into the more leisurely Palm Beach life-style. They placed him as the head of the department's small homicide division. He managed to stay busy, and for the year he had been in West Palm he had not regretted the decision.

The Saab's tires squealed as he took another curve.

"Slow down, you're gonna get stopped!" Gabe screamed and turned to face him with a scowl.

"Okay! Relax, we won't get stopped. All the patrolmen

15

know my car." He shifted down and the engine whined as the car slowed to just over fifty. He could see the turnoff to the intracoastal bridge coming up.

The car was Andy's toy. The sleek aircraft-like interior of the Saab had appealed to him immediately and he'd juggled his borderline finances to afford it. Gabe still drove her nondescript dark blue Toyota.

"Seventeen-twelve Seabreeze. Should be a right on Ocean Boulevard, then about ten streets." Gabe had picked up a map. She would always refer to one to give Andy exact directions. He preferred to find things by guesswork, which annoyed her. Andy picked his speed back up, placed the revolving blue light on the dashboard, and turned it on. Gabe gave him another annoyed look, but he just grinned widely like a boy with an expensive new plaything.

They crossed the Flagler Memorial Bridge and drove along Poinciana Way, both of them glancing quickly over to the pristine gardens, office buildings, and fountains and marveling at them. Andy goosed the Saab through a red light and onto the oceanside roadway. Gabe was counting off streets on the map, calling them out to Andy, getting ready to tell him where to turn. He was ignoring her, passing cars that pulled over for the blue light, knowing that if a homicide scene was anywhere on this decorous and sterile island, he would be able to find it.

Lieutenant Andy Amato pulled in behind the unmarked Plymouth that he guessed must be from the medical examiner's office. He surveyed the scene stretched out before him, framed in Palm Beach sunlight, ocean breeze, and immaculate surroundings: four Palm Beach PD patrol cars, one a supervisor's; three detective cars; the M.E.'s car; a detective sergeant's car; a detective lieutenant's car; and an ambulance.

Gabe had once asked him how he could tell who all the

different unmarked cars belonged to. He told her it was a feel, it was in his blood. He could look at a guy, or a car, and he just *knew*. He was never wrong. She thought it was spooky.

His eyes finally caught the person in charge of the crime scene, a short and lean man in a tan suit who was walking quickly around, barking out orders, conferring with uniformed officers, writing on a pad. They got out and walked past the ambulance, then under the crime scene tape, flashing their West Palm badges at a young officer with mirrored sunglasses and an immaculately pressed uniform.

"Lieutenant Amato, West Palm PD. I'm looking for your detective lieutenant."

"Right over there." It was the short guy in the tan suit, confirming Andy's guess.

They walked over, both Gabe and Andy flashing their badges at him.

"Lieutenant, I'm Lieutenant Andy Amato from West Palm, and this is Sergeant Gabe Amato, my partner."

The man looked them over. "Parker. Gary Parker. Thanks for coming down. Walk over here with me." He didn't extend a hand, only nodded at each of them, then walked off toward a black Lincoln. They followed behind.

"I appreciate you coming down here so quickly. I know this is an unusual request. I've heard about you two at meetings, in conversations. I know you were involved in a lot of organized crime and Mafia stuff down in Dade County."

"Some. Mostly mob homicides," Andy said.

"Good. I need you to take a look at this. I've never seen anything like it before in all my time on this island, nothing even close. We've got two bodies, one in the car, the other over in that mansion." Their eyes followed as Parker pointed to the Lincoln, then over the eight-foot wall of 1712 Seabreeze. Gabe took out her pad and started taking notes.

"An old woman was walking her dog about seven this

morning," Parker said. "She went by the Lincoln and saw the body slumped on its back with blood everywhere. She screamed and ran to neighbors; then we got the call. Later, when we started canvassing, a patrolman noticed that the alarm panel to Seventeen-twelve over there is usually on, but was turned off for some reason. He found a break-in through the back patio doors. We went in. There's the body of an old man, maybe mid-sixties, in bed upstairs. Shot once in the head, through the mouth, and once in the chest. Not suicide, even if that were possible with two wounds like that, because there's no gun anywhere. The house isn't ransacked, no sign of a burglary."

"Alarm wires cut or bypassed?" Gabe asked.

"No. He used a key. I'll get to that. It gets more complicated."

"What about this car? The New York plates?" Andy asked.

The three walked toward the Lincoln. A crime scene man was busy dusting for prints all around the body. All the doors were open and the trunk was up. The body lay slumped on its back, head on the passenger floorboard, feet on the driver's seat. Andy admired how well the dark businessman's suit hid the bloodstains.

"Plates come back to a New York leasing company with a Manhattan address. We've been unable to make contact. The stiff had a wallet with plenty of cash and ID. A New York mobster, I think, but I wanted to run it by you." Parker held out the driver's license from the man's wallet. Andy didn't recognize the name, but it was Italian, and the address was from an Italian neighborhood in Brooklyn.

"I don't know the name. But the mob would be a good first assumption," Andy said, handing the license back.

"Right. There's more. Come over to the trunk."

The three of them walked over, with Gabe and Andy glancing ahead, approaching cautiously, hoping it wasn't something gruesome.

18

Gabe looked inside first, relieved. Then she wrote again on her pad.

"Gun, silencer, burglar tools, gloves, the alarm key, and a clock we think is probably from the house," the Palm Beach lieutenant said, pointing at the items.

"Everything was locked when you found the car?" Gabe asked.

"Right. The stiff had the ignition key in his hand, he was still clutching it. All the doors were locked, the trunk was locked. We Slim-Jimmed the door, then opened the trunk using the button in the glove box."

"Any other clues inside?" Gabe asked.

"Nothing so far. We're working on prints right now."

Andy stepped away and looked over the wall toward the house.

"The old man was killed with a twenty-two auto," Parker continued. "Through the roof of the mouth. We found the casings. One in the mouth, one in the chest. The M.E. people are up there now along with a couple of my detectives, trying to get me more clues. It looks like the gun and silencer in the trunk here might be the murder weapon, meaning this is the guy who killed the old man in the house."

"Then who killed *him?*" Andy asked. "That's the big question, isn't it?"

"Exactly. The wound in this guy's head is at least from a thirty-eight, maybe larger, and it came in from behind the left ear at close range."

"Do you mind?" Gabe asked the lieutenant, motioning that she wanted to inspect the body in the front of the Lincoln.

"No. Go ahead. We haven't taken pictures yet, so just try to keep the body in the same position."

The crime scene man was working on the exterior of the driver's window, slinging black carbon powder all over the glass. Gabe went around to the passenger side and began poking around with a pen, looking over the body, making notes.

"No ID on the guy in the house?" Andy asked.

"Another mystery. This is where it *really* starts to get bizarre on us. Our records show that the house belongs to a Gregory Languiss, a New York book publisher. It's usually vacant for the summer, except for a part-time housekeeper. We checked with her, but she says that she was let go by the owner two weeks ago, without an explanation. Meanwhile, we're waiting to get in touch with Languiss, to see what he says."

"He'll deny anyone's supposed to be here," Andy said. He was looking Parker over, trying to size up the man.

The lieutenant nodded. "Maybe. Meanwhile, our old man has no ID, but he obviously has lived there for at least a few weeks. There are groceries and clothes in the house, and he had a stash of cash, jewelry, watches, and some pictures. Just nothing with a name or address, nothing to cross-reference."

Andy nodded. "What about a car?"

"None on the grounds. Someone had to be picking him up or taking care of him—it's a long way from here to a grocery store."

"What about the owner—a New York publisher? Anyone know of any ties to organized crime?"

"We thought of that. I really doubt it. He's here with his wife all winter, then they go back to Long Island in the summer. Typical part-time Palm Beachers, service clubs, Republican club, all that. We'll check with NYPD on him, but I really can't see it."

"There's nothing you're not telling me? A mob hit is still what you're zeroing in on?" Andy asked.

"Right. About three A.M., judging from the condition of the bodies, a Mafia hit man turns the alarm off, breaks in and kills the guy in the house, for some reason steals the clock, then goes back to his car."

"And gets whacked. At three A.M. in Palm Beach. Coming back from whacking somebody out." *Just when you thought you'd seen it all.*

"That's the way it looks," Parker said softly.

Andy continued, almost to himself. "A double Mafia kill. They want one guy whacked out, so our stiff in the Lincoln breaks into the mansion and does it. He's ready to start the car and leave, then someone else comes up and whacks *him* out." He shook his head.

"Or maybe there were two guys sent to do the hit? And one of them secretly had a contract to take out the other one after the job was over . . . ?" Parker said.

Andy thought a moment. "No. Possible, but unlikely. It would draw too much attention, leaving them like this. The mob doesn't like its bodies found, or at least not till they're good an' ripe. He would've driven the guy away, dumped the body someplace, and no one would've been the wiser. Besides, the hit men wouldn't have come in separate cars."

Parker nodded. "See what I mean? I'm starting to flip out over all the possibilities in this one."

Andy smiled. "Don't. Actually, it's going to be clear-cut, once you have all the details worked out. Don't sweat it—it'll fall into place, they always do. And the bottom line is that you've probably got two dead New York gangsters. So, how they got dead, in a coupla days no one will give a shit." Andy thought of the bagpipe player at the Mallory docks, seeing himself again sipping on a large Key West Rumrunner.

"Right. You're right, it could be worse."

"Yeah. You could have one of these innocent millionaires with his brains blown to bits."

"That would be a problem."

Andy stayed silent. He looked at the short Palm Beach lieutenant. He figured this was probably the second or third homicide he'd ever investigated, if that many.

Gabe came back under the yellow crime scene tape and walked over to the two men.

21

"Find anything?" Andy asked.

"Professional hit man. No question. The suit's a straight black, very uncommon. Dark blue shirt, dark tie. He didn't want to be seen. The jacket and pants are custom made with extra pockets, all double deep for hiding objects. He has all the ID a cop could ever ask for, all in perfect order. All of it obviously forged to look important and legitimate. Finally, his watch. This is where I can tell he's definitely a pro. He timed himself and didn't reset the hands. Ten minutes, almost exactly. He timed how long he'd be. This was obviously not his first hit. Maybe his fastest. Definitely his last."

Both men took in the facts, Parker writing the information down on his own pad. He looked closely at the license Gabe Amato proclaimed as a phony.

"And it had to be a surprise—a big one," she continued. "Couldn't have been someone with him. Looks like he was seated on the driver's side, ready to start the car. Someone came in from the open driver's door at the last second, pushed his head to the right, and shot him. He was dead instantly. The body slumped down to where it is now. Then whoever it was locked the door and took off."

"Why couldn't the stiff have been a passenger, and the driver reached out and shot him?" Parker asked.

"Sorry. After the bullet impacted, the head hit hard against the dash, just to the left of the glove box. If you look closely you can see the indentation. That impact would have been impossible if the guy was seated on the passenger side."

Parker looked astounded. Andy Amato beamed with pride, knowing that his partner would come up with clues to confirm his statement. He winked at her, but she ignored him.

"Let's go in the house," Andy suggested. Parker nodded and led the way to the open gate, under the tape, and into the manicured compound.

Gabe and Andy took it all in. Gabe made meticulous notes at the point of entry. Once inside, she pointed out to Parker the outline of the clock in the dust atop the fireplace. They went upstairs, dodging the Palm Beach detectives and forensic people, and stood back and watched as one of the M.E. team took photos of the dead man from every conceivable angle. Andy finally went up and examined the entry wounds, looking around the rest of the bedroom. Gabe did likewise. All three walked around examining the rest of the house and finally went back outside.

"That's the twenty-two from the trunk, no doubt. Scrambled the old guy's brains for sure," Andy said.

"Mob style. Head first, then one in the heart, for good measure," Gabe added.

Parker nodded, leading them back out to the street.

"Definitely a Mafia contract hit. No doubt about it," Andy said. "Everything fits, the twenty-two with a silencer, the custom clothes and fake ID, the leased Lincoln with New York plates."

"But what was the old man doing here, and how did the hit man catch a thirty-eight in the back of the head? Where'd he get an alarm key? It just doesn't make any sense to me." Parker seemed exasperated and overwhelmed by the investigation he knew was to follow.

"Like I said, it'll all fall into place," Andy said.

A car turned off Ocean Boulevard onto Seabreeze. It was a black Grand Fury, all tinted windows. No spotlight. It had an antenna for a cellular telephone and another short one for a 800-megahertz radio. Two men in business suits were in the front seat. The car pulled up next to Andy's Saab and the three detectives stood silently, watching as the men got out and walked past the ambulance.

"Who the hell are they? They're not with my department," Parker said.

Andy looked over the car. "Miami FBI. We may start getting some answers to your questions, Lieutenant." He stepped forward to face the two men as they lifted up the crime scene tape and flashed their credentials.

The lead agent was tall and lean, the second shorter, with a bulldog scowl and a crew cut. The taller man extended his hand to Andy and a smile came over his face, a smile of recognition.

"Andy! Andy Amato!" He shook Andy's hand and slapped him on the shoulder.

Andy pointed behind him to Gabe and Lieutenant Parker.

"Gabe! Hello. Fancy seeing you both here," the agent added. Gabe smiled but remained stationary and silent.

"Phillip Wesley, FBI," the agent added. "This is Agent Donald Gruen, supervisor from the West Palm office. He escorted me over here," Wesley explained. "You were working the Overtown Caladega homicide last I heard from you, Andy. Everything been going okay?"

"Fine. We put that guy away. Dade grand jury came back with an indictment—he's doing life in Raiford right now."

"To what do we owe the pleasure?" Parker finally asked, both curious and worried.

Gruen spoke just as Wesley was about to. "We're here to tell you that this is now a federal case. We've been monitoring your transmissions, that's how we found out about the killings. This matter now concerns the federal government and we have priority."

Parker was silent, staring at Gruen.

"My, how subtle," Andy said. "I see nothing's changed since I last dealt with you guys."

Gruen gave him a pompous look. "You may continue to work your state crimes, but we're asserting our federal authority over everything that happens here."

Andy laughed. A short distance away, five members of the press, some with cameras, were giving the officer with the mirrored glasses a hard time, but he was standing his ground.

24

"That's real cute, Gruen. Real cute. You rehearse that?" Amato added.

"Back off, Amato. It's not your case," Gruen replied.

Andy stayed silent. Parker looked at him as if he couldn't believe someone had talked to the FBI that way.

"Look, we'll try to explain as best we can," Wesley added politely. "There's a lot going on here you may not be aware of. There are important factors to consider, which local authorities are not in a position to act on."

Gruen walked over to the Lincoln, lifting up the yellow tape and walking under it. The crime scene man gave him a concerned look, then returned to dusting for prints. Gruen fingered his way through the dead man's wallet, now lying open on the passenger seat.

"Respectfully, Phil, this may have something to do with the FBI. But this is a double homicide, a local case. And in Florida, that's the electric chair. You telling me that you federal boys have got something more serious than that?"

Wesley took Andy by the elbow and led him out of Gruen's earshot. Parker and Gabe split their attention between them and Gruen, who was poking around the Lincoln, looking under seats, and reaching into the dead man's pockets. Parker was starting to appear disturbed.

"I can't tell you everything right now, Andy. I wish I could. If it were up to me, I would, you know that. We go back a long way. You did me a lot of favors, you saved my ass a few times. I did the same for you. I'd tell you. But I can't. Not now." Wesley shook his head.

Andy leaned toward him and lowered his voice. "The old man upstairs looks like a mafioso, mid-sixties. No ID, but plenty of money and jewelry. The house belongs to a New York publisher and is never occupied in the summer. Our stiff in the car is another New York mobster, a hit man. There's a twenty-two and silencer in the trunk, along with a key to the house's alarm. A mob hit, then someone whacks the shooter. On the streets of probably the richest fucking island in the U.S. And guess what, Phil? I'm on the case. As of now, I'm officially on loan to Palm Beach PD until they clear this up. So, maybe you want to tell us a little more about what's going on?"

Gabe had been listening and gave an almost-silent groan. The vacation was shot.

Wesley laughed, patting Andy on the back. "Stubborn type, that's what makes you a good cop. But you need to relax a little, Andy. You need to have trust in teamwork, you need to trust the system. This whole thing is a big mystery to us, also. We don't know who killed the guy in the Lincoln. We may not even care. But like Gruen said, something's going on that doesn't really concern local authorities right now."

"Bullshit. Don't feed me any more of that federal government 'we're more important' bullshit, Phil. I know your system as well as you do, you know that. I know how you guys think, how you act, I know the politics you live with. So let's not fuck around anymore. This is a Palm Beach homicide. They've got the scene and we're helping. We got two dead guys with their brains blown to bits. So cut the crap."

"I'm sorry, Andy. I can't. Gruen's in charge. He'll have me flown to Anchorage on an air force cargo flight tomorrow morning if I tell you anything."

"Start with why you're here. Tell me why Miami FBI drives all the way up here early in the morning, picks up this turkey at the local office, then drives over to a Palm Beach homicide." Andy pointed at Gruen, who was interrogating the crime scene man.

"It involves our office, that's why. It's an important project that involves Miami."

"Who's the dead guy in the mansion?"

"I can't tell you that."

"Who's the dead guy in the Lincoln, then?"

"I don't know. If I did, I couldn't tell you."

26

"How did he find this old guy, who was obviously in hiding from something? Why's the old man in this house? Does the owner know? Where'd the killer get the alarm key?"

Wesley just shook his head.

"This is a murder case, Phil. These are questions we'll have to get answered. We can butt heads, play rough, go behind each other's back. You know what that's like. Or you can cut the crap and stop treating us like kids. We're cops, remember?"

"I'm sorry. Not here, not now. There's too much going on. This involves Washington, not just Miami. This is serious shit. There's gonna be big problems over all this."

Andy stood back and shook his head. He had worked with federal agents hundreds of times. He was starting to understand.

The agent continued, almost in a whisper. "Come by the office tomorrow. Late, after five. Meet me downstairs, at the pistol range." Wesley nodded, then walked past Andy to speak with the Palm Beach lieutenant.

"They're hiding something, something big," Andy said to his wife, who nodded.

"I've got half a notepad of details. Some very strange facts, not all fitting together. There's not much more we can do here," Gabe said.

"There's plenty more we can do. Just not here and not now." Andy backed away, looking contemptuously at Gruen, who was now heading toward the mansion and the old, dead mafioso, Wesley and Lieutenant Parker following him. Andy felt sorry for the Palm Beach investigator. Gruen was going to fuck everything up and leave the local police in the dark.

Gabe and Andy looked at each other and silently agreed it was time to leave. But the case was theirs, even if they had to work it on their own time. They walked back to the Saab, squinting into the noonday Florida sun.

Key West was history.

Andy started the engine, then took another long look at the Lincoln and at 1712 Seabreeze. He slowly backed away from the scene and sped around the corner, squealing his tires and heading back to West Palm, trying to formulate what to tell Jacobson, and sifting through his years of homicide experience to figure out where on earth this investigation was going to lead.

2

Silhouettes

They were not nightmares—they were not even dreams. Her mind raced through the details, exhausting her, going over every item of minutiae from the double killing. First she was in the Lincoln, emptying the dead assassin's pockets; then she was in the bedroom suite, leaning down to look up the old man's mouth, trying to find the bullet's entrance wound. Then she was back at the car, staring at the pistol and silencer sitting innocently on the floor of the trunk, imagining herself sitting in the passenger seat, trying to watch, to intrude upon something as personal as a violent death, as the hand with the gun came through the door, pushed the killer's head, then shot the round that snapped the head forward and sent it crashing against the dashboard.

She was bothered by something her mind could not grasp. It eluded her throughout the night. Her imagination toyed with the face of the beautiful mantel clock, over the cut openings in the patio doors, over the alarm key sitting so benign yet deadly in the trunk of the assassin's car.

She sensed that it was none of these things that bothered

her. She knew it was something else. So her mind raced on.

Suddenly it revealed itself. It was the face of the killer's watch. The Rolex was in front of her, its sweep-second hand pushing forward, racing toward the ten-minute mark. She reached out and tried to stop it. When she could not, the analytical side of her tried to understand what it meant. It nagged at her, confused and tickled her brain like a word desperately needed but anchored on the tip of the tongue. She watched intently as the second hand moved toward its final destination, sweeping up past the forty-five mark, then fifty, then fifty-five, then . . .

She jumped up and awoke with a start. She sat straight up in bed, aware only of her perspiration, her headache from the troubled sleep, and the killer's watch ticking off and stopping at exactly ten minutes.

"Ten minutes," she said out loud. She shook her head, coming fully awake, letting the thought of the watch pass through her and away. In a minute it returned as just another meaningless detail.

She looked at Andy next to her, sound asleep. He often told her that she talked in her sleep, tossing and turning, and generally being a nuisance. She would apologize, he would kiss her and say that it was okay, that it came with taking her job too seriously.

Well, I'm back at it again.

But it was more than that, she knew. It wasn't either of the bodies, it wasn't the murders at all. It wasn't any of the routine details that every murder held. There was something about this one that frightened and worried her. Maybe the watch was part of it, but that wasn't all of what was beginning to bother her about this particular homicide.

Andy had felt it also. She was sure of it. They had gone home at their usual time and relaxed. While he cooked dinner, she made him a drink and took a long, steamy-hot shower. They ate, ran out for dessert and shopping, came

30

home and watched TV, then went to bed. There had been lovemaking, at first slow and typical, then quicker, more worried and frantic. She saw it in his hot-brown, sex-absorbed Sicilian eyes; something worried him, too. And he was more used to it, he had seen thousands of homicides, compared to her few hundred . . .

The sex. She returned to it. She gauged trouble in their lives by the style, frequency, and quality of their lovemaking; and last night had a quality of strangeness to it. It was silent, abnormally so. Not hurried, but definitely intent on something else, as if there were an important meeting each of them had to go to immediately afterward.

Maybe she worried too much, she realized. It was her style to examine and dissect everything, even their intimacy. Andy was more rugged psychologically, less impressionable, less eager to bare his persona for the sake of a homicide investigation. Because of it, he never saw all the details, where she would. He was a "big picture" man, acting out of instinct, out of feel.

He also slept better, she noticed.

She rolled out of the waterbed, causing a minimum of waves, and picked up the alarm clock. Six-twelve A.M. Too early for work, too late to try for more sleep. She walked, naked, to the bathroom. She would go in early and read the newspaper, she decided.

Andy still slept, and dreamed.

Andy frantically backed the Saab out of the driveway and purposefully cut into the early-morning traffic. He gave the town house another quick look, trying to remember whether he had locked the door, decided that he had, then revved the engine and thrilled as the instant acceleration left a horn-blaring Oldsmobile trailing far behind.

He smiled as he quickly outpaced the traffic, happy that he was able to convince Jacobson that Gabe should work the case with him. He had left her with all the dirty work—the typical next-day homicide routine of autopsies (this time two), reading reports, and checking over the endless initial details, most of them worthless. He also stuck her with the phone calls to the New York police to try and learn the whos and whys—who the two mafiosos were and why they were whacked out on Palm Beach. He was sure they would have no interesting information.

He chortled as he rolled onto the interstate, pushing seventy and cutting across three traffic lanes. He rolled open the sunroof and patted down his curly hair, cringing at the expanding bald spot, and smoothed his ample black mustache. Gabe was doing all the *fugace* work, while he was driving to Miami to *really* start solving the case. He told Gabe to tell Jacobson that he would be gone the whole day, and maybe the better part of tomorrow. He hoped Captain Barney would understand.

His first stop would be Hollywood and his old friend Carmine. He settled in the fast lane, pulling the speed back down below seventy so as not to attract the highway patrol. When he came up behind a slower car he would sometimes tailgate until it moved, or he would sometimes simply go around. He set the stereo to a soft-rock station and entrenched himself in the soft-leather seat.

Traffic was fairly light. It wasn't tourist season, so there would be no horn-blaring traffic jams by the Lauderdale airport.

He thought of Gabe, of their town house, and he wondered how his parents were doing out in Sun City, Arizona. He wondered how much longer till he was bald, and he thought about how happy he was after a year in West Palm PD. He was a third-generation Italian immigrant made good. He was happy with himself. Going bald in the back didn't bother him as much as he thought it would.

Miles went by. His mind bounced around, still soggy with early-morning lethargy. He turned up the air conditioner as soon as the hot Florida sun made its way completely through the tinted windows.

Then he thought about the murder. He did what he always did—he put himself in the killer's shoes, he gave himself the killer's viewpoint. He walked through the crime scene, doing what he knew the killer must have done. He cut the glass on the sliding doors, he looked around in the dark solitude, then he made his way up the stairs to the bedroom. He imagined the surprise of the aging mobster, the way he must have begged, and maybe even fought. He flinched at the gunshots. He *became* the killer who left the room, made his way downstairs, picked up the mantel clock. It was not hard. None of it. He could have done it, he said to himself.

"I could do it," he said out loud. Neither the thought nor the words frightened him.

He opened the door of the Lincoln as it sat on the deserted Palm Beach ocean roadway. He got in, ready to start the engine.

He winced as the bullet entered his imagination through the left rear of his head, snapping him forward, then dragging him down . . .

He shifted uncomfortably in the seat, still feeling the sharp, jagged pain that the assassin must have felt.

He repeated it to himself as if he hadn't thought of it before: the guy in the Lincoln whacked out the old man, then somebody sneaked up on him and turned his head into an overripe honeydew with a .38 at close range.

He shook off the homicide and decided to listen to the music. He was leaving Palm Beach County, barreling through Deerfield Beach, Pompano, Lauderdale, and finally coming into Hollywood. The hour trip took him only forty minutes. The killings slipped in and out of his thoughts.

He found the dog track easily, remembering the streets from only one prior trip. He was waved into the parking lot by an overweight, overage attendant with a Yankees cap and a ripe cigar. The sun was temporarily behind some low, dark gray clouds, but rain was not in the forecast. The puppies would run, he knew, and he would meet Carmine and hopefully get some answers.

He pulled in next to a carload of noisy young people and waited until they left for the clubhouse. He reached forward and switched off the cellular phone and police radio, hiding the blue light under a newspaper.

When he opened the car door, he found the air hotter than he expected for a cloudy day in June. He loosened his tie, took off his jacket and shoulder holster and left them in the car, and started out at a brisk pace toward the entrance gate.

Once inside, he stopped and bought two beers from the overpriced bar and walked slowly down the air-conditioned and marbled hallway of the Hollywood Kennel Club's VIP section. He looked toward the second-floor railing, expecting to see his old friend. The glass viewing area was empty, reminding him of the red-eye waiting area in Palm Beach International Airport. He looked around some more, finally spotting Carmine off to the left, at a table.

His father's friend was old and furtive-looking. His ears stuck out from his head, looking big because there was no hair to surround them. The eyes were deep copper. His feet and hands were large, almost abnormally so. He wore the typical retiree outfit of pastel pants, pullover knit shirt, and white, imitation-leather shoes. A tremendous overbite was evident as he smiled at Amato and reached across to pull out a padded chair. Andy sat and placed the beers down. The old man guffawed with pleasure as his large hand reached out and picked up a glass.

They were immediately friendly. Their conversation was about old times, Carmine pulling his chair close to Andy and talking to him the way a father talks to a son, about women and sex. They went from hushed tones to outbursts of

34

laughter. Andy Amato hadn't seen Carmine in over a year, but it was like only yesterday.

"I'm glad your old man's doing good. He deserves it. He worked fuckin' hard for all his dough, he deserves to take it easy," Carmine said.

Andy leaned back and nodded, letting a smile show through. "Right. He deserves it. So does my mom. They both do."

More small talk flowed by as Andy thought over what he had come to say. When the conversation slackened, Carmine D'Angelo, retired mafioso, picked up the daily program and sifted through the names from one to eight, listening closely for his mind to tell him the winner.

"Four and three. Good dogs. Perfecta. Do it for me, Andy," he said. He plucked a hundred-dollar bill from a stack he took out of his pocket and handed it to Andy. "Go in if you want. It's a sure one, I know the owners."

Amato nodded and stood up. He would have to do it to show the man respect.

The old woman in the betting cage reminded Andy of his second-grade teacher. She was short and fat with gray hair pulled back and a flowered dress that hung straight down from her shoulders. He placed Carmine's bet, and threw in a twenty of his own. He had to show confidence. *Respect.* The old woman gave him a prophetic smile as he nodded and walked away.

"Got it. Here." He handed Carmine the tickets, to show him that he believed him and had gone in on the bet. As he saw a TV monitor flash the odds on their two dogs hitting on a perfecta, it occurred to him that respect had a high price.

"You got somethin' heavy, Andy? You sounded tired and shaky on the phone. But you look all right. You havin' problems with that pretty Greek thing you married?"

Andy shook his head, smiling. "Gabe? No, she's fine."

"Somethin' personal? Somethin' on the job? They screwin' with you?"

"Nothing like that. This is official. I need your opinion on something. Yesterday in Palm Beach there was a double killing. You seen the papers?"

"Just the sports section. All that other stuff, I don't give a fuck no more, you know that."

"Right. But I know you keep up on old . . . friends of yours. I know you listen and hear. I know you don't repeat and say anything. But I was hoping you'd help me out on this."

Andy saw Carmine glance around. He was looking to see who saw them together, who could make him as talking to a cop. Andy would have felt insulted if he didn't know Carmine was a made guy from New York and had to be careful. Every time they had met it was out of the way, with Carmine looking around to make sure no one he knew was nearby. Though he was an old friend of Andy's father, he was still a mobster, and mobsters couldn't talk to cops. Andy took a deep breath and sat back and waited.

"Your dad an' me go back a long way. You know that. He was the only friend I hung around with that wasn't a connected guy. He was good to me, like a brother. He was straight, and that counted for a lot in the old days. I could trust him. I owe your old man, that's why I talk to you . . ."

Andy knew what Carmine was getting at.

"I respect you, Carmine. You're not my stoolie, I know that."

"You're A-fuckin' right I ain't," Carmine said immediately. "I ain't no stoolie. I won't take money. No way. I'll talk to you. But that's it. I'll steer you right. I owe your ol' man. But there ain't no way I'll give up any made or connected guys or any friends . . ."

"Of course," Andy said and nodded. It was a ritual they went through almost every time they met.

36

"Besides, I don't tell you everything." Carmine laughed and chomped down on his cigar with nicotine-stained buck teeth.

The first race went off at exactly 1:15. It lasted one minute. Andy and Carmine were on their feet; there was no talk, no cheering. Their first choice came in, their second was far back in the pack. Carmine tore up his losing hundred-dollar perfecta ticket and sat back down.

Andy began by telling Carmine about the expensive Palm Beach oceanside mansion, then reenacted the first killing as he pictured it, then went on to the Lincoln. He told the story with enough details to get Carmine to stare, bite down on the cigar, widen his eyes, and shake his head. Andy left off important information—things he knew as a homicide dick he couldn't tell Carmine, things only he and the killer would know. Andy leaned back and rolled the end of his mustache in his fingers.

"Describe the old man again," Carmine said.

Andy did. Carmine nodded and looked down at race number 2, a $15,000 purse for two-year-olds. More of a crowd began to pour in and a few people sat at the table next to them. Carmine eyed them suspiciously.

He and Andy finished their beers and went to the betting cages. The old man showed Andy the next race and pointed to the winner. Andy went in with him for another twenty. Then they walked back to the glass railing and stood.

"You're not really family, Andy. I can't tell you everything. You're straight, you're a stand-up cop. That's good. Otherwise I wouldn't talk to you at all."

"Right," Andy said.

There was silence, then, "You shoulda been in the FBI, but I heard those fuckers turned you down 'cause of your dad's connections. It's their loss."

Andy remained silent. The old man sucked on the cigar. Andy knew he was avoiding the issue.

37

"I can't even say this shit to you if you was your old man—not even *talk* about tellin' a fuckin' cop. Forget about it. They'd whack me out, anybody knew I was tellin' you this."

"I need this, Carmine. This is bad. Something is big-time wrong here and I've got to get to it." More ritual.

Carmine took a puff, blew a ring, then nodded. His large hand came up and scratched his bald prow as he looked down worriedly at the next race.

"I know the old man that bought it. I'm sure of it. I'm not tellin' you who, 'cause if it's him you'll find out soon enough from the FBI. It's the witness-protection stuff. It's the fuckin' marshals and the FBI together hiding federal witnesses. You know, federal witness protection program, somethin' like that. They're all over South Florida, the fucks. It's easy down here, lots of money, nice weather. They rat out somebody up in New York or Milwaukee or maybe Chicago, next thing they're down here protected better than the fuckin' president. Then pretty soon they got a new name, new ID, new house, new clothes, new job, the works. The family puts out hits on them, sometimes they get them, but most times they don't. And the fucks are still scammin' and boostin' and stealin'. That's what it's got to be."

Andy nodded.

"The old guy was in a safe house, one the government rents out from the owner. Watch an' see. They stash people there in between stops. Somebody in the mob found out and the guy got whacked. Probably deserved it."

"Who did the hit, any idea?"

Carmine turned around to check his back. He smiled and shook his head.

"No way to tell. From what you describe, the car, the plates, that could be any young wiseguy down from New York to make some money. No fuckin' way to tell. Could be anybody. If you really need to know, I have people I can ask."

"I need to know. And then who hits *him?* And why?" Andy asked anxiously.

Carmine shook his head again. Andy was annoyed but knew he couldn't show it. Respect. He had to give the old man respect to get any information.

"You got me. I ain't never seen nothin' like it. There's no way anybody in on the hit is gonna do it. That's crazy."

They turned back around. The second race was off. This time the old man clutched the tickets tightly and began to pump his fist and whisper under his breath. Andy looked at his own ticket, then back at the field of young, light brown greyhounds as they circled the final turn and headed in to the finish. At the last moment he saw their dog drop from first to third. Carmine pounded the rail. Andy stood silent, another twenty gone.

He waited for the disappointment to pass. "I figure that it was a double hit. The mob hits the old man, then somebody else in the mob has the killer hit for some other reason. Maybe one family in on both hits, maybe two families that don't know what the other's doing."

Carmine shook his head. "It don't work that way. They ain't gonna hire some guy that they want whacked out to do a hit, then whack him too. That don't make no sense. There ain't no way. The capos and the captains talk to each other, and they clear stuff like that with the big capo. And he's a friend of mine, stays down here a lot. No way that coulda happened."

Andy gave the man a disappointed look, then a shrug that asked for Carmine's own theory. The old man finished the cigar and put it out on the pristine marble floor. They moved over a few feet, farther away from the crowd.

"There's one son of a bitch I know who maya had somethin' to do with it," Carmine began. "If anybody down here did it, he woulda known about it or he maya even did it himself. He's a fat, no-good rat. A stoolie. He's also a mean killer without no conscience. No honor. He used to kill for

39

business, and he also used to kill for no good reason. I heard that a guy one time was fuckin' with cars in a restaurant he was at. Just a kid, really. This no-good catches the kid in his car, goes up and stabs him, then shoots him. No fuckin' reason to do that to a kid rippin' cars."

"Who?" Andy sounded insistent. He had to let the retired mobster know that he had to have the name. *Respect.*

"I'll tell ya. Fuck him. He's a no-good rat."

"Right. Who, and where can I find him?"

"You won't have to find him. Call the feds, they know where he is. They got him in that witness program. Benny 'Beans' Pisoli. He was a made guy that turned stoolie and was chicken on doin' time in that case where the FBI infiltrated all those pizza parlors. Remember? Lotsa fuckin' heads were gonna roll off over that one. Lotsa guys were gonna become hamburger on that fuck-up, and Benny was one of 'em. So he turned rat and decided to get in with the feds while the gettin' was good. He's somewhere between Vero Beach and Lauderdale, that's all I know. He's s'posed to have a new name, some kinda business. The fuckin' feds got him all set up, go talk to them. That fat fuck gonna have somethin' to do with your mess, I'm sure of it."

Andy repeated the name to himself. He had never heard of the guy before, but it had been a while since he had run up against any New York mobsters.

"Like you cops say, he's got a motive. The fat fuck's got lots of enemies, most who want to kill him. He turned on lots of people. Fuckin' *hundreds* of cases the government made on his word alone, if you can believe that. Maybe Benny was the guy's next stop after whackin' that old man in the mansion, so maybe Benny tailed him and whacked him first, who knows?" Carmine smiled.

Andy thought about it. It was complicated, but possible. The federal witness protection program. He'd never had any direct contact with it.

40

"What else can you tell me about this witness stuff? You know anybody in it? You know who's runnin' it?" Andy asked.

Carmine shook his head and looked back down at the program. Then there was another quick glance all around.

"You'd know better than me, you got the cop connections. The FBI, I guess. Lots of ex-mob guys in it down here, that's for sure," Carmine answered.

Andy thought over "ex-mob." He knew the penalty for being divorced from the Mafia—eventual death. Few escaped.

"I'm going to Miami after this, meeting with an old FBI friend of mine. I'll ask him. You may have hit on something."

"It's gotta be. I know who the old man was, I'm sure of it. He became a rat, so he was no fuckin' good. But I knew him, I knew his kids and his family. I feel bad for the guy in a way. But he shoulda known." Carmine took out another cigar and lit it up in deep, exhaustive breaths, filling the area with the bitter aroma. He leaned against the stainless steel railing next to the glass, looking down at the third race's entries.

Andy looked down at the gate area as handlers led the dogs onto the field. He glanced at the crowd, then back at his father's old friend. He knew that there was a lot the old man was holding back.

"Fuck it, I give up. I don't see shit on this one, Andy. You see anything on this?" Carmine pushed the program across the railing and gave out a disgusted sigh along with a phlegm-filled cough caused by the corrosive cigar.

Andy took the program in hand and gave it his full attention. Within a few seconds he spotted the winner. He took out his pen and circled the name. He would let Carmine play it; he would let the old man win something. He wanted nothing more, no more information, no more bets. It was time to go.

41

Carmine took the program back and read it over quickly, coming to Andy's choice.

"Bad Omen," Carmine read off. He shook his head. The dog was a long shot.

"Bet on it, Carmine. Bet it to win," Andy said as he turned to leave.

From Hollywood Andy drove to Collins Avenue and ate lunch at a favorite beachfront spot that overwhelmed him with Coney Island hot dogs, raw clams, corn on the cob, and tart New York beer. The waitresses dressed in tight shorts and skimpy blouses, and the loud and brightly lit interior made it a pleasant place to eat and watch the tourists. He finished the meal off with half a basket of onion rings, and left to take the leisurely route down the busy, touristy ocean road.

From Miami Beach and its south-end decay and art deco Andy took the breezy Julia Tuttle Causeway to Miami proper. He drove around, visiting spots he hadn't seen in over a year, areas that held memories of his fifteen years in Miami PD—Overtown, Liberty City, Downtown, Bayside, with the glistening water and thousands of boats. Then he drove past the new police building with its large brown façade and overdone landscaping, finally winding his way over the Miami River to the old department building, the one he knew best, the one he'd spent most of his career in. He was saddened by its abandonment and decay. He checked his watch; it was time to drive on to FBI headquarters.

He parked on the street by the old federal building just after the rush hour had abandoned downtown Miami. It was a little before six when he walked into the lobby and showed the guard his ID.

"Andy Amato, West Palm PD. I'm meeting Phil Wesley in the pistol range."

The guard was an older Cuban. He nodded, not really taking his eyes off the dozen or so TV monitors. He handed Andy a visitor's pass, which the detective clipped to his shirt.

The building was dark, but its air conditioning seemed barely adequate. Andy sensed the accumulated summer heat in the aged stucco walls. In the basement, he heard the muffled thumps of practice handgun ammunition and smelled the almost sweet nitrites from the cheap powder. He spotted Wesley through the safety glass and pushed open the door.

The agent was facing Andy, his right arm outstretched toward a target, his left arm bent, the hand gripping his hip. As Andy approached, Phil Wesley let rip six rapid-fire shots at the distant silhouette.

Andy walked up behind him and stared down the range at the purposely darkened alleyway. Wesley pulled the target in and counted out the holes.

"Again. Four out of six. Damn!" Wesley took off his amber shooting glasses and laid them and his revolver on the bench. They shook hands.

"That's not bad in the dark from fifteen yards. Four in the kill ring with just two in the hostage," Andy said. He looked over the black and white silhouette of a man holding a woman around the throat and pointing a gun at her head. An FBI innovation—Andy had never seen this kind of target before.

"Right. It's not bad. But not good. I'm trying out for an elite new squad. Hostage Negotiation and Suspect Termination. Believe that? Things are getting that bad down here. It'll be fifteen guys who can put every round from a rifle, shotgun, and pistol in the bad-guy part of the target from fifteen yards, in this lighting. So far I'm okay with the rifle and shotgun—it's just this fuckin' thing giving me fits."

Andy laughed along with Wesley. They stood back from the target aisle and made small talk.

"You used to go up to Palm Beach a lot, if I remember," Andy said. "You used to have a hideaway, right?"

Wesley smiled and winked. "Right. A house. Northeast West Palm. Still have it, just don't use it much anymore. Not as young as I used to be."

"Youth is a state of mind, I figure. I used to think I was getting old when I hit thirty. Then I met Gabe."

"You have the same questions you did yesterday. That curious look of yours, I see it in your eyes. It's not good on stuff like this, Andy." Wesley seemed nervous.

"You're right," Andy said. "It's not good. But it's the way it is."

Wesley hesitated before he spoke. "I couldn't talk in front of Gruen. He'd have had fits and reported me if I'da said one word to you about what we had there. It's top-secret stuff."

"Right. Well, Gruen sure isn't around now. And I'm on the case, that's official. So how about we start from the beginning?"

"The beginning? I'm not sure there is one. How much do you know already?"

"The old man was in the federal witness protection program. Who he is I don't know yet. A New York contract hit. Somebody who knew where the old man was exactly, that's the only way to explain the alarm key. The killer was a young up-and-coming type from New York, from one of the main families. Then somebody kills *him.* After that, I'm all ears."

Wesley walked back over to the firing lane and stapled up another paper target, a bad-guy-and-hostage silhouette. "That's good," he said. "That's more than I thought you'd have in this short time. I underestimated you."

"No problem. Keep talking," Andy replied.

Wesley pressed a button on the electronic display, which sent the target fifteen yards out in low light. "I can get fired for talking to you," he said simply.

"You have to do the right thing, Phil. This is the right thing," Andy replied.

There was a short pause as Wesley peered at the silhouette. He fingered his gun, picked it up from the bench, and loaded it. "The old mobster was Charles Portuno, a New York captain in the Genovese family. He'd had six months in the protection program. The U.S. marshals had just let up round-the-clock protection on him. He had two more days to do in Palm Beach, then he would be going off to St. Petersburg for his new identity. Fuck, Andy, I just blew my whole career if you say anything."

Andy nodded as they stared at each other. There was understanding. "What was his story? Why was he talking to the feds?"

"No choice. He didn't want to do life at hard time in a federal pen for racketeering. And we had him on conspiracy to murder, a few other things. He didn't want the slammer, it would've been his first time. This was his only way out. So he gave up his friends."

Andy mulled over the part about giving up his friends, and remembered back to Carmine talking to him when he was a teenager. *"You never give up your friends,"* the friend of his father would tell him regularly.

"Do you know who the wiseguy in the Lincoln was?"

"Yeah. Can't remember his name, not important. Just a soldier. A high-class, well-paid killer. When he wasn't doing that, his rap sheet said he was into hijacking, stolen property, all the usual stuff."

"Thirty-eight to the back of the head. Who did it?" Andy asked.

Wesley laughed. "Your guess is as good as mine. Could be anybody. Besides, that's not our problem, that's a local case. We're one less mobster, the killer is now dead. Case is closed. Who shot the guy in the Lincoln is a local problem for you or Palm Beach PD to work out."

Andy detected the insincerity in his old friend's voice. It was an indistinct coldness he had not heard from Phil Wesley before. He knew the FBI was not walking out on a case like that just because the killer's brain was scrambled. There was more to it, Andy was certain.

"What else can you give me on this, Phil?" Andy made himself sound both sincere and pleading.

"I can't give you much. It's the hazards of the mobster game, if you ask me. Getting a protected witness killed is not that common, thank God. And we're real successful at keeping bad publicity like this out of the papers. The people might lose faith in their government, all that stuff. There have been others—that's life in the mob. There was one killed in Fort Pierce maybe three months ago, and another mafioso killed in Vero Beach about six weeks ago. It's been a bad summer so far. That's the way it goes. We all know how much the Sicilian Mafia loves a tattletale."

Andy knew the reference was directed at his own Sicilian heritage. He let it pass. "Phil, my friend, I think you're holding out on me. I don't think you're telling me everything."

Wesley smiled and shook his head. He put the glasses on, stretched out and steadied his arm, aimed, and fired off all six new rounds in rapid succession. He brought in the target—four out of six in the bad guy's chest, but two more killing the black silhouette of the victim.

"Damn!" Wesley pulled the glasses off and threw them on the counter.

Andy reached over and picked up a new target, stapling it quickly on the cardboard as Wesley stepped away. He sent the target gliding silently back, into the shadows. "Charles Portuno is dead for some reason I don't think you're telling me. The killer is dead for the same reason. Now you're telling me there have been prior killings. You and the rest of the FBI have a pile of shit on your hands. Let me help you out. Level with me."

Wesley smiled the innocent farmboy smile that lit up his fair complexion and soft, light brown hair. He shook his head at Andy.

46

Amato stepped back and quickly broke his 9-millimeter free of the leather shoulder holster. He raised the gun as Wesley stepped farther away. He didn't aim, simply stepped forward and thrust the large gun at the cloaked double silhouette.

The bullets started at one a second, then increased until the last ten rounds were a continuous sputter, almost as fast as a machine gun. Andy inspected the weapon when the slide locked back, then loaded a fresh magazine and reholstered. Wesley stepped forward, still smiling and shaking his head, and brought the target in.

Andy was pleased—fifteen out of fifteen in the bad guy's chest. The pattern was slightly larger than a softball, all in the kill zone.

"Good shooting," Wesley said unemotionally. "Portuno is dead. That's tough luck on me, Gruen and the rest of the FBI, and the marshal's office. We'll catch hell for a while. Sure, we'll investigate what we can about where the key came from, how they tracked down the house, and all that. Maybe we'll get somewhere, maybe we won't. It'll all pass as other stuff comes up. It always does. Soon, nobody important will remember."

"I thought all these witnesses were guarded," Andy said in a tone more like a question than a statement.

"You've got to be kidding. Guarded by who? Not us or the marshals, there isn't enough manpower. They'll get direct protection up to a certain point, then they're on their own."

"How long has all this been going on down here?" he asked.

"Since the sixties, since the Valachi case. It's nothing new, the Bureau and the marshals just avoid publicity at all costs. There's been very little written about it. That's the way we like it."

Andy nodded. Wesley prepared to put up another target.

"Who's Benny 'Beans' Pisoli? You know him?" he asked.

Wesley was caught off guard. He stopped, smiled at Andy, then stapled up the new silhouette.

"Good choice of names. Where'd you come up with that?"

"A connection. Said the name may have a bad guy attached to it that could pull something like this second hit—the piggyback."

Wesley nodded. "Maybe. Pisoli certainly is bad enough. But he's watched. He's deep, deep into the program. Almost round-the-clock protection. He's *special.* Stuff I can't go into. I couldn't even tell you where he is now—the marshals have him. Strictly classified. He's a badass, and the government doesn't want to be embarrassed if he pulls something naughty. And he's got enough enemies to fill a small-town phone book. But he's strictly a con man and an opportunist, with an appetite for loose women. I doubt if he could pull something like this. I doubt if he'd have a reason to."

"Pisoli and these guys in the program are allowed to have guns?" Andy asked.

Wesley thought a moment. "It's like anything else. You can't be everywhere. They're not supposed to, but you can't always watch them. If they want a gun, they know where to find one."

There was silence. Wesley sent the target silently outward again.

"You want some advice, Phil? Drop the fancy stuff. Get rid of the glasses, get rid of the dumb stance. Get rid of the revolver while you're at it—try a nine-millimeter. Shooting's natural. It's an extension of the self. It's pointing and stroking, that's all. Just bend, point, and shoot—forget all the extra crap."

"I'd like to. But this is how I was taught, and this is the gun I like." Wesley raised the revolver again and rapidly stroked the trigger. Andy muffled his ears with his hands and looked down range as the muzzle flash lit up the target for an instant with each shot. When it was over he thought Wesley had done better.

The FBI agent ripped off his glasses and hearing protection. "You and I go back to a lot of cases, Andy. I'd tell you if you had something to worry about. This ain't it. This is mob stuff, and if a few mafiosos happen to trip and get boo-boos, nobody really gives a shit. You know that as well as I do. I can't say I'm getting all hot and bothered about the whole thing. It's basically the marshal's problem, anyway."

The silhouette came in. Wesley had five out of six in the bad guy's chest. The last round was up and to the right, half an inch into the neck of the hostage. The FBI agent just stood and shook his head.

"You need more practice, Phil. That isn't going to cut it," Andy said as he started toward the door. Wesley, preparing another target, grunted at his friend.

"It always used to be good enough, five out of six. Nobody used to complain. Things are getting rough. More violence. More lawsuits. Even cops are being taken hostage. Happened the other day. One cop got his gun taken away, and he was held hostage right in front of his partner. The guy was a rookie, didn't know what to do."

Andy nodded. "If they were partners they should have had a plan. You know—drop and shoot."

"Right." Wesley pressed the button and the new target went back out.

They said goodbye and Andy took the stairs back up to the lobby, depositing the ID card with the old Cuban guard. He stepped out into the Miami evening dampness and thought of Charles Portuno and the young New York wiseguy, both unlucky enough to meet one early morning in Palm Beach.

Phil Wesley was holding back, just like Carmine, he knew. As he put his key in the door of the Saab his mind left the killing and settled on Gabe and the long ride home.

3

For Keeps

He stood back and admired his handiwork. It was surreal to him, almost imaginary. He looked at it as though it was a painting he had seen hanging somewhere, twisting his head from side to side trying to make out the details through all the haze.

He trembled slightly, then his stomach jerked, surprising him. He focused on the man's face, then the hands, then the gun, then the blood. The eerie quality of the scene before him still wrenched his stomach, but with delight now, not disgust, not anything he was any longer ashamed of. He had come to understand and accept the actions that he took (not rationalizing, for that implied guilt) and he stood back, away from his latest work, feeling almost pity, almost sorrow, for the person too stupid to escape from his grip.

"Stupid," he said out loud. "Too easy." He shook his head and smiled.

He hoped the man was finally dead. He stood perfectly still, listening for breathing, and was sure there was none. He took his gun out and held it against the forehead of the man, above the blindfold, and thought to put a bullet clean into the cerebrum, just below the hairline. He didn't, wanting instead for the body to be found just like it was.

Perfect.

The man had killed himself! What a laugh. He thought of his lawyer explaining his innocence to a jury. The man had pulled the trigger all on his own and had shot himself in the head.

Technicality. Case closed. Not guilty, Your Honor.

He put his gun away, then lifted the key to the apartment out of his shirt pocket and threw it to the ground just inside the doorway. He looked up and tried to remember what the man had looked like alive. There was only a cloudy face, just like the little red-haired girl running through the field in the painting. His mind went blank.

With a hurried motion, with only a faint recollection of what he had done, he was out the door and gone.

Andy Amato ran hard, his thighs cramping and his lungs blowing out sour air faster than he could inhale. He kept up, even at one point gained some ground, but then quickly fell back. His ankles twisted too easily after the first mile in the sand, and he almost cried out to tell her to slow down.

Gabe ran intently but with less exertion. She pulled out farther in front, her strides reminding Andy of a flamingo, seeming to leap in the air as she ran. He tried to keep his mind off his own exhaustion by looking at his wife's graceful marathon, and noticing the sweat on her back, which was only half covered by her cut-off gold and maroon Florida State T-shirt. Andy finally grunted loudly. Gabe turned and slowed for her jogging partner. They matched each other, slowing down, Andy on the right by the ocean, finally able to steady his breath and continue.

In the dawn light the ocean was a flat gray and the beach cottages were covered by a fine, smoky mist. They ran past abandoned piles of planking, beach chairs, and more than one weathered Palm Beach gazebo. The sun was over the horizon to their right, straining through the clouds. There was only the slightest hint of the typical South Florida pink and blue.

The Amatos ran three times a week, always at least two miles, always at sunrise, before they went to work. This morning Andy had picked the location of their run.

"Hold up," he finally sputtered as they ran past one of the many underground tunnels leading under Ocean Boulevard to the mansions opposite the beach. Gabe ran a few more yards ahead, then turned. Andy could finally see sunlight reflecting off her shiny shorts.

"Is this it?" she asked without panting.

He stopped and bent in agony at his midsection, putting his head down by his knees. He wasn't used to running in sand, especially not on a breezeless, muggy late-July morning.

He stood back up and nodded, catching his breath. "This is it," he said simply, looking into the dark tunnel.

Gabe lit their way into the sandy grotto with a small flashlight she carried on her keychain. There was a cross-breeze, making the air bearable. The lack of an odor surprised him. It was wet, but cooler than he expected. After a minute they emerged on the west side of the tunnel, next to some hedges.

Without a word they jogged along the sidewalk, around a corner, and then along the high fence. They slowed and then stopped in front of the main gate. The monogram *GL* stood high and proud on the black wrought iron.

1712 Seabreeze. They looked over the landscaping, still able to see plenty of yellow crime scene tape around the front and side of the estate.

"This is not a normal murder," he said softly.

She nodded and moved closer to inspect the gate.

"I went and talked to Carmine," Andy said. "He figured

it out right away. Then I confirmed it with Wesley down in Miami. This was a government safe house. Run by the government to stash witnesses. The U.S. Marshals Service keeping mobsters under wraps. Top-secret stuff."

Gabe nodded without surprise and moved forward. Andy followed. They walked slowly, inspecting the grounds, peeking around corners like children in a zoo looking for a glimpse of some rare, exotic beast. Nothing had changed from two days before except that now the estate was quiet and they could inspect the location more clearly without the rush of police work interfering.

"The autopsy tell you anything?" he asked.

"What we expected. And a little more. The thirty-eight that killed the hit man didn't have a silencer. The powder burns show that much. Powerful hit—maybe a three-five-seven. Palm Beach PD had a detective there. They took the pictures and the examiner's report." She smiled at him and raised her eyebrows.

Andy's chest finally stopped heaving. He took in a long, purposeful breath of ocean air and looked over to where the Lincoln had been parked.

"Wesley has a suspect. A badass mafioso named Pisoli who's under protection down here—some kind of defector from up north, didn't want to do jail time. And something else that Phil says is 'special.' Pisoli sounds capable of hunting the hit man down and blowing him away, especially if he knew that *he* was the next mob guy on the list to get whacked."

"Right. Makes sense, I guess," Gabe said simply. She stroked her hair back to her ponytail as she looked at the house, hoping for an extra detail or some new revelation.

"There's been a couple other killings before this. Probably not by the same guy, though. Also mob hits. What makes this one different is that the killer got bumped off. Just doesn't make sense."

"I got the name of the guy in the Lincoln late yesterday.

From NYPD. Matched the prints also. The FBI already has it—he was from the Guardinaro mob," Gabe said.

"I know," Andy answered. They moved off around the corner, then walked up to another gate, this one for pedestrians only. They were able to look in from the back, toward the patio sliding doors. Palm Beach PD had them boarded up.

"The prints on the car were all smudged. Whoever grabbed and opened that door, and then shut it, wore gloves. They lifted some smooth glove prints off the driver's window."

As they walked back to the main gate, Gabe began speaking slowly, gesturing with her hands. "The alarm key. That's number one. Number two is the killer's watch. It was stopped at exactly ten minutes. He was timing himself. He did a job like that in a mansion that size in only ten minutes. All of that means one thing . . ." Gabe's voice trailed off.

"Inside knowledge." Andy finished her statement. "A mobster bought some information or was able to muscle somebody with knowledge of the guy's whereabouts."

She nodded. "Maybe some clerical help on the inside. Happens all the time," Gabe added. Andy looked at her. He had thought of it himself. Some low-level worker leaking information from inside the FBI or the U.S. marshal's office.

"Or someone dropped a dime," Andy said. It was his least favorite theory. "For some reason somebody called up the mob and told them where he was." Gabe nodded but didn't reply.

They left 1712 Seabreeze just as the sun was totally up and the horizon burst out finally in Florida orange and light indigo. They ran back through the tunnel, emerging on the beach. Sea gulls overhead barked to greet the morning light. The sea odor was strong and almost sour.

They stopped, then began running in place, Andy obviously about to say something. "We've got someone new to meet. I made the appointment late yesterday. I hope you didn't tell Captain Barney to expect us too early."

"He's going to hear you call him that one day, Teddy, and all hell's gonna break loose."

Andy laughed. Gabe gave him an affectionate bump with her shoulder. "I told him we'd come in late. But tell me where we're heading."

"Can't. I wanted to surprise you. Anyway, it's right by the station."

"I hate surprises. Tell me where." Gabe sounded like a little kid. Andy knew that she really did abhor surprises. Everything had to be orderly and predictable. He loved to frazzle that trait in his lovely but sometimes irritating wife.

"Shut up and run," he said matter-of-factly as he broke into a fast sprint, his feet pounding the sand and carrying him well ahead of his wife. She trotted after him. He held the lead for the moment, but he knew he wouldn't keep it for the mile back to the car.

The four-story building was not one that people ever noticed. Gray concrete with dull granite columns, 701 Clematis Street was marked only by one small sign: PAUL G. ROGERS FEDERAL BUILDING. It was a small structure by South Florida government standards—next to the post office, a block from West Palm Beach PD, not much of anything by itself. If you weren't looking for a U.S. government agency you could spend a lifetime in West Palm and never distinguish the building from the dozens of similar ones in the area.

The Amatos went home to shower and change, then drove over. Andy pulled the Saab in and scooted into a parking space. He placed the blue light on the dash and ignored the parking meter. He and Gabe walked quickly toward the door. It was just before nine and government workers entered at a slow pace, one or two at a time. Andy immediately compared the complex favorably to the madhouse the Miami federal building was by this time of the morning.

They were both surprised by the lack of metal detectors and armed federal guards. It was their first chance to visit the building and they were taken aback by its distinct simplicity.

Andy looked over the directory: federal courts, FBI, U.S. Attorney, Secret Service, Immigration, U.S. Marshal. He finally found the snack bar entry on the lower right. They headed toward the elevators.

The man didn't look like the picture his voice had conjured up. Andy always imagined a person's looks after a phone conversation, and he hadn't come close with Tom Sunderland. He thought the federal agent would be small and wiry, a clerk type with glasses and stooped shoulders. Instead he was a huge Swede. There was the short blond hair, the light brown eyes, the tan, the prominent but well-proportioned nose. He wore a brown suit with brown wingtips. He sat on the far wall of the snack bar stirring a large glass of iced tea.

They shook hands. Andy saw that Gabe took in the man's good looks and physique and returned an uncharacteristically girlish smile. Men's looks seldom impressed her, except the exceptionally good-looking and muscular ones.

"Thanks for meeting us so early. I wanted to talk to you first thing, before the day wore on and we got tied up," Andy said.

"Sure thing. You two grab a coffee or something." They both did. There was an old, well-dressed woman behind the counter puffing on a long brown cigarette. Sunderland waved at her to charge his account for the detectives' coffees.

"So what brings West Palm PD to our humble snack bar this morning?" Sunderland said, laughing, and Andy chuckled politely. Gabe purposely looked away and fixed their cups.

56

"We're helping Palm Beach PD on a homicide from Monday. Two homicides, actually. An old man and the young New York punk that killed him. Ring a bell?"

Sunderland smiled and nodded. "Sure. But I didn't think that was a local case."

"It is. Homicide. Death penalty, all that. Don't get worried, I know how to work with the feds. I just wanted to talk to you and find out some answers."

"I'm sorry, I can't give you anything. What I know is strictly classified government info. Not much I can say." Sunderland retained his smile.

"Right. Then confirm some information for us. It's important that we know what we're dealing with." Andy looked at Gabe.

She removed her black leather notebook from her purse and opened it, flipping backward past the autopsy notes.

Sunderland sat and listened stone-faced as Gabe read off all the details. Mafioso, .22, silencer, gloves, alarm key, stopwatch. She then rattled off all the details of the autopsies. The agent remained unfazed.

Andy mentioned Benny "Beans" Pisoli. Sunderland's eyebrows rose briefly. His lower lip pursed. Andy saw that the man was not the stone-cold foreign type he was trying to portray. He reminded Andy of a blond Arnold Schwarzenegger in any of several movies.

"You obviously have informants," the deputy marshal said.

"Obviously," Gabe replied. Andy smiled. Carmine would be proud.

"I want to talk to Pisoli. I understand he's deep in your witness protection program. Whether or not he's a suspect, he's a good place to start." Andy gave the man a friendly, brotherly tap on the elbow. The Swede's eyes became wide and he looked away.

"Not possible," Sunderland said, shaking his head.

"And I need a list of the mobsters that have gotten themselves killed in the last year while in the program down here. Then a list of those that are still in the program and are living in South Florida." Sunderland chuckled, then laughed; so did Andy. Gabe remained straight-faced and serious.

"Amato, you have balls, I swear. I've never had any local cop come in here and ask me for stuff like this. Now I know how you got your reputation. Good homicide cop, that's what everyone said. *Very* good. The best. I can see why."

"Thanks. I need Pisoli, and the lists."

Sunderland shook his head. "Not possible."

"We can go to the Palm Beach state's attorney and get a subpoena," Andy said, still smiling.

"Quashed within an hour," Sunderland replied indifferently.

"I can dig around and find Pisoli myself, which is guaranteed to really aggravate you and your friends. Or we can work together. There's nothing says we can't be friends and partners, all that jazz. We're both cops, remember?"

"Right. But this is federal stuff. We're talking a very sensitive program. More important than a few murders."

"Listen, somebody with inside information is killing your protected mobsters. I may not be a fed with a four-year business degree, but I didn't graduate from the police academy yesterday, either. You've got a problem, we can help."

"The problem will be taken care of. The U.S. Marshals Service and the FBI can handle it. Thanks for your offer. We'll pass."

"If you admit there's a problem," Gabe said, "why don't you give us more information so we can work the case, maybe get some leads? We'll keep it confidential, then turn it all over to you when we're done." She spoke without emotion, but Andy saw the sparkle in her eye as she talked to the tall, attractive Sunderland.

"The problem is not like you're used to. You locals deal

with statutory crimes that are clear-cut. There's a killing, you investigate, you arrest. Simple. Our life is more complicated. There's program security, politics, all those things we have to be concerned with in this building. You have no idea. What's going on here is not that simple."

Andy caught and held the deputy marshal's eye. He knew that Sunderland could be persuaded to tell them more.

They got up from the stools in the snack bar, following Sunderland as he motioned them down the hall toward his office. They walked through a small reception area with a secretary into a large inner office with plenty of diplomas and bookcases. Andy looked over a color photo on the far wall of Sunderland shaking hands with Ronald Reagan. In another he was side by side with Vice President Quayle.

"Why are you coming to me with this?" Sunderland asked.

"You run the local program. You're the logical place to start," Andy said.

"The FBI's heading the investigation into the killings. You should be asking them. We run the protection program, we set up these people with their ID's and new lives. But Gruen and the FBI investigate crimes and assaults on federal witnesses, not us."

"Gruen's not talking. That's obvious. I could tell after five minutes that the man is a typical overpuffed agent all proud of himself and unwilling to give local cops the right time. I'll get to Gruen, but only when I have more."

The three were still standing. Andy wanted to keep an advantage; he could detect Sunderland weakening.

"He's the man to talk to," Sunderland said. "He can give you more details. Everything I know is classified enough so that telling you will cost me my job and my pension. I like you, Amato. You've got guts, but you're not worth all that."

"Gruen is a cocksucker. Why don't *you* tell me?"

"Don't be so rough on the man. He's had a bad time. About a year ago his daughter was raped and murdered up around North Palm Beach. It was a pretty brutal stabbing. He took it hard. He has to get to know you. Give it a few days, then try him again."

The phone rang and Sunderland picked it up. Andy and Gabe didn't get a chance to react to the news about Gruen's daughter. Sunderland talked for a few seconds and hung up.

"I can find out or you can help me," Andy said. "There's nobody here but us three, and I assume your office isn't bugged. Tell me what I need to know. The prior killings— what type weapon was used? Are they related? Is there a suspect?"

Sunderland sat down with a sigh. Andy knew he had gotten through. He and Gabe remained standing.

"There were two earlier ones. The one in Palm Beach makes three. The killer getting shot is four, if you're counting him. All killings were with thirty-eights, except for the old man getting it with the twenty-two. There are no suspects, except the most obvious. The Mafia is killing off all the witnesses they can. There are lots of big cases being made, lots of witnesses. This last one confirms that the Mafia is contracting out these killings."

"How do they know where to go? How are they finding where these guys are hidden out at?" Andy asked.

Sunderland shook his head. "I wish I knew. Meanwhile we're guarding the real important ones, every one we can. We're moving people around. We're keeping tabs on the northern mobsters we spot down here. We're existing as best we can with the limited manpower we have—both we and the FBI."

"What about Pisoli? Is he 'real important'?"

Sunderland nodded.

"Are your people always with him? Have you asked him what he knows about all this?"

"Who told you about Pisoli?" Sunderland asked.

It was Andy Amato's turn to shake his head.

60

"Pisoli is scum. But he's our job. We protect him," Sunderland said with a disgust Andy had not heard before.

"I still want to talk to him," Andy said.

"Against rules. Can't happen. Not at my level. It'll take a supervisor from Washington to authorize that. Pisoli is special, he's in the elite at the top of the witness pile."

Andy nodded. "So I've heard. But try and arrange it. I can set it up, but it'll take longer and get more people involved. You do it and there'll be less people becoming suspicious."

Sunderland hesitated. "I'll try. But I doubt it." He smiled at the West Palm detectives. "You two are something," he added.

Andy didn't acknowledge the compliment. "Pisoli. Don't forget. See what you can do for us by Friday."

Sunderland smiled and shook his head again. It was a expression of amazement at the persuasive power of a local cop.

They shook hands and went for the elevator.

Andy watched the glimmer in Gabe's eye as they left the big Swede's office. Getting in the Saab, he wondered exactly what, if anything, his wife was thinking.

They rode the two blocks from the federal building to the PD in silence. Gabe had her notebook open and made some notes about the conversation with Sunderland. Andy replayed the entire investigation through his mind, centering on the talks with Carmine, with Wesley, and now with Sunderland. He was trying to get a feel for where the investigation should go.

The three-story West Palm Beach police building was tan and bright orange, surrounded with expensive tropical landscaping. It was encircled by tenements and abandoned businesses, having for company on the far west end of downtown only the post office, federal building, and Florida state office building. At night the police building became a large, isolated, brightly lit warehouse of human problems, sins, and failings.

Andy always parked in front of the building, never in the employee lot. He and Gabe got out and walked toward the entrance. Andy would always cut across the long expanse of neatly mowed grass, Gabe would walk in a square around the designated sidewalk. Then Andy would wait at the front door, holding it open for his wife, who would berate him about walking on the lawn. Andy would counter with his theory that smart architects would lay down sidewalks only after people had worn a natural pathway up to the door.

They went up the stairs to the detective bureau, finding the area deserted, much out of character for ten A.M. on a Wednesday. Andy and Gabe were heading toward their separate areas when the door to the captain's office came abruptly open and Bobby Jacobson looked at each of them in turn with a concerned scowl.

"In here. Both of you." Jacobson was holding the phone, stretched from the desk to the doorway. He said a few more words into the mouthpiece and then hung up. Andy and Gabe came dutifully in behind him, mock concern on their faces.

"We were following up, Captain. Sorry we're late. I thought Gabe told—"

"That's not it. Sit down, both of you," Jacobson snapped.

They sat, and Jacobson leaned back in his chair and closed the blinds, shutting out the sun and leaving only the dim light from a single ceiling-hung fluorescent lamp.

"I've been on the phone all morning. First the deputy chief, then the FBI, then the U.S. marshal. I had a lot of uncomfortable questions to answer. That's okay, that's my job. Things like why we're investigating a murder out of our jurisdiction. Things like how the Amatos are getting in the way of a federal investigation. How Andy is sticking his nose in something that's none of his business . . . ."

Andy almost countered but the phone rang. Jacobson looked at them with a smirk and hit the button for the speaker-phone.

"Captain Jacobson," he answered. His secretary's voice came across with a name from an unrelated case. Jacobson told her to take a message.

"I thought that would be Gruen from the FBI again. He's called twice. He doesn't want you nosing around this thing. He says you're known to be friendly with a *Herald* reporter. He's afraid the press will get in on it and relate it back to their witness protection stuff. They can't have that."

"There *is* no federal investigation, Captain. It's all mired up in politics and personalities. And Palm Beach can't really handle it by themselves. I was just trying to get the ball rolling—that's what you sent us over there for."

"Well, the ball's rolling. The feds got it. What Palm Beach does isn't our problem. You two write up a final report on where you're at so far and we'll file it and forward it to all the right people."

"Somebody in the government is leaking information, Captain. There's no doubt. If you go over the facts we've got so far, you can't dispute that someone's getting information to the mob on the whereabouts of these people. That's maybe why the feds *aren't* the boys to be handling this."

Jacobson shook his head and his eyes showed disbelief. Gabe opened her notebook and gave him all the details about the alarm key, the stopwatch, the method of entry, and how the hit man did the killing. Andy told him about the two prior killings that the feds were trying to keep hushed up.

"It's not our case," Jacobson repeated.

"We have the expertise. We may be the only department in this area with the ability to follow up, besides the feds, who may have a leak." Andy leaned forward onto Jacobson's dark oak desk.

"And I'm supposed to say what to the deputy chief? That

you've decided or we've decided to spend our resources on something that isn't our case, when the feds want us off it? Because the feds *may* have a leak? Think, Amato. Use your brains."

"That's politics, Captain. Not brains."

"You two are off the case. Get back on the other ones you have holding. You have just three working days till your vacation. I want all the loose ends tied up."

The Mallory docks at sunset in Key West flashed into Andy's mind, then quickly out again.

"This is a regional problem, Captain. We're the biggest city in the area. It affects us. Not directly, not yet. But we can't ignore it. There's a lot here we can't put our fingers on yet. Just let us look at a few more things until Friday."

Jacobson shook his head. "Off," he muttered. The phone rang.

Jacobson listened and wrote on his calendar–desk mat. He rolled his eyes at Andy and Gabe and smiled. "Good. Something to keep you two occupied for a day or two. Keep you out of trouble. How fortunate you got back just in time." He hung up the phone.

Andy wanted to argue to be left on the Palm Beach case. He almost did. Gabe came up next to him and pinched his shoulder, cutting off his first word.

Jacobson, still smiling, looked at Gabe, who was ready with her notepad. Andy was slumped in his seat, the hurt look of a disappointed little boy on his face.

"Looks like a suicide. Patrol isn't sure. Strange one. It's on Executive Center Drive, just south of the baseball stadium, off Congress Avenue. Have Dispatch give you the address. They say it's messy and they can't rule out foul play, but it looks like somebody just got fed up and blew their brains out. That'll keep you busy the rest of the day."

Gabe closed the notebook and tugged at Andy's arm. He rose out of the chair slowly, still frowning at the captain. He almost said something again.

64

"Teddy, let's go," Gabe said, cutting him off.

Jacobson gave them a smile of victory and waved goodbye to them as they backed out of his office.

Suicide, Andy thought to himself. *We're homicide detectives. How degrading.*

He kept turning around, about to say something to Jacobson, motioning with his hands that he was going to yell something back, but Gabe kept tugging until Andy followed behind her down the stairs and back out to the bright morning sunlight.

4

A Way to Go

It wasn't a suicide. Andy saw that right away, as soon as they walked past the young patrol officer guarding the outer perimeter and ventured into the living room where the body was still sitting upright, a gun taped into its right hand, and a bullet in its head.

Blood was everywhere. The man had been shot five or six times at least, Andy saw. But none of this meant anything to him. What he *felt* when first walking into a crime scene was what he went by.

The gun and the corpse's hand were wrapped with heavy silver duct tape; the arm and hand were heavily taped to his head so that the gun pointed at the man's brains and nowhere else. Andy saw the man's finger on the trigger.

Suicide? Andy thought again.

He looked at the dead man—an older man in a business suit, slumped back in the chair, and he knew it was a homicide. It was a quick decision, but he had made his mind up, and that was how he would proceed.

People committing suicide didn't tape the gun to their

hand and then the hand to their head. They didn't shoot themselves all over before the coup de grace to the head, either. But Andy kept studying the unearthly scene. He shook his head. He almost wasn't sure.

Andy made snap judgments and stuck by them; Gabe did not. He was right in all the cases he'd ever worked, and all the ones they'd worked since being together. He knew of no exceptions; his first instincts, his first impressions, always turned out to be correct. Sometimes details were missing, but he knew where to start. Gabe would analyze, summarize, retrace, and scrutinize before deciding. It drove him crazy— he sometimes couldn't be near her or participate in her analytical sessions; he preferred to investigate a homicide by feel and touch, by gut reaction. Gabe treated them like trigonometry formulas. She knew how Andy worked and so she would remain quiet, never insisting that he mull over the details along with her. He would ask her for a particular fact and she would give it to him—never anything more. And she would never ridicule his instinctive methods—she knew his batting average.

Andy knew that he could work on his own—had worked most of his career on his own—but he preferred being with Gabe. Her scientific insights sometimes came in handy. But he also believed that without him, she would have made a competent but mediocre homicide detective.

In fifteen years Andy had walked into the worst crime scenes the city of Miami had to offer. He'd seen drug executions, castrations, bludgeonings, electrocutions, firebombings, hackings, drownings, and every other method anyone could use to kill another human being. He'd worked homicides in the heyday of the Mariel boatlift, when Miami skyrocketed to number one in the nation for murders.

Shootings were commonplace; stabbings a close and obvious second. In most cases he found the suspect at the scene or nearby, very often ready to surrender and confess. These were the most routine, the ones that a homicide detective could do almost asleep—the domestic argument, the drug rip-off, the angry boyfriend/girlfriend/lover. For these Andy and the others followed a simple formula called the "24-hour rule." For the first twenty-four hours after the homicide you concentrate all your efforts and resources on investigating the prior twenty-four hours of the victim's life, and within twenty-four hours after that your suspect will be delivered to jail and a taped confession squirreled away, ready for overworked prosecutors to rave about. For Andy it had become simple.

But then there were the other cases, and Andy could feel those, too, when he first walked into the scene. These were called "whodunits" or "mysteries," because a good detective just *knew* that it wasn't someone the victim knew or had dealings with—it wasn't someone who was a part of the victim's everyday life. In this case, the 24-hour rule didn't work, and a seasoned homicide detective knew to try another approach.

Andy walked closer to the body and almost touched it, reaching out, but stopped short when he heard the crime scene sergeant groan that he was too close already.

He backed away and stared in amazement. Andy knew it was a whodunit, and knew also that he had never, in all his experience, ever seen anything like it.

Not even close.

Gabe walked over to the forensic homicide specialist, a sergeant who was wearing a navy blue jumpsuit already soaked with sweat and covered with fingerprint powder. He had a large, round face and old-style black-frame eyeglasses.

Gabe smiled at him. He just shook his head and looked back down.

"I trust you have this mess all figured out," she said dryly. The sergeant was on his hands and knees, using a magnifying glass and a sketch pad to document blood spatter evidence. He stopped and looked up.

"Sometime late yesterday," he began matter-of-factly. "There are six bullet wounds altogether, all probably by the same gun he's holding there, that thirty-eight revolver. I've already tested the top of his hand for gunpowder residue—just in case that wasn't the gun that shot him. It was positive. He did it himself, all right. He fired at least one of the bullets, probably all of them. The head shot is a contact wound—the gun was taped right up there and pressed in, then he pulled the trigger and shot himself. He's got a tight grip on the gun, a death grip. He must've been frightened something awful." The man looked back down and continued with the magnifying glass.

Gabe wrote it all down. She saw also there was no sign of struggle in the house. No forced entry. A key on the carpet. She noted the time, the temperature and thermostat setting, even the early stage of fly larvae development; she guessed that the body had been in the apartment a day. Then she walked around the apartment, careful not to touch anything, looking through the too-neat furnishings for some idea of what monstrous thing had gone on. Finally she walked into the small bedroom and began speaking with a uniformed patrol sergeant.

Andy finally took his eyes off the bloated, contorted face of the dead man. He looked over the body again, cataloging the wounds. His stomach churned and his chest tightened when he realized what had happened.

Andy spoke under his breath, describing the body to himself, pointing at each bullet puncture as he did. "One in each kneecap, one in the left arm, one in the shoulder, one in the goddamned nuts, right in the balls, blowing them to kingdom come. Someone else fired them. But then they taped the gun to his head and had him finish it off."

Andy carefully looked at the revolver. There was only one

spent cartridge, the one right under the hammer. Whoever shot him in the testicles used another gun or emptied that one, leaving the man only one bullet to kill himself with. Andy shook his head in disbelief and confusion.

Not a suicide, Andy knew. No way. Someone made him do it to himself. Torture-murder. Blew the guy's balls off, then forced him, above all the pain, to end his own agony with a shot to the head. Probably holding another gun on him. "Sick fuck," Andy said out loud about whatever kind of crazed lunatic could think of such a demonic way to kill someone.

From behind him in the dimly lit apartment electronic quartz flashes went off, giving the body an eerie illusion of movement and making Andy imagine the torturous pain inflicted on whoever it was still seated before him.

The round-faced sergeant walked all around, taking pictures from every angle. The camera's motorized film advance allowed him to shoot the whole roll in less than a minute as Andy stood and watched the strange ritual, peculiar to homicide scenes.

Feeling alone, Andy turned and looked for his wife. He saw her off in the small bedroom, standing with the patrol sergeant, discussing the contents of a large envelope. In her free hand Andy saw her carefully holding a small automatic pistol.

"Is that his ID?" Andy called out. He already knew the answer, he'd already figured it out.

Gabe turned to him but didn't speak. She had a "how did you know?" look on her face, as did the sergeant. She walked toward him, holding the envelope out with the flap torn open, a blank look of amazement still her only expression.

He took the envelope gently from her outstretched hand but did not immediately look inside. He already suspected what he would find. Gabe shook with nervousness over what she was thinking.

70

"Is there any food in the refrigerator?" he asked his wife, knowing by that time that she had looked.

She shook her head.

"Who's the apartment rented to?" he asked.

"A phony Delaware corporation. Patrol just found out," she replied.

"Who called this in? Who found the body?"

"Anonymous call," she said simply.

There was a pause as Andy looked at the body's groin area. Gabe looked over as well, realizing also what had taken place. He knew she was beginning to understand what he was thinking. Her pen shook in her hand.

"Any clothes in the closet?" he asked.

"None. Only an unpacked suitcase in the room."

"And this envelope was in the suitcase, right?"

She nodded. "Right. Along with this gun."

He looked in the envelope, then he walked to the kitchen counter and dumped the contents, spreading it all out. He glanced at the body, stepping to one side to view the face, then looking back at the papers. In the envelope was a Florida driver's license, a social security card, bank account card, Visa card, American Express card, voter's registration, and a birth certificate. All new. The license belonged to the partially covered face sitting in the chair with its brains blown out. The name was something made up by a Washington bureaucrat, one that didn't come close to fitting the dead Italian mobster, Andy knew.

Gabe put the cheap .25 auto down next to the papers. It was a "street gun," one the man had picked up without ID for about thirty dollars. Andy checked to see if it was loaded. It was.

The .25 and the .38 both belonged to the mobster, Andy knew. A protected witness. Someone had made the man commit suicide with his own gun.

"Call Sunderland," Andy said. "Tell him to come over.

71

Tell him to bring the FBI." He spoke calmly to his wife, who was already moving toward the phone.

Gruen lit a cigar and ignored the stern look of the round-faced sergeant. Andy also gave the agent a sour look but the man looked away, then walked over and examined the blood-covered corpse.

Sunderland was next to the kitchen counter looking over the fabricated pieces of identification and the cheap handgun.

The marshal shook his head in disbelief. "He was a mid-level guy, somebody who isn't even important. We've been moving him and issuing him new ID for the last month. In a day or two we'da had him settled. Now this."

"Where'd he get the guns?" Andy asked. "What would he be doing with them?"

"Like I said before, these are criminals—killers, many of them. They like guns. When we find them with one, we take it away, try and hassle them. It's hard to stop."

Andy looked at the large man in the chair and felt pity for him. Then he looked over at the FBI agent. Gruen was laughing.

"What the fuck is so funny?" Andy asked.

The agent looked toward him, his expression still one of amusement.

"They blew his balls off! What a twist. The Mafia can always be counted on for a few laughs, right, Amato?" He chuckled again, then walked to the kitchen sink and spit out some brownish phlegm. He looked up at Andy and smiled, small pieces of cigar shining on his lower lip.

Sunderland took out a notebook and started to read. "Thomas Ripaldi. Fifty-five years old. Been in the program just under a year. Testified in the murder trial of—"

"Don't give them that! That's classified stuff!" Gruen yelled out, walking toward them.

It was what Andy had been waiting for.

He moved to the agent, meeting him just in front of the body. Andy got up close, invading the man's personal space.

"This is West Palm Beach. This is a homicide. This is my jurisdiction, Gruen. You've got nothing to say. I'll have all the facts or I'll find a way to get you transferred to North Dakota where your sorry ass belongs."

There was silence. Gruen stared. Gabe shuffled her feet, looking down, embarrassed. Sunderland started to read from the file again. Andy got no response from the agent, only a cold, uncaring gaze. He backed away.

"He testified in a Chicago murder trial," Sunderland continued. "Then went under our witness protection program. This is the first breach of security we've had on him. There's no family to speak of. This apartment was a new addition as a safe house; no one should have known it was here."

Andy moved back another foot from Gruen. The agent clearly showed that if he was challenged an inch further he would swing at the West Palm detective. Andy knew he would win, but it'd be a bad scene.

"This is a West Palm case," Andy began again, looking at Gruen. "We're on it. And we're gonna stay on it. Go ahead and make your phone calls. You got friends high up, so do we. You're not going to shake us off of it by being assholes."

"I've got nothing to hide," Sunderland added sternly.

Gruen cut him off. "Let him talk. Let him bury himself," the FBI agent said.

Andy grinned. "I want a list of every one of the witnesses you have in the area that are unprotected. I want an address on each of the safe houses. It won't be photocopied or distributed to anyone else."

"Forget it," Gruen said.

"And I want to talk to Pisoli. Benny Pisoli. Wherever you want me to meet him, I don't care. I want to talk to him. If you won't let me, I'll have to find him, and I don't care whose toes I step on to do it."

"You're out of line, Amato. You talk big for a guinea homicide detective," Gruen sputtered.

Gabe came over and pulled her husband back just as he moved toward the FBI agent. Andy did not resist. He walked sideways, guided by Gabe, into the small bedroom. Eventually, he dropped his stare from the bulldog face of the FBI agent.

"You were going to punch him," Gabe said. "That would've been a problem."

"No. I was going to choke him. I was going to put my hands around his fat little neck and choke the shit outta him."

"Bad for interagency relations," she said. Andy smiled.

They both looked toward the uniformed officers in the room, who they knew had heard every word. The sergeant looked up but then continued carefully searching the carpet with a flashlight for any minuscule piece of evidence he could find.

Sunderland approached the dead man in the chair. Andy watched through the doorway as the deputy marshal inspected the body, counting the bullet wounds, just as he had done. Sunderland shook his head.

Gruen lit up a second cigar and blew smoke toward the body, obviously trying to cover the developing stench. The identification sergeant got up off his knees, walked over to the agent, removed the cigar from his lips, and dropped it into the sink. Gruen accepted this silently, only grinning at the ID man.

In the bedroom Gabe gave Andy a concerned look, one he seldom saw except when the most pressing of details hung on his wife's mind. It was her look of worried confusion, Andy knew.

"I've never seen anything like this before, Andy. How

could this happen? How could this be a murder? Why didn't he just shoot whoever was in the room with him when they put the gun in his hand? Why kill himself?"

Andy shook his head. "Whoever did it searched the place and found the guns. He shot the guy all over and blew his nuts off. Then he gave him the gun, taping him up, telling him to finish himself off with a shot to the head. He held a gun on the guy, ready to kill him himself. Obviously, the guy decided to do it." Andy thought of his own testicles. It was something only a man could understand.

Gabe couldn't conjure a logical explanation. Without logic to work with she was lost. She shook her head at her husband. Andy understood, silently nodding. He himself knew many people capable of such cruelty.

"Someone's giving the mob information," Gabe said. "Somebody from the inside. It's got to be."

Andy nodded.

"There was no forced entry," Gabe went on. "They found a spare key on the carpet, just inside the front door. Whoever it was had a key and used it to open the door with this guy inside."

Andy didn't say anything. He thought of the .25 auto found in the bedroom, remembering that it was loaded.

As Sunderland came into the bedroom, Andy heard the front door open and saw the back of Gruen's suit as the agent quickly left the apartment.

"I told him to wait downstairs," Sunderland said. "This is a U.S. marshal safe house, and I'm in charge. He was in the way, I could see that. He wasn't helping any. I apologize for his behavior."

Gabe nodded. Andy looked toward the uniformed officers and gave them a tilt of his head. The sergeant grumbled something and he and the patrol officer moved out of the bedroom. Gabe shut the door behind them.

Sunderland looked relieved. He let out a sigh and re-opened the small notebook.

"I'll have the list to you by tomorrow close of business. I'll get permission from Washington and give it to you."

"Thanks," Andy said.

"Something's going on. We've had staff meetings all week. We're calling in extra men from all over the country, just for protection of the witnesses down here. Five dead. There's no obvious pattern. They didn't know each other—they're not from the same case or the same crime family. There's no explaining it. They're all Italian mobsters, all middle-aged or old, all in our witness program. Those are the only real similarities."

Andy said nothing. He was inclined to trust the tall Swede. He wanted to point out a few things, but decided against it.

"Pisoli. You can arrange a meeting," Andy said.

Sunderland nodded. "I can. But he's being watched. He's been under direct observation for the last three days. He couldn't have done this."

Andy nodded. "He may know something. He may have hired somebody. Or he may have slipped by your men. It's too early to rule anything out."

Sunderland nodded, agreeing with the West Palm detective. The man looked profoundly worried.

"Pisoli is an animal. You won't like him, and he won't tell you anything of value. He has no redeeming qualities whatsoever. He's a pathological liar. But he's one of the FBI's best informants. They treat him like a king. I can't stand to be around him. I don't even like to think about him."

"Good. I'm used to that. He'll tell me what I need to know, then," Andy said.

Five minutes went by. Andy stepped over to the apartment window and looked out over the city. Gabe conferred again with the ID sergeant, scribbling furiously on her notepad.

The door opened and the patrol sergeant peeked his head through. "Dispatch called on the radio for you, Lieutenant.

Captain Jacobson wants you to call him at the office immediately." Andy nodded and the door closed.

Sunderland looked at him and shook his head.

Andy began. "It's Gruen. He's already called Jacobson to complain. I'll handle it. You just worry about the list and Pisoli. We'll put an end to this shit, I promise you."

"I hope so. Soon," Sunderland said.

Andy opened the door and walked out. Gabe caught the good-looking Swede's eye and smiled at him.

Andy Amato walked up behind the body. It looked new to him, as if he hadn't seen it a few minutes earlier. It was the new angle, the new perspective on the man clutching the gun taped to his hand and his head, in some evil ritual whose meaning he didn't know.

Something came to the tip of Andy's mind but then withdrew. It was a brief memory from long ago, something he had seen once, something that he thought might hold the answer to the gruesome murder sitting in front of him. He opened his mouth as if to say it, but it was gone. It was a mystery, just as big a mystery as the killing laid out in front of them. Gabe put her arm around him and kissed him behind the ear.

He walked past the body, his wife at his side, resolving never to look at it again. He would work from the photographs and the crime scene report. He would put the pieces together from there.

The elusive thought came back, but only for an instant, and again was gone. But he had grasped some small meaning from it and held on to it. Still he would not look back at the body. The answer was not there, he knew.

Gabe continued to hold him, leading him out the door of the apartment by the arm like an old woman leading her infirm husband.

The image of death was gone. Andy's only thought was about how someone could have gotten a copy of the key.

5

The Best Advice

Back at the station, the glass door to the captain's office was closed, and Jacobson had his executive chair turned around, facing the back window, looking out at Datura Street.

It was midafternoon. Andy knew Jacobson hadn't gone to lunch. He hadn't had his after-lunch cigar, and he'd been talking on the phone either with the chief or the deputy chief. In only a year of working for Jacobson, Andy could easily spot the captain's moods. Jacobson was annoyed.

Andy and Gabe walked slowly toward the glass door and hesitated outside.

Jacobson shut the window blinds and turned around. His light-mauve shirt was rolled up to the elbows. Homicide and robbery case folders were stacked neatly all over the desk. He had obviously spent the morning and early afternoon painstakingly reading through them.

He waved the Amatos in. Andy entered without flinching, Gabe right behind him.

"How ya doin', Captain?" Andy asked.

"Fine, Lieutenant. Fine. And you?" Jacobson's lusterless

monotone contradicted his words. Andy could tell Jacobson had already gotten the call.

"Captain, you hear the one about the old lady got her house broken into?"

Jacobson only stared. Andy continued.

"She wakes up and goes to work. When she gets there she gets fired. She's all upset, right? She leaves for home, and on the way she gets into an accident, and her car's wrecked. Now she's frantic, right? Well, she gets a cab home and goes up to the door, and she sees the door's kicked in and the place has been ransacked. Now she starts screamin' and the neighbors call the police. One of our canine guys gets there right away to search for the burglar. He gets the dog out of the car and on a leash, and he runs up to the front door. The cop says, 'Watch out, lady, I'm goin' in to look for the burglar.' She steps back and the cop and the dog run in past her. Then she looks up at the sky and says, 'First I get fired, then I wreck my car, then my house gets robbed, then they send me a goddamned blind policeman!'"

Andy laughed. Captain Jacobson looked down at his desk, and then smiled. Gabe shook her head; she'd heard Andy tell the joke ten times. She took out her notepad.

Jacobson wiped the smile off. "The first call was from Gruen at the FBI. Then the deputy chief, who had to listen to the chief scream. All because Andy Amato, hotshot homicide detective, likes to step on the FBI's toes. What's the matter, Andy? You can't get along with the feds?"

"Sure I can. They just like to get in the way and be horses' asses. Gruen's there at our crime scene, smokin' a cigar and generally makin' a nuisance out of himself. Ask the crime scene sergeant, he'll tell you."

"The chief's got the word, Andy. This may be our homicide case, but the bigger investigation belongs to the feds. They want no problems, no publicity. They're going to run things their way. They have the authority to take charge of the case, if they want."

"Wait a minute, Captain. Feds or not, I've never had any problems dealing with another agency until Gruen came along. There's the two C's—cooperation and coordination. No problem. But now they're more a nuisance than a help. And it's maybe not all their fault. All these killings been going on—they're undermanned. They're spread out real thin, trying to track down what's going on, trying to protect as many of these witnesses as they can."

"Strange. That's what they said about you. A nuisance. There's pressure to get you two off the case and send you on your vacation."

"But now it's a West Palm case. If we don't solve it, the feds sure as hell won't. They've got nothing to work with. They don't have the manpower to cover it. Not even with the marshal's people."

"Right. So it happened in West Palm Beach, so what? These are still gangsters, still federal witnesses. What do you think a local detective can uncover? You think you have the intelligence and computer files they have? Like I said, they're gangsters, so why should we get bent out of shape?"

"That's all too simple, Captain. There's a lot more to it than that. There's a lot going on that we're just starting to figure out."

Jacobson frowned at Andy and gave him a knowing, helpless shrug. "That's the way it is, Andy. They want you off. The deputy chief told me to look into it and do the right thing. That means, probably, keep the FBI happy. We have to work with them, after all. Try and do bank robberies and lots of other things without them. We can't. We have to stay friendly."

"We're still talking *murder*. That's worse than bank robbery, last I checked. And just because these guys getting killed are Italian gangsters don't mean we should just shrug it off."

"That's not what I'm saying, Andy. You know it." Jacobson let annoyance show through in his voice.

"We have to keep going. Keep us on the case," Andy said. It was almost a demand.

"And piss off the deputy chief, the chief, and the fucking FBI? Why, Andy? Can you tell me why, when all this is is a couple of dead mobsters, one not even in our city, and all of it basically a federal problem? Huh, Amato? Can you tell me?"

Andy looked back at Gabe. She smiled, looking over the massive notes she had taken in shorthand.

"Wait and hear before you decide, Captain. Then after, if you say to get off the case, we'll get off. But at least hear some of what we got here."

Jacobson shrugged again, looking noncommittal.

Gabe began by reading him dates, times, victim and background information. It was her typically methodical, organized summary. The captain leaned back, showing moderate interest, staying attentive.

When the foundation was laid Andy smiled broadly and, like a circus ringmaster, stepped back, bowed slightly, and motioned with his hand, as if introducing a new act. Jacobson waited, having seen this type of presentation from the husband-wife team before.

Gabe ignored Andy and continued. "The killer has intense knowledge of the federal witness protection program. We think it's someone in the program, maybe even a plant from northern organized crime families—someone who's worked his way into being a protected witness and who is now either selling information back to the Mafia or possibly carrying out the killings himself or with associates. At the Palm Beach mansion the first killer used an alarm key to shut off the alarm, and took it with him. It would have appeared later on that the old man simply forgot to set the alarm, if we hadn't found the key in the trunk of the Lincoln. We checked with the alarm company—those tubular keys are not

81

common to other alarms, and can only be duplicated through a code number on the inside of the interior alarm panel. Any refined locksmith could have done it from that number. Then there's the killer's wristwatch. His timer function was stopped at exactly ten minutes. He was a professional who was timing himself. He went in, defeated the alarm, cut the glass, did the killing, and got out in ten minutes. That's a twenty-room mansion. He had to have studied a map and some floor plans. Otherwise it would have taken him closer to twenty minutes, maybe more."

Jacobson nodded, looking impressed.

"Someone on the inside gave someone the key code and floor plans. That's the only logical conclusion to draw," Gabe said, finishing.

Andy picked up. "Then there's the killing in the city this morning. Another protected witness. Some sicko shoots a guy all over five or so times, then blows his nuts off. Then he tapes the gun to the guy's hand and the gun and hand to the guy's head. Then—bingo. The guy, who's bleeding to death and knows he's gonna die anyway, pulls the trigger and puts himself out of his misery."

Jacobson for the first time showed concern and shock.

Gabe continued. "On the carpet inside the front door was the key to the apartment's deadbolt. It was a professional copy, a high-security key—and not a master. Inside the bedroom was a suitcase with federally made identification for the man's newest identity. The apartment was a safe house for a few days until the guy was transferred."

Jacobson looked over at Andy as if to ask what the point was.

"These guys are not stupid, Captain. They're hiding out under threat of death. They know that the mob's been whacking them out all over South Florida. So this guy's gonna let somebody just walk in on him like that? He's not gonna be carrying a gun? He had two guns, probably kept both in easy reach."

Jacobson's quizzical look remained.

Andy continued. "If the guy heard a noise at the door, he'da brought out his gun, maybe only a small twenty-five, but enough to ruin somebody's day. So whoever it was used a key to get in quietly and surprised our victim. Again—it's the same thing as the one in Palm Beach. But this time they leave us the key. They don't care that we know. They're making it obvious. They *want* us to know. Someone from the mob is getting inside information on this federal program—addresses, names, house plans, even keys."

Jacobson was still unconvinced.

Gabe continued. "Sunderland from the U.S. Marshals is going to let us have a list of witnesses and a talk with a prime suspect. Some mob guy who's been in the system down here awhile, some badass who's supposed to have the kind of stomach it takes to do this kind of stuff."

Jacobson nodded. "So, who killed the hitter that shot the old man?" he asked. "Who's getting all the information on the houses, alarms, keys, and all that? I don't understand."

Andy paused. "We don't either, Captain. Not yet. This is your basic mystery, with lots of pitfalls, and stuffed-shirt FBI agents gettin' in the way."

Jacobson leaned back. Andy saw that he was probably thinking of the promise he had made to the deputy chief to get Gabe and Andy off the case and out of the way of the feds.

Gabe turned on the charm. "You have to let us continue, Captain. There's too much here. Something isn't right and you have to let Andy and me find out what it is." She smiled at the senior commander when he turned toward her.

The phone rang. Jacobson let the secretary pick up. He looked worried. Andy wanted a vacation, but he was hoping that Jacobson would listen to Gabe's pleadings and leave them on the investigation.

"Okay. Stay on it, but only to the end of the week. Then we'll have to reassess it, if you've come up with anything."

"Thank you, Captain," Gabe said in her sweetest of voices.

"Low key," he added. "Very low key."

Andy nodded.

"Maybe it's not that complicated," Jacobson continued. "Maybe it's something simple. Maybe the FBI will solve it by then and we can be done with it. Maybe it's not a big, complicated pile of shit after all," the detective captain rationalized. "Maybe you can have it wrapped up before Saturday." He looked worried; he knew he would have to answer to the deputy chief because of his decision.

Gabe smiled wide and began to back out of the office. Andy smiled also, nodding his head. He caught Jacobson's eye and identified the perceptive look of a police captain who had knowingly been bullshitted, with his own full permission.

Maybe it's something simple, Andy repeated to himself. *Maybe the FBI can solve it. Maybe you can have it wrapped up by Saturday . . .*

They were out the door. Jacobson picked up the phone and Andy knew he would be calling the deputy chief.

Maybe the pope is a fucking Protestant, Andy said to himself, laughing and shaking his head, following Gabe over to her desk.

Andy slept late the next morning. It was a shallow sleep, taking him all the way to ten o'clock, but giving him little respite from the massive speculating and investigative planning he and Gabe had done before going to bed. As they always did when working together, they had spent their evening talking about the case they were working, going over every last detail. He used that time to learn intimately what Gabe, the meticulous interviewer and investigator, had uncovered. He told her his gut feelings and what he projected onto the case. He told her what he felt, and where they should go from there. She listened with the same attention and respect as he paid her.

84

They made love afterward, almost at midnight. As it often was, it was like their first time, after a few months of working cases together in Miami. Being so enmeshed in a homicide case meant that even while they were giving and receiving pleasure they were thinking about death, and they could see this in each other's faces. They fell together, deeply entwined, hips moving rapidly and mouths kissing, not wanting to give up the moment but realizing that it would soon be over, and that their bodies and minds would return to the work that they themselves chose to be in. The sex was active but never rough; experimental but never kinky. There was nothing they would not do for each other's pleasure. And when the whirlwind was over Andy would withdraw, kissing Gabe all over, loving her and licking her and telling her how great it was; then they would both lie there on their backs, catching their breath, finally truly separating from each other and returning to the homicide.

Andy knew the dip in the road was coming up; he gassed the Saab up over seventy so he would sail right over smoothly. It was almost noon on the Julia Tuttle Causeway to the beach. Traffic was light, letting Andy easily weave in and out, passing the slower cars. The sun was baking down on the roadway, glittering off the pavement and the car's hood. He sped up again, pushing the sunglasses up on his face, finally coming to the last few miles where he could glide into South Beach on a thin part of roadway surrounded by calm blue water. He geared down to third and pulled the clutch in at the first traffic light.

Gabe was back in West Palm Beach, doing the follow-up, day-after homicide work. Andy had sent her to interview locksmiths further about the key, to canvass neighbors in the apartment building about what they may have seen or heard, and to attend the autopsy. And he knew Gabe would find her own areas to follow up on. He didn't feel guilty about leaving her behind; he knew that she wouldn't want to leave important investigative work undone to make a business trip to Miami if it was just to talk to someone.

Andy drove down First Street, then turned south. He slowed, looking at boarded-up businesses, hotels, and rooming houses. It made him shake his head. So much had changed in a year.

South Beach was dying. What was once the modest, middle-class home of Jewish retirees at the far south end of Miami Beach had become rows of abandoned hotels, businesses, and shops. The older people seldom walked in the streets anymore, day *or* night, and seldom sat in front of their retirement homes after dark, sharing life histories or medical problems with each other.

South Beach was now the home of crack cocaine addicts and burglars, purse snatchers and graffiti artists. Like other South Florida inner cities on the decline, the police force was losing ground to the hundreds of new and repeat offenders whom the overburdened jail facilities couldn't house. They roamed the streets, doing nothing illegal when police were around, but carefully staking out and preying on the old people and the middle class who still lived in the newly formed ghetto or even just drove through it.

Lieutenant Andy Amato of Miami PD homicide loved to go to South Beach to track down a Marielito homicide suspect whose possible address was given as either Collins, Washington, Meridian, or one of the other famous South Beach streets. He would find the location to be bogus or the suspect long since moved away. Then he would search through the ghetto cantinas and bars for the suspect or an associate, sometimes getting lucky, more often finding that the trail led nowhere. Finally, he would wander the area, making contacts, eating the food, enjoying the people.

Andy grew to love all of Miami Beach, but mostly the south end. It reminded him in many ways of the New York neighborhoods he visited as a youngster, with his father

86

showing him where old friends or family had lived. Although South Beach was across Biscayne Bay and out of Miami, Andy drove over for lunch, or would find an excuse to visit the Miami Beach police department, looking for a suspect photo or copy of a report.

Now he drove over to Joe's Crab House at First Street and Collins. The landmark had just reopened for crab season after a particularly hot June vacation. As he pulled up to the pink stucco building he saw the typical crowd whose upper-class and touristy automobiles jammed the parking lot. He admired the recently painted black, wrought iron trim and the bright red Spanish barrel-tile roof. He pulled across the street, into a metered parking space next to a Latin grocery, and put his blue light on the dash, along with his West Palm Beach police ON DUTY sign.

Andy ignored the line of people outside and pushed into the crowded lobby. He found a familiar face by a wooden podium and held out his hand and business card.

"Hello, Lieutenant Amato. How have you been?" the tall Cuban asked. Not waiting for a reply, he said, "Your friend has already arrived and is seated in back." Andy saw the annoyed look on the face of an older local resident as he was ushered in ahead of him.

Carmine was seated alone at a big table. He didn't get up, but only nodded at Andy when the tall Cuban had left.

Andy's friend was dressed indistinguishably from the dozens of other retirees in the large, crowded dining room. He wore his favorite bright blue pants with a light pink shirt open at the collar. His cigar was already lit and half burned. He was looking at the racing section of the *Miami Herald.*

Andy sat and smiled. Carmine smiled back, his brownish buck teeth fully bared.

"Glad to see you. An unexpected surprise," Carmine said

87

in typically hushed, New York gangster tones. "Any word from your old man? How's he doin'?"

"Talked to him last week. He's not tired of that Arizona desert out there yet. Said him and Mom are doin' fine. Lots of bingo and card games, some trips to Vegas. Give him a little while longer, he'll be down to the swamp pretty soon."

An awkward silence followed their laugh. Carmine seemed distant to Andy—definitely uncomfortable about something. Then there was small talk about dog and horse races, about the Miami Dolphins' upcoming roster, about a major league baseball club for South Florida. Andy knew that Carmine was more interested in the betting angles of professional sports than he was about the sports themselves.

The waiter finally came and Carmine ordered a clam bake special. Andy stuck with the deep-sea stone crabs, freshly caught by the restaurant's fleet. The restaurant was named for the dish, which was the biggest tourist draw.

"I read a small article about your case in this morning's *Herald*," Carmine said, turning to the page and pointing it out for him. Andy quickly skimmed through the half-column article. It was the typical few-facts, police-won't-comment piece. "It's another hit, right?"

Andy nodded. "Another witness in the program. This one a torture killing. With a unique way of ending it—he forced the guy to kill himself. I haven't seen that before." Andy could only tell Carmine so much and no more. The retired mobster usually understood.

Carmine showed untypical surprise at Andy's description of the killing. He asked probing questions, and Andy did his best to answer. He would be careful not to reveal too many details, ones that the police were reserving just for themselves and the killer, such as the kind and color of the tape, and exactly where the body was seated.

When Andy was done with as much as he could tell his old friend, the mobster leaned back, disgusted. He threw the paper down and began speaking louder than was his habit. He waved his hands in the air in typical Italian fashion.

"I can't believe this shit! Where has the honor gone? Where is the self-respect? Used to be you were whacked out fast. Clean and simple. No big torture, there was no need for that. That was the way it was. A coupla shots and it was all over. I'd like to know myself who in the hell is behind this. I bet they don't have approval for this shit. I bet whoever's behind it is off on their own, or the family doesn't know how this stuff is being carried out."

The waiter came back with the drinks and a basket of sourdough biscuits. He dropped them on the table and walked on, obviously in a hurry.

"There were more rules in the old days, remember, Andy? Remember how it was back in the sixties and seventies? Now there's more of this kinda shit goin' on. Remember when you was a kid, Andy? Remember Joey Gallo gettin' hit at Umberto's on Mulberry Street?"

Andy nodded. He thought about being twelve years old, down in New York's Little Italy with his father. Carmine and his dad were in an Italian coffee shop playing cards. He and his older cousin were down the block when they heard the gunshots and ran to stand outside the famous Italian restaurant, the ill-famed hangout of ruthless Sicilian mobsters. The two boys watched people running, watched the New York police get there, watched for hours as the cops half-heartedly worked the crime scene, knowing that it was only Crazy Joe Gallo who had caught the bullets.

Carmine pointed at Andy and cocked his thumb. "That was the way it was. Bang! You caught one right in the head or the heart and it was all over, nothin' to worry about. The boys would even watch out for the guy's family afterward. Give them a little somethin' to get by on for a while. Everything was decent. Nothing personal. It was nothin' personal, all business."

Carmine went back to the racing pages. Andy thought about the old man's words and how he seemed committed to what he said. It still frightened Andy to think about the culture he had grown up in but somehow escaped.

The waiter finally came back with their orders, and replenished their drinks and biscuits. Carmine gave the young man a disgusted look, shaking his head. The Cuban ignored him.

"You could used to talk to the waiters in this place. They were friendly and took good care of you. Mostly old Jews or guineas. These fucks don't hardly even speak English," Carmine said when the waiter walked off.

After almost an hour of slow eating and idle conversation, mostly about gambling and sports, both men pushed their dishes aside. Carmine lit another cigar. The lunchtime crowd was thinning out; it was almost two o'clock.

Andy knew what he wanted—what he came down to Miami for and what he had to have. It was the end of the lunch ritual, and he was wondering if he would have to come out and ask Carmine for it. He decided to give the old man a few more minutes to come out with it on his own. *Respect.*

The talk went on—about food, about restaurants, and again about sports. Carmine knew Andy still loved baseball, was still a Mets fan. Carmine tested his knowledge about their pitching staff. Then, when the old man seemed to sense that Andy was growing weary, he went into his pants pocket, pulling out some folded notebook paper. He opened the pages and glanced at the handwritten notes. Then, looking carefully around the half-empty restaurant, he pushed the papers across the table.

"This took me all of last night, after you called. I had to reach out to people, make a lot of calls. Some people will be wonderin' why I was askin'. I hope you appreciate it," Carmine said.

"I do," Andy replied. He paged through the ruled paper, making out the names. It was the list he had asked Carmine for, but it had more than twice as many names as he'd thought would be on it. There were both sides of four pages, almost two hundred mobsters.

"Those are all the wiseguys who have disappeared after testifying, or after giving the Justice Department or FBI information about our business. And those are just the names of people the family feels are being hidden somewhere in Florida. It may not be down here, you understand. It could be Tampa, Orlando, Jacksonville, even Tallahassee. But South Florida is a good bet—that's where the action is. And all these boys *love* action. Especially that fuck Benny."

Andy looked on the second page and found Benny "Beans" Pisoli's name underlined. Andy had asked the old man to highlight the names he thought could be doing the killings or masterminding a plot to buy the names from a leak inside the federal government. He'd done so only to Benny's and a handful of others.

Carmine looked around suspiciously as Andy continued to read through the pages. Soon they were the only ones left. Restaurant people were beginning to clean up and rearrange the dining room for the early dinner crowd.

Andy realized why Carmine was watchful. Giving this list, or anything else, to a cop could cost his father's old friend his life. And Andy wouldn't have to pay a penny for it, only pick up the check at the expensive restaurant.

"Who's the killer, Carmine? Can you tell me?"

There was only a brief hesitation. "I can't answer that, Andy. You know that. If I knew, I couldn't tell you if I knew or not. And if I knew, I couldn't tell you who. I ain't no rat."

"Of course not. That's not what I want. But I need to know if you *really* don't know. With all the connections you still have, with all your knowledge of the business, if you *really* don't know, that tells me something important right there. Telling me if you really don't know who it is won't violate anything, will it?"

Carmine thought it over. He brushed his side hair back and dabbed his crown and forehead with a white silk handkerchief. The man appeared hot, even in the air-conditioned restaurant.

"I really don't know, Andy. And if I *did* know, I wouldn't tell you. I'm sorry, but that's the best I can do."

Andy smiled at the gangster doublespeak, then read through the list once more. Carmine uncomfortably began to gather up his things. With each name on the list there was the Mafia family that the wiseguy belonged to, what the guy had done to force him into the witness protection program, the approximate date he disappeared, and Carmine's best guess as to what part of Florida he was likely hiding out in.

"I appreciate this," Andy said simply when he finished reading.

Carmine nodded and smiled. There was no need to answer.

Andy took out a red pen from his pocket and circled the names of the witnesses who he knew were already dead. He found the first three easily. He circled the name of Thomas Ripaldi, the unfortunate victim from the day before. He pictured the killer shooting the mobster in the balls, then the man pulling the trigger to put a bullet through his own brain.

Andy scrutinized the list again, the red pen hovering over the names, trying to guess who would be next. There were too many choices. He folded the list and put it in his pocket, and both men walked silently out of the almost-deserted restaurant.

Phil Wesley had said he would meet Andy at 4:15, on the north side of the Bay River Club and Spa. Andy pulled into the lot just before the time and cast his eyes on the building and Biscayne Bay beyond.

He could see a raised deck and pool on the north side of

the club, overlooking the racing and charter boats that were crisscrossing the bay. There were a dozen tanned and bikini-clad women, all apparently in their early twenties, walking, talking, and going in and out of the pool. The men were all tanned and muscular, all short-haired and clean shaven. On the far north side was a tiki hut with a Jamaican bartender blending daiquiris for the happy-hour crowd coming out from the weight room.

Andy admired one woman in particular. She had very light hair, a bronzed, curvaceous body, and oversized breasts. She walked to the bar and back, then set her drink down and climbed back into the pool. Andy got out of the Saab and stood by the driver's door, keeping his eyes on her. He didn't see Wesley come up to him, carrying a gym bag, wearing only an open-collar dress shirt and gray slacks.

"Nice scenery, Andy? Love them boats, don't you?"

"Oh, sure, great boats. No wonder you come here a lot."

"It's great for the mind and body. Gives me a rest from the daily federal grind. It's expensive, but worth it."

"It looks it. Get in." Andy got behind the wheel. Wesley walked around and sank into the deep leather passenger seat.

"It's been bad, Andy. Very bad. Today was the worst. The Washington bureaucrats are in town, and some politico who reports right to the director. We have big problems. Thank God the press hasn't figured it out yet."

Andy started the engine and threw the air conditioning on full blast. "I count five murders, Phil. The two before that I've read about, now the three in Palm Beach. And I'm on the one in West Palm, at least until Friday. The pressure's on from the FBI, Gruen in particular, to get me and Gabe off the case."

Wesley showed no surprise. "Don't be offended. That's standard with cases concerning the witness program. Local agencies usually don't have the savvy to keep this stuff in perspective and keep it out of the papers. Gruen's just following orders. I think he knows about you and that reporter—"

"I got nothing goin' with no reporter, Phil. Don't start that shit on me again."

"Fine. Whatever you say. But Gruen's just doin' his job."

"He does it with a special knack. You know me, Phil. I respect the FBI. You guys are top notch. I never in all the years you knew me got in your way. Then in two days, *wham!* Gruen's all over my case, making phone calls behind the scenes . . ."

"This is different. We never had anything like this when you were down here. This is heavyweight stuff. This involves politics on the national level. You're gonna have to tread water and play the game as it comes. And if they pull you off, so what? What makes you so concerned about a few federal witnesses, anyway?"

Andy stared ahead at another colorful sailboat, then looked over the pool, becoming mildly disturbed when he was unable to find the blonde with the big boats and the tight bikini.

She came back into sight as he took out Carmine's folded handwritten list and handed it across to Wesley. The agent unfolded the pages and glanced through the names, looking progressively more fascinated and disturbed.

"Where did you get this?" he asked Andy in a calm voice, one blocking out nervous concern.

"A friend. Someone who knows," Andy answered.

"It's good. *Very* good. Most of these names are in the program down here."

"Like I said, it's someone who's been around. He helps me out, that's all. Not a paid snitch, just someone who'll talk to me."

Wesley continued to look over the list. Andy stared off at the tiki bar, keeping his eyes on the blonde.

"I'd like a copy, Andy."

"Can't do it."

There was more silence. Wesley shook his head, then folded and handed the list back. Andy knew his friend wanted the list to trace his informant through a handwriting comparison. He couldn't get Carmine involved.

"Tomorrow I get a list from Sunderland," Andy continued. "Every one of these assholes in Dade, Broward, and Palm Beach will be on it. All the way from Homestead to Jupiter. With addresses. But I needed this list from my friend. It has more information. Besides, I don't trust you guys not to conveniently leave off a name or two."

"I'm surprised the marshals are letting you have it, but it makes sense." Wesley trailed off, lost in thought.

"Look closely at the list, Phil." Andy handed it back. "Read the information on the four witnesses who are already dead, not counting the hired killer. Tell me what you see."

The FBI agent studied the information on the mobsters whose names Andy had circled. Then he looked back up at Andy and shrugged.

"There's no pattern, Phil. Not a thing. Different mob families, from different parts of the country, testifying in different trials. Probably never heard of each other. Now they're all dead."

Wesley looked at the five again. He glanced back at Andy with the same blank stare.

Andy took the list back and put it away. "Something's wrong. I know it, the FBI knows it, and I'm going to find out what it is. I'm also talking to my only suspect to date, Mr. Pisoli, hopefully soon. I'm going to get to the bottom of it, Phil—whether or not Gruen gets my department to call me off."

Wesley nodded. He gave Andy a look of understanding. "You think he did it? Pisoli? You think he knows what's going on?" Wesley asked.

95

"Sounds like he's my best bet. The sheet I've seen on him tells me that he's got connections all across the families, all across the country. If any of these guys have figured anything out, Pisoli has. Believe me, I know the type."

Wesley nodded. He patted Andy on the knee and opened his door. Carrying his gym bag he walked to his black Dodge Diplomat on the other side of the lot.

Andy saw the Jamaican bartender pour a glass of thick red liquid from a blender into an oversized plastic cup. The blonde picked it up, smiled in Andy's direction, and bounced off toward one of the clean-shaven men with muscles.

Andy watched for a few moments as a raceboat with a skier in tow hooked a hard left in front of the pool, spraying ocean foam almost up to the patio deck. The blonde jumped and laughed. Andy put the Saab in reverse and slowly pulled out.

Gabe pulled in to the guest lot of the Executive Center Drive apartments and walked briskly toward the building. It would be her last effort in a long and tiring day.

Without Andy her days were often joyless. She missed his humor, although she never admitted this to him. She missed his dramatics and flair, and most of all, she missed his intuitive insights into complicated cases. She would always write those down next to her own more scientific observations.

The autopsy earlier in the morning gave her nothing. She had stood and watched, dutifully making her notes, feeling empty. The medical examiner's personnel were clean and efficient, sometimes pleasant, telling the expected off-color death-and-gore jokes as they cut, chopped, and weighed. Gave learned only what she already knew. After an hour she drove from the M.E.'s office back to the downtown federal building.

Sunderland had been there at noon, just as he promised. He gave her the complete background on the dead Thomas

R. Ripaldi. He retraced the mobster's steps. Gabe wearily wrote the information down.

Ripaldi was fifty-one, divorced with two grown children. He had run the skimming operations for Las Vegas and Atlantic City casinos in his younger years, then graduated to soliciting labor union contracts and kickbacks from their pension funds. He was indicted the previous fall for racketeering, bribery, and extortion. Instead of at least twenty years and a half million in fines, Ripaldi chose to testify against a dozen mobsters from Denver to L.A., putting all of them in jail. He was allowed to keep most of the small personal fortune he had amassed. Such were the deals being made.

It meant nothing to her. She concentrated instead on the dark-brown eyes of the deputy U.S. marshal and his impressive build and strong, soothing voice. They spent a half hour in his tiny office, another forty-five minutes in a local restaurant talking Mafia and federal witness protection over precooked Mexican food. He was always the gentleman, mindful of his speech. She caught him only once admiring her body.

The apartment building where the killing had taken place was large but there were only six units on each floor. Gabe planned on interviewing each of Ripaldi's five neighbors and each of the renters whose apartments were on the ground floor facing the main elevator.

At the three apartments near the elevator, she found only one person home, a teacher living with her husband and young daughter. She had seen no one at the elevators the prior day.

On the third floor, Ripaldi's apartment door was still covered with yellow crime scene tape. Gabe checked the deadbolt—locked.

Patrol officers had knocked on nearby doors not long after

the body was discovered and she and Andy had arrived. She remembered them saying that no one was home.

At the apartment just to the right, she rang the doorbell. When there was no answer, she knocked and waited.

First there was a long silence, almost enough to send her to the next door. Then a baby cried, and Gabe heard someone coming toward the door. It opened quickly, without any questioning, and without a security chain.

She held up her badge. "I'm Sergeant Amato from West Palm Beach police. I'm doing some follow-up work on the body that was found in that apartment yesterday."

The woman was very young, barely twenty, Gabe guessed, with dark hair, most of it carefully pulled back in a bun. She wore an old but clean blouse, no bra, and tight-fitting yellowish shorts. The infant was cradled in her right arm, resting on her hip.

The woman looked at the gold badge, nodded, but said nothing.

"I'm hoping you can recall seeing something on Tuesday, probably late afternoon or evening. Maybe a man loitering in this hallway? Maybe someone putting a key in that door there?" Gabe was going for broke—it was always possible.

The woman hesitated, using her free hand to brush a few strands of hair from her eyes. The baby cried.

Gabe put away her ID. She felt sorry for the woman, in a way, but also a twinge of envy at a woman who could stay home and take care of a kid.

"I didn't see anyone," the young mother finally answered. "Not anyone. I heard something from outside that apartment, though. I remember hearing loud knocking, then voices. I remember it because that place has been vacant for so long, you know? I remember thinking how odd it was to hear voices coming from there. Two men. There was just some talking, then they closed the door."

"Did you see anyone?"

98

She shook her head. "I kept the door closed. For some reason I was frightened."

"The voices, could you make out what was said?"

"No, just one that was loud and demanding."

"Did you hear any gunshots?"

She shook her head. "I don't think so. There's so much noise late at night, and these walls are pretty thick. I can't be sure."

"This was Tuesday?" Gabe asked. The woman nodded. "What time?"

"Late evening, I guess. Before eight. My husband works construction and gets home at eight. It was before then."

Gabe took the woman's name and phone number and thanked her.

Gabe underlined everything the woman had told her. It was the truth, she decided. There was no reason for her to lie, not standing there and holding her kid. She had heard the knocking and the two male voices. And it was late Tuesday. She checked her autopsy notes. Ripaldi had shot himself in the head no later than eight P.M.

Gabe wrote the words *Key on carpet* in her notebook, then underlined it and put a large question mark on both ends. Then she wrote, *Who knocked on door?*

There was no one home at the other apartments. It was just as well, she thought to herself. She knew that she had found what she came for.

6

A Place to Meet

Charlie Aiello walked out of the expensive town house on the lake and strolled slowly, carefully, toward his car.

He took a moment to enjoy the early-morning warmth, something he was not used to back home, even in the summertime. Then he walked on, half admiring the well-manicured lawn and bushes, half wondering if his appointed killer was hiding nearby.

He liked Boca Raton better than Detroit, of that he was sure. Even under the current circumstances he preferred the well-landscaped flatness, the wealth, and the year-round heat to the garbage strikes and the smell of northern urban decay. Boca had treated him well. He had it all, and just a ten-minute drive north of Ft. Lauderdale: a hundred-grand town house, plenty of free time, and a good cash flow to gamble with.

He would rather have been alone, but under the circumstances the U.S. marshal strolling along behind him was not exactly unwelcome. He had read the papers and heard the talk. Something bad was up—the heat was on, and people were dying.

He was happy that his testifying days were over. His mob

100

enemies were long since put away and he believed, in his heart at least, that he was small potatoes and the wiseguys who had once hunted him had undoubtedly gone on to bigger fish.

Still, he was worried. More so than usual. There was a return of the paranoia from years back, when he began his testimony and started pointing fingers at mob bosses in Detroit, Chicago, and Milwaukee. The new killings worried him. He looked over his shoulder; he awoke in the middle of the night, frightened at every little noise.

And he bought a gun.

But now his illegal pistol was in the house, safely hidden from his marshal friend. The tall lawman had lived with him for three days, and the two got along, but just barely. He had struck up many conversations but he found the skinny southern officer mostly dry and overcommitted to his job. In many respects, he was glad of that.

He rounded a corner in the parking lot and spotted the jade green Porsche parked exactly as he'd left it. The windows were fogged from the dew and the sun was already bright enough to make him and his bodyguard squint. He walked a few more feet, then stopped. The marshal stopped behind him. The tall lawman glanced around, hand on the military Beretta 92F 9-millimeter under his jacket.

Aiello took out the remote starter from the small valise he was clutching. The device was just slightly bigger than a pocket calculator, with a thin silver antenna pointing out one end. He aimed the device at the Porsche, flipped a switch, and pushed a recessed button on top of the panel.

There was a click and a low grinding, then the starter took over and the well-honed engine burst into life. He loved the sound of the magnificent, expensive turbine as it mixed gasoline with air and churned out more horsepower than any other car on the road. He smiled and walked to the automobile.

The marshal walked with him, to his assigned car parked behind the Porsche. He would follow Aiello down to Pompano Beach for some shopping, then to lunch, then to the harness track for the matinee races. The day was strictly planned and would allow for little deviation. He would stay close by and in radio contact with the local FBI frequencies.

Concealed, from a block away, he watched the mobster and the U.S. marshal split up for their separate vehicles. He eyed the green Porsche, waiting for the man to open the door, get in, and start to drive away.

It was less than a minute, but the man seemed to be taking forever, as if he expected something. But then he put the key in the lock, opened the door, and shut himself inside.

He was originally going to wait until the Porsche was clear of the parking lot and out on the main street where more people could see and traffic would be blocked for miles, but he decided not to. He waited only for the car to lurch backward out of the parking spot, then creep forward and pick up speed. The white Impala from the marshal's office stayed about a car length behind.

He took out the remote control and flipped the large red switch. A red light started blinking, then glowed steadily, arming the hidden device. He admired the car for the last time, then looked down and pressed a button.

He heard the explosion, heard the metal doors ripping away. When he looked up he saw the body flying over the top of the car, engulfed in flames, and land on some grass by the side of the pond. The Porsche's gas tank exploded next, ripping apart the rest of the bright green metal and filling the air with black smoke and burning oil and gas.

He waited long enough for the marshal to pull over, excitedly get out of his car, and make a dash for the burning body on the side of the pond. Then he put his car in gear and drove slowly away.

Sunderland called West Palm PD and told the Amatos to meet him in Boca Raton at the scene. They had rushed straight out to the wealthy Boca West golf course development.

Andy now was standing by the wooden gate of a nearby town house. Gabe was over speaking with Boca Raton PD investigators. The tall U.S. marshal with the southern accent was being treated by fire-rescue for burns and smoke inhalation. The only thing left of the Porsche, Andy saw, was some charred metal low to the ground, a broken and scorched chassis, and an engine that looked like a pile of black, burned marshmallows.

Donald Gruen and his team of West Palm FBI agents walked among the scattered debris looking for clues. Andy knew that Phil Wesley would be on his way up from Miami, a team of Washington FBI bureaucrats in tow.

He was having a feeling of déjà vu, and it finally occurred to him why. Almost fifteen years earlier, when he was a rookie Miami cop, there had been an airplane crash—an L-1011 down in the Florida Everglades. He had helped the county police inventory the bodies.

It was the same feeling of death and destruction, on a smaller scale.

Bits of the car were thrown over a full acre of land. One of the car doors, its jade green metallic paint intact from having been thrown far enough away from the blaze, lay on its side against a tilted fire hydrant about a hundred feet from the wreckage still smoldering in spite of having been doused repeatedly by the Boca Raton Fire Department's four trucks on the scene.

The body lay twisted and burned at the side of the small lake, the medical examiner's khaki-colored plastic covering it from the probing camera shots of the news media gathered across the parking lot. Andy took it all in, disturbed and

103

sickened. He watched Gabe, aware that this was the most hideous explosion the two had ever investigated. She did not react well at the sight of the black, charred bones of the latest mobster. He had glimpsed a small break in her efficient composure, but then he saw her take a breath and walk off, the cool look of a competent female detective slowly coming back to her.

Sunderland walked up to him from across the lot where a spokesman for the U.S. Marshals Service had issued a brief, cryptic statement to Palm Beach and Broward County newspapers. They were keeping television cameras far back, away from the lake. The worst had happened, Andy knew. Newspeople were everywhere, asking questions, wondering why there was a car-bombing in ritzy Boca Raton and why U.S. marshals and FBI agents were swarming the area.

"How is he?" Andy asked, motioning to the injured marshal by the rescue truck.

"Fine. He'll have some scarring, but it's minor. He was far enough back when the thing went off. He was hit with some hot metal from the second blast, and has some hand burns from trying to move the body. He tried his best. It was a bad scene."

Andy nodded. There was nothing to ask and very little to investigate. Whatever the device was, one of the most powerful he had ever seen or heard of, it had blown all evidence of itself up along with the Porsche.

"This witness had one of our remote starters. Either the bomb was planted to go off a few minutes after the car started, or it was set off by remote control by somebody watching nearby."

Andy nodded again and cataloged the fact about the remote starter in the back of his mind.

Sunderland was openly disturbed. His calm, businesslike composure was evaporating right in front of the West Palm Beach detective lieutenant.

Andy spoke slowly and almost in a whisper, as if he

was revealing a secret. "This makes *six,* Tom. All connected. And what's worse, he didn't leave you a bit of fucking evidence."

Sunderland smiled but the rest of his composure was gone. Andy decided to push even further.

"I brought my own list with me. Your list will be good, but I want to know what the Mafia knows. This guy here has been in the program for almost ten years. This was somebody fairly low level. He was history. Nobody should've even remembered him. Any idea who'd try and kill him after all this time?"

Sunderland shook his head. The tall Swede looked over at the khaki-covered body by the pond.

"No pattern," Andy continued. "Except it's all happening in South Florida, and mostly in Palm Beach County. Nothing else connects. And you haven't a clue, I can tell. And what Gabe and I have so far, I'm afraid, isn't exactly hopeful."

Tom Sunderland's hands were shaking. After a moment he regained his composure and took out a folded envelope from his coat. He handed the list over to Andy.

"Everything is crumbling," he told Andy. "The shit's hit the fan in Washington. They want answers, we can't even figure out the questions. There are hundreds of protected witnesses down here. They're all in danger. We're outnumbered—we can't protect all of them, we're not even sure where they all are. And even when we're there, this happens. It's out of control. And the FBI won't admit they're in the same boat we are. They're pushing forward like this is some routine investigation. They don't have any leads, either."

Andy opened the envelope. He saw a list of names followed by long, numeric codes for addresses.

"The code is explained on the last page. Then destroy it. Don't tell anyone."

Andy felt honored, but didn't let it show. Carmine's list along with this one finally gave him what he needed.

"For some reason I trust you, Amato. You're good. You'll

help us. No one else in South Florida has that list—not even the FBI. We don't cooperate as much as people think. Just me and you and some people in Washington have it. Not even Gruen or your friend Wesley. It's highly classified. Why they let me show it to you, I'm not sure."

"Like I said, I have friends, too."

Andy opened his coat and gave Sunderland a copy of Carmine's list. "You might find this interesting. This is what the mob knows about your program. I wanted it to make sure I had all the names—that you weren't holding anything back."

Sunderland looked at him questioningly.

"Don't worry, it's from a friend," Andy said. "Someone who couldn't have had anything to do with this. Someone who used to be in the mob and is now down here, retired."

The marshal nodded and looked over the handwritten pages. "There's one last thing," he said, putting Carmine's list in his pocket. "About Pisoli. I checked into it and he hasn't been watched as closely as I thought. But he is now. He couldn't have done this this morning, but he could have masterminded it. And we can't be one hundred percent sure he didn't take part in the earlier killings."

Both men watched as personnel from the medical examiner's office loaded the bag of charred remains into the rear of a black station wagon. Andy glanced over at Gabe, who was still busily interviewing bystanders and making notes.

"We're desperate, Amato. We're spread too thin and there's too many witnesses, too many people to protect. We never planned for anything like this. Whatever you can do to help . . ." His voice trailed off, almost trembling.

"I just hope it's not too little, too late," Andy said.

"Whatever you need, just ask. One of my men has been injured. It's getting closer to home and I want it stopped. Just ask."

Andy nodded. "Pisoli. I'll begin with him. No later than

106

tomorrow night. Set it up. I need to have a chat with our prime suspect. I need to get some things straight."

"You got it. Tomorrow night, no later. I'll set it up and be in touch."

"Make it somewhere he and I can talk alone. No wires, no FBI, no marshals or bodyguards. They can stay nearby but we have to be out of sight and earshot. That's the deal."

"No problem. I understand," Sunderland said, then walked off.

Andy glanced around the death scene. Some media people were walking off, having taken their fill of photos and heard enough official denials and "No comment"s.

After a few more minutes four black Dodges pulled into the town house area from Glades Road. Andy recognized Wesley's car and saw each of the three others packed with agents in suits. They were older men, most likely FBI bosses.

Andy walked away from the remains of the Porsche, ready to go get Gabe and leave.

Gabe and Andy were in the Saab, the motor running. It was an eerie scene for Palm Beach—five or six police cars, all lights off, completely surrounding all entrances and exits to the small city beach. Two more were at each end of the ocean roadway, turning back traffic without offering explanations. A uniformed Lake Worth sergeant talked into a radio, then motioned Andy and Gabe forward. Andy drove slowly by, getting questioning looks from the uniforms standing guard at the outer perimeter, policemen who were unsure of what was going on.

It was Saturday, a few minutes after midnight, and the beach was long closed. Towering Palm Beach condominiums were on either side of the small park, along with a radio station antenna bursting up from the ground. There were only a few streetlights still burning. Andy opened a window as he started up the small rise that would take him around to the oceanfront. The breeze was steady. He immediately heard the breaking waves and could smell the ocean.

At the center of the beach was a large restaurant and pier complex, flanked by lifeguard stands and soda machines. Andy spotted the Impalas from the marshal's office forming a wedge at the entrance to the complex. There was only one uniformed officer, a Lake Worth lieutenant, who stood far back of the marshals, off by the sidewalk leading to the ocean. The beach and small pavilion were in the city of Lake Worth, bought from the ritzy oceanfront town of Palm Beach in the 1920s.

Sunderland walked over quickly as Andy and Gabe got out of the Saab. Five other marshals stood to the rear, blank expressions on their faces and automatic machine guns at the ready. Andy hadn't seen such firepower openly displayed since the last presidential visit to Miami.

Sunderland offered his hand to both of them. Andy gave him a confused grin, shaking his head at the heavily armed marshals.

"Sorry for the late hour and all the mystery," Sunderland said. "This was the only way I could get you to see him privately."

They nodded their understanding.

"There was paperwork to clear. Bosses up in Washington had to be called. Everything had to be approved, and then approved again. The FBI protested, but I finally got it through. He's here, out on the end of the pier."

"What makes Pisoli so special?" Gabe asked. Andy wanted to hear also. He only knew what he had heard about the man's reputation.

Sunderland hesitated just a moment, looking back at his men.

"Pisoli is not your normal mobster," the marshal began. "Ever since he came down here we've been having to put up with the drain of providing the extra manpower. It wasn't long before the mob up north knew he was in South Florida, and it wasn't long after that that all the death threats started. We heard from sources that big contracts were out. There were tails and surveillance on U.S. marshal operations spotted all up and down the coast. He was on his own for a while—he's had plastic surgery and he has four sets of ID, all legit, all with backup from the government. People don't realize what kind of manpower is involved in setting up round-the-clock protection for these people. They don't realize the detailed paper trail you have to have. to make it work. It all takes time. Anyway, he's been back under direct, armed guard only the last few days."

"What did he give the government to justify all this?" Gabe asked, astonished at what she was hearing.

"He gave the federal prosecutors more than they ever had before. He gave them more than Valachi and every other mob stoolie ever dreamed about, more than any other U.S. mobster in history ever spilled. We're talking *hundreds* of felony prosecutions, including murder, on this man's word alone. And I can't even count how many wiretaps, fugitive captures, and other leads. He was in the mob, near the top, for over ten years. He knows everything there is to know about everybody important."

"What does he do down here? Does he just live off the government in one of your safe houses?" Gabe asked.

Sunderland laughed quietly. "Not exactly. These people usually have money, and are allowed to keep some of it. Pisoli has maybe one, two hundred thou he was allowed to keep in investments. Enough to keep a steady cash flow, but not much more. He can't hold down a job. He can't travel or go to the high-profile spots like the racetracks. He just hangs around, watches television, and meets with prosecutors. Every once in a while he still flies up to Washington to testify."

"Has anyone made an attempt on his life in all the time he's been in the program?" Gabe asked.

"Threats, but no actual attempts. Like I said, he's been

moved around a lot. His face is nothing like it used to be, even his hair is totally different. But we think all these killings may actually have *him* as a target. With everything he's done for the government, that's a natural assumption."

"Or he's behind it all? Is that possible?" Gabe asked.

"We're looking into that. We just don't know. He's got no friends, and everybody that's been killed, including the bombing yesterday, could be called an enemy of his. It's all speculation. The mob is too secretive and we don't have the investigative funds or manpower to go after this whole mess."

There was a minute of silence. Then there was some radio crackle as the Lake Worth lieutenant talked to the officers on the beach's perimeter. The ocean beyond the restaurant was dark. Looking out over the dimly lit pier, Andy could make out the faint outline of a man lighting a large cigar.

"What will you be asking him?" Sunderland requested nervously.

"I'm like you. I think he's either the target of all this or he's actually at the center of it, carrying it out. Why? Like you said—speculation. Maybe he has plans of his own you're not aware of. Like having his enemies killed off, then leaving the program and going back into the mobster business under his new name. Maybe somebody owes him something and this is his way of trying to collect. With the Mafia, there's no telling. Whatever it is, at the center of it is greed or revenge. Those are the only two things they operate by."

Sunderland nodded, agreeing. He turned and led the two West Palm detectives through the phalanx of armed marshals and up to the door of the restaurant and pier. They stopped at the side of a large outdoor aquarium built into a wall. Turtles and red snappers looked at them through greenish water and algae-stained glass.

"I need your gun," Sunderland said quietly as he turned toward Amato. "Regulations. No one but marshal's person-

110

nel and FBI near him with a gun. His protection, and yours."

Andy nodded. He removed the Smith & Wesson 9-milli-meter from his shoulder holster and handed it to Gabe.

Sunderland opened the restaurant door with a key and locked it again after Andy had passed through. He walked through the dark restaurant to a door marked PIER BAIT AND POLE RENTALS. In the small bait store, refrigerators were humming and glass cases were packed with lures and tackle. He walked through a turnstile, then a cheap, wooden door, and finally out to the pier. The ocean breeze had picked up and was blowing steadily from the north. Gabe and Sunderland left him to wait by the cars.

He saw the figure plainly at the end of the old pier. There was a dim light over a fish-cleaning counter and sink, and the man stood just beyond that, arms crossed, leaning back against the railing.

Andy walked up confidently. The man was just as Andy pictured him: late forties, black hair set cleanly against a clean-shaven face. The body was big but not imposing; six feet, maybe six-one, at least 260 pounds. The face was simple and open, a boyish replacement of what Andy thought must be the true, hard-grown face underneath. Pisoli was dressed in expensive jeans and an Adidas pullover knit shirt. The cigar was a long, fat Italian one that Andy recognized as very expensive.

Both men nodded, sizing each other up.

"You wanted to talk to me, Amato?" Pisoli finally said.

"Right."

"Well, get on with it. It's late and it's fucking cold out here," Pisoli snapped. There was a typical Brooklyn accent.

Andy walked closer. Pisoli remained with his arms crossed, back to the ocean.

"I've heard a lot about you, Benny. I wanted to come see for myself if it's all true or just more Mafia bullshit."

"Whatever you say. Get on with it."

111

"The killings that have been going on. Tell me what you know and what you've heard," Andy said in a demanding tone.

"Why should I?" Pisoli shot back.

"Because we're all alone out here. I'm not wired and neither are you. Nothing can be used against you. Besides, you've got nothing better to do."

"I know what you're thinkin', Amato. You figure since I'm a stoolie once I'll always be a stoolie. You're like the rest of them, think you can come up and ask any fuckin' thing and I'll just roll over and start talkin'. Well, it ain't like that."

Andy watched some wind-driven waves break, then looked back at Pisoli. "Get this straight right now. I don't care about you or your past or your business. All I care about is homicides. I don't care what you tell or don't tell to whoever the fuck you tell it to. I just care about my cases. I'm a typical cop. That's all."

"They sent you to talk to me 'cause you got a reputation down here. And you're Italian. I know what they think they're doin'. Well, don't expect me to be impressed."

Pisoli took a long, slow draw on the cigar and inhaled the smoke into his lungs. Andy moved a step closer, a move Pisoli obviously resented.

"I think you know something about the killings. In fact, I'm *sure* you do. You were too high up, too important. I'm sure there are a few people still loyal to you, people you still talk to. I'm sure you've reached out and done some checking."

"Maybe I have. So what? Maybe I've learned some things for my own protection. So why the fuck should I tell you?" It was an important question, Andy realized. He would have to answer it or turn around and walk back along the deserted pier. "You gonna give me money, Amato? You gonna threaten me, or what? What the fuck can you do?"

"No threats. You don't need money. What I can do is save

your life. The way I figure it, something's going on that's way too big for you, Benny. Even if you're somehow connected to the killings, this thing's gonna somehow eat you up and swallow you whole. It's too coincidental that all this shit is falling down around your head. You help me, I do what I can to help you stay alive."

Pisoli laughed, then coughed up some phlegm and spit it out.

"Look around, Amato. Who the fuck are *you?* Some West Palm Beach detective gonna solve my problems? I got the marshals and the FBI. I'm so big, if I sneeze a couple times they're likely to call out the fuckin' Marines to come protect me. You gonna do somethin' for me that they can't?"

"Six dead, Benny. All mobsters, all in the protection program, just like you. One even had a federal bodyguard. Somebody is telling the mob where all the fucks are and somebody is taking you out, one by one. And you ain't Superman, Benny, just another fat fuckin' mobster that somebody wants to kill."

Pisoli laughed again but Andy saw a change in the man's attitude. He knew how to read mobsters. He could tell from eye contact, from their mannerisms, whether they were clean or dirty, and whether they were holding out information. Pisoli had reacted. The laughter was to cover up a weakness, Andy knew.

Pisoli stopped laughing. He looked out over the ocean and drew another puff. "What do you want to know, Amato?" he finally said quietly. There was no human being in sight, and only a few sea gulls far overhead. Still, Pisoli knew it was a dangerous remark to make to a cop.

"Do you know who's doing the killings?"

"I think so, I'm not sure. Let me say I've got a strong suspicion."

"Is it you? You behind it?"

Pisoli shook his head. "No way. What the fuck for? I've

113

got too much to lose. Things have been too easy. Soon they'll be done with me. No more trips to Washington to testify with a fuckin' bag over my head. I could clean up some money I got layin' around and be the fuck on my own again."

"Who, then? Who's behind it?"

Pisoli shook his head. "I'm not tellin' you, Amato. One, I'm not sure. And two, if I was, there wouldn't be a fuckin' thing you could do about it."

"I'll decide that. Tell me what you know. It doesn't get out where I got it from. I do everything on my own. No statements, no court. You have my word."

"Word? The word of a cop? An *Italian* cop? You think I'm stupid, or what? You cops are all on the edge. With enough reason, you can be pushed. And you're like me, Amato. You're a fuckin' gangster, you just happen to have a badge."

Andy didn't show his anger. "That's crap. This isn't New York. You have nothing to be afraid of and everything to gain by cooperating with me."

"Not that simple. You wouldn't hear what you're expecting to. It's nothing you can handle. Go back to West Palm Beach, Amato. Leave me the fuck alone. I'll figure something out."

Andy went into his coat pocket and took out a copy of Carmine's list. He walked forward and held it up to the moonlight, just over an arm's length away from Pisoli. He opened it and let him step forward and read some names.

"So what?" Pisoli backed up.

"So tell me who's next."

"I don't know. It depends."

"On what?"

Pisoli gave him an exasperated look and shook his head. "On lots of things."

Andy changed his tone. Pisoli was tough, and only respected toughness. "I could make life difficult for you. I could try that. Or maybe I could find out where they're keeping you and let some people know." Andy put the list away.

Pisoli smiled. "You're bluffing," he said simply.

Andy knew he was, but didn't show it. Pisoli would have no way to know.

"Let's just say life as you know it will get a lot more difficult without your cooperation. I can do it."

"Fuck off, Amato. One word from me and the marshals'll keep you so far away you'll be talkin' fuckin' Spanish. I'm hot stuff. The Washington FBI boys in the suits love me. Nobody can get close. I ain't worried."

"You're worried. I can tell. You're fuckin' worried that you're the next guy gonna buy a bullet in the head, or maybe a bomb in your fuckin' car. Or maybe they'll firebomb your house. You'll burn up like a big, fat piece of pork, layin' in bed."

Pisoli nodded and held the cigar to his side. "That works two ways, Amato. I already know a lot about you, too. That's the way this life is. I know about your cute cop wife, about your car, about your town house out by the Palm Beach Mall. I got feelers out on you, too. You get in my way, I make some phone calls and you could have a rough time, too."

Andy didn't dare betray surprise or distress. He smiled and moved forward casually, without hurry. "Tell me who's behind this, Pisoli. You know, so tell me. Let's stay friends. Let's avoid complications in our lives."

"Beat it, Amato. You're makin' me sleepy. It's late, and you're startin' to be like a pain in the ass."

Andy moved in closer. The mobster made two fists and brought them up to his waist. They stared at each other, a minute of silence interrupted only by the screech of a sea gull and the far-off horn of an ocean liner. Pisoli started to relax and bit down on the cigar between his lips.

"One last time. No more games. Who's doing the killings?"

"Your mother, Amato. That's the fuck who."

Andy moved in again and stopped. Pisoli moved his hand slowly up to his mouth and took the cigar between his fingers. They stood just a few feet from each other.

"I'm tired, beat it," the mobster said and flicked the cigar butt at Andy, hitting him square in the chest.

Andy's left hook in the upper chest that bounced the man back against the railing and then forward. Andy caught him again with a right elbow to the stomach, then a quick knee to the groin. Pisoli fell to his knees, a look of disbelief on his face.

Andy backed up and took the small revolver out of his ankle holster. Pisoli looked as if he wanted to scream, but couldn't. He stared wide-eyed at the out-of-control detective.

Andy moved up and grabbed Pisoli by the hair. Since they were out of sight he held the small revolver a few inches back, aimed between the man's eyes. There was a moment of silence and then Andy cocked the hammer back.

Pisoli finally cried out, but not loudly. Andy didn't know if the men on the beach had heard, and didn't know what they would do if they did.

He moved the revolver closer, placing the small barrel in one of Pisoli's nostrils as he gripped the man tightly by the hair.

"You come near my wife or my house and you're a dead man. *Anybody* comes near us that I don't like, you fat piece of shit, and I find you and kill you. You understand me?"

Pisoli nodded. Andy drew the gun back and let go of the man's hair. Pisoli tried to get up but Andy kicked him in the shoulder, sending him toppling to the wooden planking. The man lay there motionless, unhurt and unbruised, Andy knew, but not wanting any further abuse.

Andy bent down, decocked and replaced the small revolver into his ankle holster, then covered it with his pants leg. He turned and began to walk. Pisoli was slowly picking

116

himself up. There was no noise, no crying out, no commotion. The man would tell no one, Andy knew. It was clear that Pisoli knew he would live, that Lieutenant Andy Amato was not going to shoot him, not on a pier surrounded by cops.

"You can eat shit, Amato," Pisoli called after him.

Andy kept walking.

7

The Killing Facts

The rest of Saturday went by without another body turning up. Andy spent all the time in the office making phone calls and reading lab and patrol reports. Gabe quietly pored over her notes. They didn't speak more than a few words to each other.

Each time Andy's phone rang, he ignored it. Gabe came by once while he was near the water cooler, and picked up the phone. He watched her closely—no news would be good news. She said a few words, smiled and put the phone down. He caught her eye. She shook her head, then went on to her own desk.

Pisoli haunted him. The man *knew*—he had said as much. He knew and was keeping it a secret. Andy believed that Pisoli's silence foretold something strange, something hidden and ominous. The man should have spurted it out. Unless . . . Andy went round and round with all the possibilities.

In West Palm Beach the end of July was drawing near, and the worst of summer was beginning. Andy looked out the window near his desk and saw pedestrian traffic moving slowly: well-dressed men with their ties loosened, carrying their jackets; women hurrying into the building, anxious for the air conditioning. It hadn't rained in weeks. The front lawn of the department was quilted with patches of brown, dead grass.

There was another call on Andy's line. Gabe, just as she was passing by again, picked it up. It was from Tom Sunderland. Andy had overheard her half of the call. The marshals and FBI were also waiting skittishly, that much was apparent, and were scrambling to protect whomever they could, especially all the obvious Mafia targets. Andy watched closely as Gabe hung up, but she didn't look his way. Pisoli had obviously said nothing about Andy's putting a gun up his nose, or Gruen would be complaining to Jacobson. Gabe, knowing Andy's preoccupation, walked quietly off.

Gabe and Andy went right home and had a quiet dinner. Andy caught an hour's nap as Gabe cleaned up.

Groucho came along and woke him up. The cat was Andy's from before he and Gabe had lived together. She was big, about sixteen pounds, and all white except for large patches of black fur above her eyes. To Andy they looked like hairy eyebrows, so the name fit.

He wearily put on a robe and walked into the oversized den. The room had two large desks, each taking up an opposite wall. Around Andy's desk were stacks of books, magazines, and yellow pads. Scattered about were boxes atop boxes containing everything from old homicide case files to copies of tax returns to photo albums. The bottom half of the four walls was covered with short bookcases, and the upper half had certificates and photographs.

Gabe's half of the room was much neater. Her files were in a vertical divider on her desk, surrounded by organizers for her stationery and supplies. She was turned away from him, facing a computer screen against the far wall. "Hi, Teddy. Welcome back to consciousness."

He gave a grunt and looked at the screen. She batted her eyes at him, smiled, and turned back.

"This is the data base on the killings. I was just adding the facts from the bombing yesterday. I've got six in here altogether now, all the South Florida killings. There's a lot of information, and this helps me analyze it all."

He nodded. He had seen her elaborate computer program before. He didn't understand it, and wasn't really interested in learning how to use it. She seemed to be happy with it, and that was enough for him.

He watched as she entered commands, hitting the ENTER key. Different sets of facts scrolled by. Andy watched not only names, dates, and times but also technical measurements, time-of-death estimates, weapons used, and details of the particular M.O. in the killing. Gabe's feminine hands glided over the keys and the computer responded with the screen showing list after list. She would nod, make a note or two on a pad, then enter more commands. He admired her methods, even if he found them boring.

"This is a relational data structure," she said. "It's something fairly new. It uses artificial intelligence, A.I. Besides listing all the things you put in, in any order you want, it'll actually answer questions you put to it. Some of the answers aren't much yet, not with only six killings. But with enough information, this computer could actually open up a lead or point to a set of facts we might have otherwise overlooked."

Andy tried to look impressed for Gabe, who he knew took all this computer stuff seriously. Groucho came in and jumped up on a short bookcase, rubbing against the wall and purring loudly enough for Andy to hear. He walked over to scratch her. Gabe continued feeding lines of questions into the computer and watching the screen change. Then she reached up and turned on the computer printer. She was engrossed in her operation, Andy saw. He was fatigued and ready to call it a night. His hour's nap had only served to give him a headache and make him want more sleep.

Gabe, though, was happy and alert. "You really have to learn how to do this," she said. "This is the wave of the future. Police work will be all computers in a few years. There won't be any handwritten notes or reports; everything will be on disk. Eventually, computers will be figuring out all the crimes."

"Right." Andy shrugged and grunted, shaking his head.

She looked back at the keyboard and typed in a series of commands:

> LIST EVERYONE DEAD
> LIST HOW THEY DIED
> SHOW WHAT'S UNUSUAL
> QUESTION: TELL US WHO'S NEXT

She smiled. Andy shook his head, obviously skeptical. "I've also typed in all the names from Carmine and also the U.S. marshal's list. Everyone is in here, with as much verified information as I can add. When I punch this ENTER key, we'll see if I get any results."

She hit the key. The printer came to life; it took only about a minute before it ejected the first page and went on to the next, pushing up the list. Gabe stood up and ripped the sheet from the computer, holding it next to her so they both could read it.

> 1. Eugene Ferrigno, mobster, .38 back of head, killed while walking nearby his Vero Beach condo. New ID and face. No marshal protection.

2.   Arthur Veniziano, mobster, .38 in chest, killed late in evening after parking car and walking toward his Ft. Pierce oceanfront town house. No marshal protection.

3.   Charles Portuno, mobster, .22 to skull, killed in burglary, assassin is victim #4, had key to alarm and house plans for mansion. Killed in his bed of Palm Beach mansion rented by marshal's service. No marshal protection.

4.   Gary Corrizi, hired mob assassin and killer of #3, .38 to back of head while seated in Lincoln outside Seabreeze Ave, Palm Beach. Had just completed mob contract killing of #3.

5.   Thomas Ripaldi, mobster, shot repeatedly while tied to a chair in his W. Palm Beach apartment. Gun taped to hand and tortured, forced to commit suicide with self-inflicted gunshot to head. Killer left key to apartment on carpet inside. Neighbor heard voices at victim's door just before shooting. No marshal protection.

6.   Charles T. Aiello, mobster, blown up in vehicle while leaving his Boca Raton town house. Had U.S. marshal protection and remote starter for car. Killer used start-delay or remote activator for high-powered bomb.

Your question: Tell us who's next
Your answer: Unknown, most likely possibles from data as follows:

Gregory "Gene" Salisi, Delray Beach
Fred DiPietro, W. Palm Beach

Anthony "Spike" Fillipi, Jupiter
Benjamin "Beans" Pisoli, address unknown

Andy read over the computer list twice, amused by the listing of Pisoli as one of the next possible victims.

"It's not purely scientific," Gabe said. "It's based on all the variables I put in, with a value for each based on importance. The computer is mathematical and logical, not intuitive like a human brain. But it can sometimes put logic where humans think there is none."

Andy tightened his robe. Groucho jumped from the bookcase to the desk and rubbed up against him. Andy's headache pounded away, but he was able to concentrate fully on the list.

"Maybe one day you'll have to teach me," Andy said. Gabe smiled at him.

Groucho came up to Gabe and she gave the old cat a polite but uninvolved petting. Andy read down the list once more.

Gabe turned back to the keyboard and entered more commands. She tried ages, mob families, dates of birth, known associates, and every other variable she could think of. Each time the screen would scroll through the information and both Andy and Gabe would watch intently, as if the final and deciding clue was about to pop up in front of them. To Andy, at least, it always came up just short. There wasn't quite enough. But he feigned being impressed.

Pointing at the page, he said, "There's an obvious pattern. And number three is the obvious exception—killed with a twenty-two, not a thirty-eight. And obviously by number four—who's now dead. And whoever killed number four killed everybody else with his thirty-eight, or a different one. And now a bomb."

"Very good," Gabe said.

"So. Nothing new. I could've told you all that."

"Right. But there's more. It's leading somewhere. Can't

you feel it? Can't you just tell that there's something missing, something we can almost put a finger on?"

He nodded. He *did* feel it. And he was surprised by Gabe's obviously unscientific, emotional reaction.

She continued. "If you ever need to use this and I'm not here, just type in MINDSCAPES to get into the program, then try English commands. If you ask it for something, you might be surprised, it just may answer."

He nodded again, politely. The headache was still nagging. Gabe kept talking while she punched in more commands, taking notes on the side. He admired her long hair and the way she looked in the bright print dress. He stared for a while at the fine dark hair on her arms and the ever-so-faint and only slightly dark mustache on her upper lip. She was beautiful, he said to himself once again. The facts on the killings left him. He put aside the list of the four mobsters who the computer thought were next to die. Trying to forget the headache, he put his hands on her shoulders and began a gentle massage.

Gabe looked up at him and smiled. Then she reached over and shut off the computer.

Andy would sometimes sleep without dreaming, but this was rare. He remembered his dreams, and remembered also when he was not having them. Most were jumbled conversations and activities, always involving active cases. Some made sense, some were just random drivel, and were soon forgotten.

He was deep into a dream. It was a conversation between himself, Jacobson, Gabe, Phil Wesley, and Benny Pisoli. They were walking along, he was not sure where—maybe a beach, he remembered thinking. The snatches of conversation he strained to listen to made no sense to him.

The shrill electronic phone buzzer canceled the dream and brought him almost to consciousness. He was back in

Miami, he thought. It was the once- or twice-a-week mid-A.M. wake-up call from a detective sergeant. It was another drug killing, or maybe a domestic fight taken to its limits. Maybe a badly decomposed body on the edge of the Everglades, or in a Liberty City rooming house . . .

The loud electronic buzz hit his ear again, this time like someone slapping the side of his head with a strong, flat palm. His eardrum rang.

He turned over, awake, picking up the phone and throwing off the sheet covering his naked torso.

"Hello."

"Amato. Sorry to call so late. I have to talk."

It was Sunderland, almost whispering. Andy snapped away from the dream.

"Yeah. Hi. Go ahead."

"Pisoli. What did you say to him?" The question came rapid and direct.

"Why? What happened?" Andy wanted to sound surprised.

"What did you tell him? What did he say to you?"

"Is there a problem?" Andy replayed putting his revolver in Pisoli's nostril.

"Everything. As if the killings weren't bad enough. As if the fucking collapse of the witness program weren't enough, now this shit happens."

"Tell me what you're talking about." He looked over at Gabe, who was still asleep, breathing in with a low snore, more of a hum.

"There's big problems, Andy. Gruen's after me now. He wants to know what was said, what you did." Sunderland's voice was deteriorating. He was talking quickly, almost in a mumble.

Andy took a deep breath. "Tell me what you're talking about," he insisted. He looked at the bedside clock; it was just before three A.M.

125

"Pisoli's gone. Just like that. Around midnight he comes inside from a walk. There's two marshals in the place, guarding him. He tells one he forgot something from his car. My man, in a pair of shorts, walks him out there, even has a gun ready." Sunderland trailed off, voice sounding tired and drained.

"Keep going." Andy could feel the pressure in his gut.

"Pisoli got in the car, a maroon Mercedes, like he was looking for something. Then he started it and drove off. Just fucking took off. My men went for their car keys, then they took off after him. He was gone. He took off, just like that. No clothes, just what he was wearing, and just his wallet and some cash."

Andy gave a groan of relief that Pisoli was not blown to kingdom come. "Where would he go? You try his girlfriends? His hangouts?"

"They did. Give me a break, Andy. It wasn't because the fuck wanted to get laid. We have that all prearranged, he wouldn't take off for that. This was something else."

"What about local descriptions over the police frequencies? Let a patrol car pick him up. There aren't that many maroon Mercedes out in the middle of the night."

"We can't. Those frequencies are monitored by the press. Even if we lied, someone might catch on. It's just going to be us and the FBI out looking for him."

Andy leaned back against the headboard, letting out another deep sigh. He reached up and clicked on a lamp.

"Who knew where he was? Did he suspect someone had gotten his location? Maybe he was afraid."

"No. He was just moved, orders from Washington. Only me and the two men knew—not even the FBI. Even the list I gave you was outdated. That wasn't it, he was nested in there real safe."

"I don't think I can tell you anything—"

Sunderland interrupted. "You have to help me on this,

126

Amato. Gruen's out for my ass. He was against your meeting. Now he's talkin' like you're behind it. Like you said something or did something to cause this."

Andy closed his eyes and shook his head. He thought for a moment that maybe *this* was a dream, then realized it wasn't. "There was nothing. I didn't tell him anything. And he didn't say anything to me. Only that he knew, or thought he knew, who was behind the killings."

First there was silence. "Why didn't you tell us?" Sunderland finally asked, pleading.

"There was nothing to tell. He wouldn't give a name. No facts. Nowhere to go with it. He was sticking by the Mafia code. *Omertà.*"

"Where is he, Amato? Do you know?"

"Not a clue."

"Give me a hint. Somewhere to start."

Andy thought. He would tell Sunderland his best instinct, his gut reaction, what he *knew,* but couldn't prove. "Okay. Pisoli's out looking for the killer. Or he's running away from him. I think he knows exactly who it is and is going to try to get him first."

"My God . . ." Sunderland moaned, then became silent.

Andy was wide awake, realizing he would not be going back to sleep.

When he slammed the door of the oceanside condo, he heard only overactive crickets and the equable, serene sound of the waves. There was no moon. A much needed rain had finished an hour before, leaving the pavement and grassy areas wet, making everything look and smell clean and new and fresh.

It had been easy. It was like the first time he had killed, but this time with much more emotion. He got to know his victim. They talked. He tried to believe the pleadings, only they didn't shake him back to reality. He *felt* something. But

127

he knew what he had to do. It was not Pisoli, it was not who he wanted, and the man could not help him. He had kept his gun straight out, pointing at the man's chest.

He found the devices and forced the man into them. Then he forced the man to masturbate. In the end, with the man's coerced, robotic climax, he held the Magnum up, pulling the trigger and hitting his target square in the chest. There was the explosion, the revolver kicking back, the thud from the bullet, the spurting of blood, the tensing of the muscles, and then death. The hands and fingers twitched but then stopped, and the eyes looking out from the mask had glazed over.

So the crickets sounded okay. Better than the man's pleadings. They were constant, predictable, almost melodic. The ocean, too, was a comfort. It soothed him. The rain-cleansed, early-morning air relaxed him as he took in deep, effortless breaths. He looked at his hands—there was no sweat. He listened for any voices. All was quiet. In the dead of night, neighbors had slept through it. There were the predictable sea gulls high overhead, and if you listened for it, traffic noise from A1A less than half a mile west.

He lifted the list out of his pocket. He crossed out the address. It was number six. But it wasn't the one he wanted. He knew that. There would be another night, and another chance.

He replaced the list, pushed the Magnum deep into his waistband, and walked back to his car.

8

Deep Throat

Andy was thinking about murder. His memory launched into a recount of one of the hundreds he had investigated; it was like an endless-loop videotape, one scene from one case passing into another scene from another case. He remembered faces, weapons, clues, and suspects. It wasn't something morbid—at least he felt it wasn't—it was just something that went with the territory of the homicide division. He thought of it as an occupational oddity, nothing more, not a perversion or something that was a psychological flaw. For some reason, lately, he found himself viewing his more memorable Miami cases over and over: the boyfriend who dismembered his girlfriend and tried feeding her to an alligator; a pair of armed robbers who killed a Publix supermarket manager when he refused to open the store safe; the weightlifter who hired two cronies to hold down a cheating girlfriend and pour Drano down her throat; the two Miami PD vice agents who rolled a Colombian drug dealer out of a moving department car—at seventy miles an hour.

The call came in just before ten, just as Jacobson was

lighting his second cigar of the Monday morning and getting near the end of the *Wall Street Journal*. Andy was typing a report. Gabe was across the building at the ID lab. The ringing interrupted him mulling over the Miami case of a Pakistani store owner frying a burglar on an electrified steel grating.

"Lieutenant Amato," he said quickly into the phone.

"Another one," was all Sunderland replied.

Andy paused. "Pisoli?"

"No. That's what I thought, too. It's not. It's somebody we didn't think would get hit. A third-rate nobody. But he's dead, just the same. Jupiter, by the ocean. Can you get up here?"

Andy said he could. He took down the address on a piece of pink "While You Were Out" paper and put it in his shirt pocket.

Andy thought of Jupiter, a small city in northern Palm Beach County, and he didn't think of murder. He thought of Burt Reynolds Dinner Theater, Harpoon Louie's Seafood Restaurant, clean, white beaches, new and airy shopping malls. He thought of his second wedding, to Gabe at the Jupiter Hilton, chosen purposely because it was so far from the maddening Miami crowd. It was the northern limit of where Andy would run to get away from it all. To him, a murder in Jupiter was a sacrilege, something he took personally.

Jupiter, he thought. *Shit.*

He said nothing to Jacobson, but only snagged his jacket off the chair and headed off to get Gabe.

Andy showed his gold West Palm PD badge to the deputy at the door and accepted the officer's curious nod without comment. The deputy was tall, very military looking, with a crew cut and wearing an impeccable sheriff's-green uniform.

Gabe walked in behind him. The building was a small,

newer prefab condo just off the ocean. There were about three dozen apartments side by side, some two-story, some one-story, twisting around a common parking lot. Palm trees surrounded the complex, and to the east was only driftwood, white-sugar sand, and then the Atlantic Ocean.

Sunderland was in the small living room. A sheriff's detective was talking in bothered, hushed tones on the phone in the kitchen. Andy saw Gruen and a younger FBI agent by the door to the bedroom.

"He's in there," Sunderland said. "It's incredible. I can't believe it. I never would've thought I'd ever see something like this." The U.S. marshal looked pale, almost ready to puke.

Andy had to push in past Gruen, saying nothing to the squatty, unlovable agent.

"Back for more, Amato? Super Guinea Sleuth gonna solve this one for us, too?" Gruen smiled, showing yellowish teeth.

Andy ignored him and walked into the bedroom. Gruen turned around to find Gabe giving him a cold stare. The other agent, a much younger man, was probably right out of Quantico, Andy figured, and was just there to observe.

A gym bar was suspended by two chains from the bedroom ceiling, hanging from large U-hooks bolted into the studs. Around the bar were two thick leather straps drooping downward. Dangling from the straps was a naked man. He had one belt looped into the back of a black leather girdle that was pulled tight around his back and groin. The other held up his head. His chest was crisscrossed by a thinner strap with metal studs. His head was covered by a black executioner's mask, only his eyes and mouth peering out from behind the ebony silkiness. The eyes were glazed over and staring.

The sheriff's ID team was alternating between taking pictures and using tweezers to pick up evidence. The man was thin, with black-frame glasses and greasy hair. His partner had red hair and was too heavy for the green ID jumpsuit they had given her.

The body had a gaping chest wound and a puddle of blood had dripped downward onto the pile carpeting. Near the blood was another substance, looking to Andy like melted wax. He looked back up and saw the man's half-flaccid penis, now discolored and crooked, drooping downward toward the caked blood and the dried, tacky white fluid.

Gabe looked away. Gruen laughed and walked back to the living room. Sunderland started to talk to Gabe but stopped, and joined Andy at the body. The dead man dangled freely, moving slightly, almost imperceptibly, with the rotation of the earth.

"Anthony Fillipi was this guy's name. From the Genovese family in New York. Nickname was Spike . . ." Sunderland's voice trailed off.

Andy nodded. "How long?" he asked the ID people.

Six to ten hours, they told him, then went back to their clinical doings. Gabe walked into the room.

"We figure the thirty-eight again, right in the chest. Right after the guy . . . uh . . . right after he came on the carpet there." Sunderland pointed and kept his eyes looking away from Gabe, who didn't react.

"No forced entry, is that right?" Andy asked.

"Right," Sunderland answered.

Gabe took out her pad and started her notes.

"Find a key?" Andy asked.

"No," Sunderland mumbled.

"This . . . stuff, these items. This outfit, it all belong to him?"

"Right. In the closet. This was his hangup, we knew about it. He was a kinky son of a bitch, but harmless enough. He'd bring in girls from Riviera Beach or West Palm. That much we knew. We understand he liked to get whipped."

"How long was he in the witness program?"

"About six years. He was selling information to the FBI in New York. He got caught. It was low-level stuff. We got him the hell out of there. He's had no problems ever since then. There was no Mafia interest in finding him."

Andy looked at Gabe. She was ready to tell Sunderland all about Fillipi appearing on her computer list as a next likely target. Andy shook his head slightly, telling her not to.

Sunderland continued. "We can't protect all of them. He was calling in to us every morning at nine sharp. At nine-fifteen we called him and got no answer. Then we sent the sheriff by."

Andy walked closer and examined the chest wound. The eyes were open, a glazed-over sky blue, staring straight ahead like a fish on ice in a deli case.

"What about Pisoli?" Andy asked. "Could he do this? After he took off, you search his place good? You find anything out?"

"We did. We found nothing. No notes, no letters, not a clue."

Gruen spoke up. "Do your homework, Amato. Pisoli doesn't have a gun. He's a knife man. A knife, always a knife."

Andy looked behind at the FBI agent, then back around at the body.

"Yeah, well, people change. The last week can hardly be said to be normal. Something's up with the mob. They're on a rampage. Pisoli's at the heart of it. He's got something to do with all of this. This is number seven. And now Benny Pisoli's missing. So don't tell me about homework, Gruen. Somebody's got a final exam comin' up, and we'd better be ready for it." The men glared at each other.

The ID woman got up and walked to the east window. She pulled up the shade and pushed up the glass. Yellow sunlight came into the room, broken up by a hint of shimmering blue.

"I hate the fuckin' smell in here," the woman said, and

returned to searching the carpet for hair and fiber evidence.

"When's the last time he brought a girl up here, do we know?" Andy asked.

"No way to tell. He wasn't monitored that closely. He'd drive down and pick up a streetwalker, usually. They knew him, he was a regular," Sunderland answered.

"No whore did this, Amato," Gruen said roughly from across the room.

Andy didn't look at him. "Of course not. But one may have left just before this. She may have seen something."

"Whores never see anything," Gruen said.

Gabe scribbled in her notebook. She made a sketch of the room and the body, and listed all the chains, whips, and belts she saw. She walked to the other side of the small bedroom. The closet door was open, and a large wooden chest with its lid off revealed more of the leather S and M devices. There were also vibrators, jellies, and magazines.

Andy spoke out loud, mostly to himself. "The killer left us something. Just like the rest of the cases. We have to find what it is."

"No forced entry," Sunderland said quietly. "Again. Somebody he knew?"

"Or a key," Andy said. "This time taking it with him."

Gabe was looking at the items in the closet. "These things. They're our clue," she said. "All these items. Whoever killed him knew he had these and where he kept them. Forced him into them, then killed him, just like this. Forced him to masturbate, then shot him."

Sunderland nodded. "The question is *why*? This guy was a *nothing*."

Gruen lit up a cigar and chortled. "Why? Because the Mafia hates a stool pigeon, right, Amato? Worse than they hate cops. They don't care how long it takes, eventually they catch up to you. That's their motto—it's on their fucking corporate logo, for Christ's sake."

134

Andy looked at him. "Right. That's true. But some-body's caught on to your program. None of your witnesses are safe."

Sunderland nodded.

The crime scene technician got up off her knees, picking up her three small plastic bags of trace evidence. Her partner was finishing up, using a scalpel to place the dried blood and sperm into separate tubes and capping them.

"Put the cigar out, will you please?" the fat ID officer said.

Gruen smiled, nodded, and walked back out of the cramped bedroom.

Andy had been waiting almost a full half hour. He stretched out on the hard wooden bench, shifting his weight to find a comfortable position. He felt stupid for waiting so long for the man and cursed because he knew he had to. He had loosened his tie and taken off his jacket, revealing his shoulder holster.

He looked over at the statue again, taking his eyes away from the Flagler Street Bridge and the intracoastal. The tarnished copper and bronze was of a woman and her two scantily clothed children standing beside the rubble of a mid-twenties wooden Florida shanty. The metal plaque beneath the statue announced that it was in remembrance of the 1,800 victims of an unnamed South Florida hurricane that struck West Palm in September 1928. Andy looked away, duly impressed by the numbers.

He would often choose the east side of the West Palm Beach Municipal Library for a meeting place. It was near downtown, but away from the gin mills and singles bars that other detectives used for an encounter. Andy had met snitches and miscellaneous other contacts behind the old gray building many times. But most of them had arrived on time, and Andy Amato didn't like to wait.

He finally saw the man out of the corner of his eye, walking along the sidewalk to his right. The figure weaved in and around the palm, ficus, and hibiscus trees on the south side of the library, just off the busy downtown street. In the late-evening sun the man's wrinkled brown suit cast a purple sparkle.

"Hello, Andy. Mind if I sit?"

"Please do," he replied, moving over on the bench. They didn't shake hands.

"Sorry I'm a few minutes late. Your directions were good—I just get lost in new cities. And it took a few minutes longer than I thought to drive up from Miami."

Andy nodded. The man took a pack of Juicy Fruit gum from his pocket and offered it to Andy. Amato shook his head, and the man unwrapped a stick and popped it into his mouth. He leaned back on the bench and looked around.

"Nice spot. Not secluded, but not crowded. And not noisy. Nice view. Good selection, you always could pick them."

Andy nodded and smiled. The man still looked like G. Gordon Liddy to him, with the receding hair and the dark mustache. But his companion was much smaller, not even five-ten, he guessed.

"What's it been, a year? Two? I bet you didn't think you'd see ol' Fogarty again, eh, Amato?"

"Wrong. I knew I would. Somehow I knew. Know what I mean? Like somehow you just *know* that you can't shake something off of you?"

Fogarty laughed and unwrapped another stick of Juicy Fruit, folding it into his mouth along with the first one.

"Nice city. It's no Miami, but it's quaint. Nice big buildings, nice shops, just not the crowds."

"It'll do."

"Right. Me, for one, I wasn't all that surprised when you left the Magic City to come up here. You and your second wife, uh . . ."

"Gabe."

136

"Gabe. Right. The gal from the department. I wasn't all that surprised like everyone else was. You were down there a lot of years. Lots of killings to investigate. And then all the changes. It gets to you."

"Nothing to do with it, Larry. Homicide's my business. I'm good at it. There are killings up here, too."

They looked at each other. Andy was wondering what the *Miami Herald* reporter had called him for, why he wanted to meet. He was hoping it was nothing to do with the witness killings. It was an unreasonable wish, he knew; Fogarty was too sharp for that.

"Right. Well, I know how you feel. All the fuckin' Cubans, the Haitians, Liberty City, Overtown, AIDS, all that shit. You and Gabe wanted to make a clean break."

"Maybe. There's that stuff up in West Palm Beach, too, just less of it."

"Right. Gotcha. Well, anyway, nice city. Hope you're getting along okay at the police department."

"Fine. Just fine, Larry. Everything's going real smooth. About five years to retire, and Gabe can do it in about eight. Then we want to buy a fuckin' motor home and see the country. Okay? Now, you happy?"

Fogarty reached in his mouth and grabbed the wad of gum. He threw it to his left, in the grass beside the statue of the woman and her two ragamuffins.

"How's Andy Junior?"

"Fine."

"And Gloria? She remarry?"

"Yep. About a year ago. A fuckin' Irish lawyer, you believe it?"

Fogarty shook his head and laughed. They fell silent.

"There's something I know you're good at besides homicides, Amato. Something you're famous for. That's why I'm up here."

"Yeah? What's that?"

137

"The Mafia. Cosa Nostra. The Mob, as the FBI calls it. You were always the man they talked to, always the man with the connections. I helped you out on something before, and the way I figure it, you still owe me."

He owed Fogarty. He was ashamed to admit it. It was something only he and Fogarty shared. Gabe didn't even know about what had happened.

It was the mid-eighties. "Miami Vice" was the rage. People were taking Ronald Reagan seriously. Gloria Amato had just divorced Andy, and Andy Junior just turned two. Gabrielle was still a year or two off from being assigned with him. The Liberty City riots were out of the news, and the city was quiet. Then-Sergeant Andy Amato had just been teamed up with a new detective, a Colombian, Detective First Grade Roquito Mandella Alejandro. Everyone called him Rocky because of his first name but also because of the squareness of his head and his fighter's nose.

They had been hunting for a juvenile gang member, a particularly vicious killer who had set a store owner on fire. When they found him he had fired a .45 at them. Rocky chased him into a housing project, into an apartment where the kid killed the woman who was living there. Andy ran into the apartment in time to find the kid's .45 empty and Alejandro beating him to death. Andy tried but couldn't stop his deranged Colombian partner from executing the boy, sending a bullet into his chest. Larry Fogarty had followed both the detectives up the stairs and into the apartment. Andy had turned and found Fogarty snapping pictures. Andy took the camera, exposed the film, and he and Fogarty had an interesting conversation. A deal was made. They were "friends" for life.

Lawrence Fogarty wrote the follow-up story on the case: At the last second, after a fierce struggle, the young gang member had pointed the pistol at the young detective. Not realizing the .45 was empty, the detective shot him once in the chest, killing him instantly. After finding that the gun was empty, the detective suffered severe psychological problems and retired from the force.

There would be no scandal, no riots, no indictments. Sergeant Andy Amato had made sure of it. He studied for his lieutenant's test, passed it, and got his promotion.

Larry Fogarty called him at home from time to time. They would talk about life, about their jobs, and about that very special bond between them, and about all the great news stories yet to come.

Andy remained silent and watched as an old man led a small boy by the hand on the sidewalk in front of them. The man had on an old and stained Yankees cap with the bill turned up and was wearing loose-fitting, stained yellow shorts. The five-year-old was tugging his grandpa back toward the library.

When the pair had passed Fogarty said, "Lots of bodies been showing up around here. There was that spectacle down in Boca, with the car blown to bits. The two dead guys near the Palm Beach mansion." He paused and waited, but Andy was silent.

"Miami FBI won't say shit," Fogarty went on. "Dade Metro police is disavowing any knowledge of the cases, just like the U.S. marshal's people. Palm Beach PD and Boca PD won't even return my phone calls. The paper's lawyers don't want to get involved yet, they say the public records law is kinda useless when it comes to active homicides."

"Yeah? Oh well, you know how it is."

"Right. Well, it's mob related, that much I know. There's been at least one I'm sure about in West Palm Beach, and the way I figure it they've *got* to have you involved."

"Maybe."

"Andy, you owe me."

139

"And will keep on owing you, I guess. Forever. I came up here, thinking maybe just a little bit, Fogarty, that I'd get the hell away from you. Thinking what the hell can happen in Palm Beach that ol' Larry Fogarty could possibly give a shit about."

"Somethin' big is up, Andy. I can smell it. The other papers are waitin' for it to break officially. You know, little know-nothing stories, waiting for your bullshit, typed-up release. I'm not. I want a sense of it *now*, even if you make me hold off on printing any of it."

"And I'm the first guy you run to? You figure I'm involved, right? Lucky me."

"Right, and other departments aren't gonna cooperate with me like I know you will."

"They won't cooperate with you, Larry? No shit. Wonder why. Don't suppose it has anything to do with the way you wrote up the McDuffie killing and Liberty City riots in the seventies, do you? Or Overtown and Alvarez, or maybe the way you blasted the department over the Miami River cops stuff? Or the Overtown riot when the cop shot the kid on the motorcycle? You think maybe you're not too popular with the law enforcement crowd?"

"Right. But you know better, Amato. Lieutenant Andy Amato knows better 'cause Larry Fogarty helped him out of a jam once, right, Andy?"

"Right."

Andy sighed and fell silent. The sun was almost down. He looked at the old man and kid heading down the sidewalk, toward the water, the Yankees cap still turned up and the little kid still pulling the other way.

"I got one for you, Larry. A good one."

The reporter's eyes lit up. "Go ahead."

"This cop goes into a bar down in Miami, right? He's at one end of the bar, and at the other end there's all these women falling all over these tacky-dressed guys with squinty glasses and absolutely no class. So this cop, he's kinda jeal-

140

ous, he's used to gettin' all the action, right? He asks the bartender what's going on, and the bartender says, 'Those are reporters. This is a reporters' bar, and those guys over there are reporters, and the women love them.' So the cop goes home and thinks about it. He comes back the next day after making himself up to look like a reporter, all nerdy-looking in a polyester suit with glasses, right? He goes to the end of the bar and this beautiful babe hits on him right away, and he tells her that he's a reporter for the fuckin' *Herald*. She gets all excited and they go back to her place. He's in the sack with her, boinking her, screwing her brains out, when all of a sudden he starts laughing hysterically, this cop does. So she stops and asks him, 'What's so funny,' right? So you know what he says? He says, 'What's so funny? I've been a reporter only ten minutes, and already I'm fuckin' somebody!' "

Larry Fogarty laughed—lightly at first, then louder. He hit Amato on the shoulder. His dark mustache bounced up and down.

" '. . . and already I'm fucking somebody!' Clever, Amato, very clever. Cute. I'll have to remember that. I'll reverse it and give it to the next cop that gives me a hard time."

Andy laughed. He hated Fogarty, but over the years he had come to tolerate the man, even have feelings of congeniality. It had been a year, maybe longer. Fogarty had called him on his last Miami case, a prostitute washed up near Dinner Key Auditorium with her hands sliced off. He had dodged the phone calls and never given him a story. He wondered if Larry remembered.

"Down to business, Andy. I know a lot already. I won't waste your time. The injured U.S. marshal means that the feds are protecting these people. We know about five so far, including the one yesterday that's still a big hush-hush. I'd say five's a pretty good indication of a problem . . . a trend. Something big."

"Seven. There's been seven. There were two up north,

141

Fort Pierce and Vero Beach, before the recent Palm Beach ones."

Fogarty scribbled on a pad he took out of the brown coat pocket. "What about it? They're related, aren't they, Andy?"

Andy held his breath. He knew he had to tell him. "Definitely."

"Same guy? Same killer?"

"Or same group of killers."

"What was the story in Palm Beach, on the ritzy island?"

"An old guy gets killed by a New York hotshot, then the hotshot gets killed as he's about to drive away. A contract killing of the old man, then . . ." He trailed off.

"What?"

"I don't know. It's too confusing. Too many facts."

"Right. I didn't come here for the facts. I came here for the *feel*. What does Lieutenant Andy Amato *feel?*"

"What's gonna be in the papers, and when?" Andy asked cautiously.

"Nothing now. My editor wants to cooperate and keep this quiet a while longer. If it was me, I'd have it in the headlines in the morning."

"No shit."

"Right. That's the way I am. There won't be anything right away. And I won't use your name. You'll be the 'unnamed source.' You know, the deep throat stuff. Now, I need what you *feel.*"

"What I feel's got nothing to do with this one, Fogarty. The feelings are still all jumbled up. Too many twists and turns, too many pieces up in the air and not fitting together."

"Who, exactly, are all the victims? What do they have in common? We can't even get the feds to release any names."

"Mafia. Protected witnesses. Stool pigeons down in Florida for a better life. New licenses and credit cards, new names, sometimes new faces."

Fogarty didn't look surprised. "If they're protected, how is the mob finding out where they are?"

Andy nodded. Both men stayed silent as a young couple, arm in arm, the woman's head buried deep into the boyfriend's shoulder, walked through the hibiscus trees along the sidewalk. They disappeared in the darkness, toward the intracoastal.

"The million-dollar question, Larry. Maybe there's a leak. Other possibilities include someone buying information, maybe someone breaking the feds' computer codes, getting the information that way."

"Don't give me a list, Andy. Tell me what *you* think."

"What do I think? You want to know what I think?"

"Right."

"I could lose my job for even talking to you, Fogarty. And look how close I am to my pension."

"You love danger. Tell me."

"I think more people are gonna die before we even get close to it. It's that scary. All these mobsters, and we're talking *hundreds* of them, are being protected by maybe *thirty or forty* federal agents. Even with what some local agencies can spare, even bringing FBI agents and marshals from other areas, they'll never protect everybody. There'll be dozens on their own, unprotected. They're sitting ducks for professional hit men."

"Who's behind it? Is it one family in particular? Is it some mobsters down here? Is it someone out to ruin the federal protection program?"

Andy shook his head. Pisoli, he thought. Pisoli was at the center of it, but he wasn't about to tell Fogarty about him. Fogarty had obviously not heard the name yet. There was no need to tell him. "Those are possibilities. And you're right, it might be a giant mob conspiracy to ruin the feds' program. To shut up all the future wiseguys who may think of turning stoolie. They won't be so certain they can retire down in Florida with a nice, cushy bankroll and an ocean-front condo."

"You'll confirm for me, then? The killings are all related? The victims were all in the feds' protection program? It's some kind of conspiracy? Seven dead so far, possibly more to come? You'll confirm that? Officially?"

Andy recognized the broken, excited urgency in the dedicated reporter's voice. Fogarty's inflection changed from friendliness to officiousness. Andy could already read the headlines.

"You have me over a barrel, Fogarty. I know you. Whether I answer yes or no, you'll swear it was yes."

"My credibility is everything, Amato. I couldn't do that." He smiled, showing his yellowish teeth.

"This won't break any time soon?" Andy insisted. "My name won't be mentioned? You'll swear that to me, you old scumsucking dog, you?"

"I swear. Nothing soon. We want a scoop, but we're not that close to a good story. Not yet. You'll confirm?"

"I'll confirm if you'll swear."

"I swear."

"I don't believe you, but I'll confirm."

"Thanks."

Fogarty closed his notebook and was off the bench, walking hurriedly toward his car. Andy decided to spend a few minutes in the early-evening darkness watching the brightly lit boats cruise along the intracoastal.

The electronic buzz hit his head again. It was loud, and the artificial chime caused Gabe to sit up, then turn over, taking the covers with her. Andy came awake with the second ring. He sat up and stared at the phone. He was trying to train himself to let it ring, let it bring him fully awake. He didn't like mumbling incoherently and then forgetting half of the early-morning conversation.

144

As the phone rang for the fourth time, he was able to focus his eyes. The clock radio said 3:51. He reached over and picked up the receiver.

"Lieutenant Amato," he said wearily.

"Pisoli. They found his car." It was Sunderland.

"The Mercedes?" It was a stupid question, Andy realized. The kind of question you ask when you're not fully awake.

"The Mercedes. Bullet holes and blood. But no body. On State Road Eighty, halfway to the Everglades. Highway Patrol's got it. That's all I know. I'm heading out there."

"No body?"

"No body. Just blood. Can you go out there with me?"

"Sure. How far out?"

"They said about fifteen miles. I'll look for the trooper's lights."

"Okay. I'll be there."

Sunderland hung up. Andy wanted to bury his head back in the soft pillow, back in the warmth of the waterbed, but he managed to swing his legs out and onto the carpet. Groucho jumped off the bed, complaining loudly, and scampered out of the bedroom.

9

The Belly of the Beast

Lieutenant Andy Amato put down the driver's window of the Saab and pushed in the switch to kill the powerful air conditioner. Gabe opened her eyes and lowered her window a crack. The cool western air from the Everglades swirled in as Andy pushed the car to over eighty on the deserted two-lane road. He saw the rotating blue beacons of the Highway Patrol up ahead on the deserted roadway. He could also make out other taillights. Sunderland and the usual crowd had already arrived, he figured.

"How did it go with Fogarty?" Gabe asked. She had been asleep when he finally got home.

"Fine. Same stuff. You know."

She nodded.

Andy pulled in behind a Chevy from the Marshals Service. He could smell the burning sugarcane wafting in from Belle Glade, just a few miles farther west. The sugar mills were just starting to crank up for the harvest season, and the first few tons of green, raw cane were being fed into the gargantuan ovens.

The trooper was black, probably six-six, Andy estimated.

146

His tan uniform was impeccable, shoes shined, gun belt glossy, badge sparkling. There was a straw-colored Stetson perfectly capping his short Afro. He had a clean-shaven baby face and bright eyes.

Andy showed his badge to the trooper. The man nodded and watched as he moved past him, toward the Mercedes-Benz.

Sunderland detached himself from a group of six or seven men, all in suits, and came toward them. Andy saw Gruen with the young agent and Phil Wesley, along with at least one more FBI man whom he recognized as a Washington supervisor. The others were deputy marshals.

"Thanks for coming out this time of the morning. I realize it's late and you've got to go to work in a few more hours."

"We're used to it," Gabe said wearily.

Sunderland nodded. The men in the suits were standing behind the highly polished trunk of the maroon Mercedes. The trooper stayed back, uninvolved, appearing happy to guard the outer perimeter from mosquitoes, lightning bugs, and the occasional rubbernecking motorist who wanted to pass by too closely and gawk for too long.

Sunderland looked at his watch. "Trooper here found the car just under three hours ago. He ran the tag, found our wanted message on the car. He checked inside and found it just like it still is."

"No sign of Pisoli?" Andy asked.

"None. The sugarcane is too high on either side of the road, he couldn't have gone in there. Another trooper checked the road from West Palm to Belle Glade. Nothing."

Andy looked at the canal.

"We'll have to call in a diver as soon as it's light," Sunderland added.

Divers. Murky, brown Florida canals, submerged cars, alligators, dead bodies, alligators, sometimes some evidence, and more alligators. They could keep it.

147

"First come look at this. Tell me what you make of it."

Sunderland led the way around the driver's side of the Mercedes. Wesley smiled at both of them. Gruen puffed on his cigar and walked around the passenger side, squinting in. The other men whispered, seeming uninterested.

Sunderland shined a powerful flashlight in from the open driver's door. Their faces contorted at the sight of so much blood. At least a pint or two was soaking the leather and cloth bucket seats and some had congealed inside a wooden cup holder on the transmission hump.

Andy grunted. "No one walked away from that," he said instinctively.

Sunderland nodded. "We know. Someone had to take the body away from here."

Andy bent inside the driver's side and found two bullet holes in the seat. He looked further and found two more. He looked up at Gabe, puzzled.

"We're waiting on the sheriff's office crime scene people. They're gonna dust the inside for us, take some of the blood for typing. Maybe we'll find out who was in there with him."

Gabe walked around and carefully opened the passenger door. Gruen mumbled something, which she acknowledged, and backed away.

Andy looked over the body of the Mercedes. It was still shiny and spotless—no damage. There were no skidmarks on the pavement. It didn't look like Pisoli was forced off the road by a second car.

"We figure something went wrong on the drive out here," Sunderland said. "A fight, something like that. Whoever was in there with Benny pulled a gun and shot him."

"Why not leave the body?" Andy asked.

"Not sure. Keep us guessing, believing maybe it wasn't him. But if it wasn't Pisoli that got shot, why leave the car here? Benny wouldn't leave the car here if he was still alive, that much I can tell you about the man."

148

Gabe looked in closer, poking a small AAA halogen flashlight almost completely into one of the bullet holes. She was maneuvering carefully, not wanting any blood on her clothes.

"Too much blood," Andy said.

The marshal was taken aback. He looked in at the brown, shiny liquid covering the seats.

"You mean more than one person . . . body?"

"I'm not sure," Andy said simply. He stared in at the seats, watching as Gabe started poking around with a pair of tweezers.

"Not messy enough. No signs of dragging the body out. It's all just sort of *sitting* there, congealing. Little pools coming from nowhere, doing nothing."

Sunderland was surprised. The experienced federal investigator was obviously not too well versed in the minutiae and nuances of homicide.

"Super Guinea Sleuth doing it for you again, huh?" Gruen called to the U.S. marshal. He stood off near the passenger side, smiling, holding his cigar away.

They ignored the FBI man and continued watching Gabe.

Gabe grunted, pulled, and finally forced a glistening copper bullet out of one of the holes. There was blood on one side of the bullet. She turned the projectile to look at the tip and the clean side.

"Nine millimeter, thirty-eight, or three-five-seven. Hard to tell. Intact. A hollowpoint, no expansion."

Andy smiled. He knew what it meant.

Sunderland looked quizzically at all of them.

Gabe held on to the bullet and stepped out of the car. She showed the projectile to Gruen, then the other FBI man, to Wesley, and to the Washington supervisor.

"What's it mean?" Sunderland finally asked Andy, who was staring into the car.

Gabe looked over the roof at them. "The blood is five or

six times more than would come from a single body, even with three or four bullet wounds. There are no smears from where the body would have had to be moved around to get it out of the car. No blood on the doors, handles, or the ground outside. The bullet is an undistorted hollowpoint, but our shooter couldn't have missed the body from this distance."

Sunderland looked down at his feet, down at the white shell-rock and gravel. He was catching on and feeling a little stupid.

She continued. "This bullet is an intact hollowpoint. A thirty-eight, nine millimeter, or three-five-seven. A high-speed hollowpoint like that can't go through a body, into a seat, and not expand and deform."

"Maybe that was one they missed with. Maybe four or five bullets hit him, and a few missed." Sunderland looked official and concerned.

Gabe shook her head. "Not from where this was. Someone wants us to *believe* that the bullet went through the body. This much blood could only come from an exit wound facing down."

Andy said, "A body with bullets inside of it doesn't bleed like this. And the wounds would probably be facing up. We'd find a little pool of blood on the seat, some smearing, and some blotches here and there. A bullet that goes clean through a body, a hollowpoint, has to be deformed."

Sunderland was silent, then nodded. "What are you saying?"

Gabe continued. "This whole scene is a fake. Right down to the bullet holes and blood. Someone shoots into the seat a few times, then pours in some blood. Wants to make us believe that a body was dead in the car, then removed."

"Who? Who would do it?" Sunderland asked.

"Most likely the person whose body is supposed to be here, but isn't," Andy added.

"Fat-ass Pisoli, who else?" Gruen chimed in.

150

"Someone who thinks we're stupid," Gabe continued. "Someone with limited knowledge of forensics, someone in a hurry, someone who wanted to dump the car and get a-way fast."

"What about making it look like this on purpose?" Sunderland asked. "All these mistakes? Making it look this way, knowing we'd figure it out and not believe that Pisoli's dead. What about that?"

"Possible," Andy said. "But not likely. Pisoli did this. With what little he knows he tried to get us to believe that he's got to be dead, and that for some reason they took his body so we couldn't ever find it."

"Like fuckin' Jimmy Hoffa," Gruen said. "Fuckin' ham-burger meat Hoffa, just like that."

"He's alive, and wants us to believe he's dead? That's what you think?" Sunderland asked no one in particular.

"He's alive," Andy answered. "Somebody's trying to kill him, he's trying to throw them off by making believe he's already pumped up full of lead and has bled to death like a Christmas turkey."

"Who? Us? Who's he want to believe that?"

"Us, so we'll stop looking for him. And whoever is doing these killings, so they'll stop, too," Andy said.

"Wouldn't he know the lab can analyze the blood? Find out it's not his?" Sunderland asked.

"He's hoping we wouldn't. That we'd just accept the obvi-ous and believe it. At least for now. That would buy him enough time."

Sunderland hesitated. The trooper was walking down the middle of the road, waving frantically in the dark at a Cadil-lac full of Mexican field laborers who had slowed to look at the Mercedes.

Andy noticed that the smell of burning sugarcane was getting stronger, almost overpowering, as the darkness began to give way to the first hints of dawn.

The Washington FBI supervisor looked wearily at Gruen

151

and the others. He walked back to a black Diplomat and got in the passenger side.

"Then whose blood is it?" Sunderland finally asked.

Andy shrugged. Gabe looked up from the bullet, didn't reply, then took her tweezers steadily in her hand and bent back into the car after another one of the projectiles.

10

Utmost Assurances

They got into the office early and parted silently as the elevator opened, Gabe going off to her desk and files, Andy going to start some coffee. It was barely seven A.M.

He put down the box from Dunkin' Donuts, took a Boston creme, walked over to his desk, and spread out the copy of Tuesday's *Miami Herald.*

He could see through Jacobson's office window that it was still dark outside. The area, which usually clamored with voices and phones, was so quiet that Andy could hear the overhead lights humming. The coffeepot made the only other noise, a constant, thick stream of pumping liquid, then a grumble and a burp as the pot filled up. He filled his favorite mug and went back to his desk to read the local news section.

He liked the *Herald* better than the local papers because he wanted the Miami and Ft. Lauderdale news as much as he did the Palm Beach stories. He liked to stay up on the corruption stories of Miami PD, and the *Herald* was religious in reporting those. Besides, the *Herald* would report more

153

crime stories and suicides and other seamy, tabloid-type news, enough to keep Andy abreast of what was going on crimewise all up and down the Gold Coast.

A Broward sheriff's deputy working in the jail was indicted in federal court for accepting bribes from an inmate in the Pompano Beach stockade. The man was a drug dealer, and the deputy had allowed him to keep on operating. Andy grunted and bit the doughnut.

In Delray Beach a surgeon's wife was found murdered in her kitchen while her husband was at the office. Andy thought of calling down to the Delray police. If a doctor's wife was killed, he knew, the husband was the one who always wound up doing it. Always. He'd investigated at least a dozen. When a doctor's wife died, grill the husband first. Long and hard—he would be clever in covering up. Andy finished the doughnut, got another, and warmed up his coffee. He forgot about calling Delray PD. They could figure it out for themselves.

There were lots of campaign and candidate stories and ads already started for the local September primaries, and here it was only early August. He turned the page.

A crane had fallen and crushed a construction worker in Riviera Beach. Two inmates had escaped from the state correctional facility in Lantana. A motorcyclist had died after going at high speed and skidding, striking the median, on the Lake Worth intracoastal bridge.

He turned the page again, scanned some sale ads, finished his second doughnut and decided against another.

No Miami PD corruption stories. *They're slipping,* he thought.

Town of Palm Beach officials were fighting with Burt Reynolds over tying up Worth Avenue traffic as he filmed a movie. Someone, probably kids, had planted a chlorine and acid bomb in a high school cafeteria in the north end of West Palm, damaging a stove and a freezer.

He finished his coffee. At the other end of the detective area, somewhere off by the Missing Persons unit, he heard the first morning phone ring. Andy knew that soon other detectives would start reporting in for work. Jacobson, usually early, would be there within thirty to forty minutes. Outside the captain's office window the coal-black sky was fading to a pale blue.

He had avoided looking at the front page, but now it was time. He went for more coffee, came back and put aside the local news section.

There it was, the whole lower half of the front page. He glanced at the story and forced himself to scan the banner at the top of the page and the two lead stories. The Palestinians had started more violence in some little town he couldn't pronounce and the Israelis had crushed the revolt, killing six. President Bush was fighting with Congress over trade legislation. He got into a few paragraphs of that story, then gave up. He moaned, inhaled deeply, then went down to the bottom half of the paper and read the story under Fogarty's byline:

MOBSTERS DYING; FBI AND MARSHALS REFUSE COMMENT

Lawrence Fogarty
Herald Staff Writer

West Palm Beach—In the last month, throughout South Florida and in the northern Treasure Coast towns of Ft. Pierce and Vero Beach, relocated federal witnesses have been murdered, anonymous sources have confirmed. The murders number at least seven, and appear to be related. Many of the cases have gone unreported in the media due to FBI and U.S. Marshals Service secrecy, but at least five of the cases have been in Palm Beach County, and involve two torture-murders, a car bombing, and a killing-for-hire where the gunman was then mysteriously executed.

To date, the FBI and Marshals Service refuse comment on any of the cases. This may be due to the secrecy of the Federal Witness Protection Program (FWPP), an official system started in the sixties to protect important witnesses who cooperate in prosecutions and then face death threats against them or their families. U.S. Marshals Service Supervisor Thomas Sunderland, when confronted outside the Paul G. Rogers Federal Building in West Palm Beach, confirmed only that an intensive investigation was underway, and refused further comment.

Herald reporters, meanwhile, have uncovered witness accounts that show federal agents from all over the country coming to the Palm Beach and Broward County areas, beefing up security for the remaining witnesses in the FWPP, estimated to number easily in the hundreds. Although a suspect in the killings has not yet been identified, an unnamed source has confirmed that local and federal authorities suspect Mafia involvement and possible penetration of the secret witness lists maintained by the federal government.

Fucking Fogarty, Andy thought. He put down the paper and went for another doughnut.

* * *

156

Jacobson went right into his office and shut his door. Andy saw that his usual copy of the *Wall Street Journal* was missing. He had, instead, a copy of the *Herald* under his arm. The captain's phone rang almost immediately, before he could even hang up his suit jacket. He sat down, picked up the receiver, and turned his chair to face the window.

Gabe came around the corner, stacks of files in her arms. "Anything yet?" she asked Andy.

He handed her the paper and pointed toward the captain's office.

Gabe read the story, then looked back at Andy.

"The team reported back on the Ripaldi murder over on Executive Center," she told him. "They followed up everything you gave them. There are no local leads. Nobody's snitch has anything to say. It wasn't involving any criminals from the West Palm area, or they'd have heard *something*. They're at a dead end. After today, after their typed reports are in, Jacobson said they're off the case. We're it, and I don't know how long he's going to leave us on it."

He nodded at his wife. For the first time that morning he noticed her well-done makeup, perfectly combed hair, and the new, cobalt blue dress she was wearing. He had been in a tired daze when they went home to change after inspecting Pisoli's Mercedes. "That's okay. It's what I expected. The answer to the whole riddle wasn't gonna be sittin' in that one case, anyway. It's all of them. The answer's gonna come from the whole picture. The total picture, and not necessarily the sum of all the parts." He tore off a piece of Boston creme and chewed.

"You still suspect Pisoli?" Gabe asked.

"I don't know. The faked butcher scene in the car was too obvious. He's still alive, and he's gotta believe I know that. He's gotta know I'm gonna break my ass to try to find him. He knows who's doing all the killings. He's the key to this whole mess, that's for sure."

In his office, Jacobson turned in his executive chair and gently hung up the phone.

Andy didn't wait to be called in. Jacobson had sat there, waving a pencil in the air like a conductor's wand, looking up at his certificates on the wall.

"Your phone call was about the story in the *Herald?*" Andy asked. Gabe came in behind him and closed the glass door.

Jacobson nodded. "Deputy chief. FBI supervisor from Washington called him and told him the boys in the local office think *you* are the leak. Something like it has to be you, couldn't be anyone else, so on and so on. Something about a *Herald* reporter you're always doing favors for."

"Him? Andy?" Gabe looked shocked and hurt.

"Well," Jacobson added, looking at Andy, "you deny it?"

"Of course I deny it. Why would I leak anything to the fucking *Miami Herald,* for God's sake? I hate newspapers, especially that one."

"That's just it. *Miami.* That's where you're from. That's where the reporter's from. Now you're up here, working on this, all of a sudden they're onto the story."

"And you believe that, Captain?" Gabe asked incredulously.

"I believe only that I have a city homicide division to run. You two are my top performers. But this is not a West Palm Beach problem. It's a federal problem. I understand the West Palm case is at a dead end, so I'm not really sure what further involvement I can justify for you two."

There was a moment of silence. Andy was the highest-ranking member of the homicide division, and the second-highest-ranking member of the detective bureau, grandfathered in from a larger department. He hated standing there in the captain's office, somehow feeling castigated, somehow lessened, like a child caught in a sneaky, little secret.

Jacobson seemed to be weighing his options.

158

"Captain, you hear the one about the news reporter and the angel?"

Jacobson's look said, A joke is not appropriate now but I know you'll tell it anyway so go ahead.

Gabe stood to the side, looking surprised. For once Andy was going to tell a joke that she hadn't already heard.

"Right. I didn't think you'd heard it. There's this angel, right? Down in Miami. He flies around awhile, then goes over to the *Miami Herald* building, up by a window on the top floor. There's a reporter sitting there at a desk by this open window, so the angel flies in the room, starts hovering, and only this one reporter can see him, right?"

Andy waited. Jacobson looked up and gave a halfhearted smile.

"Right. So this angel says to the reporter, 'Do you believe in God?' and the reporter looks up, all frightened, and says, 'Sure, I believe in God.' Then the angel says, 'But do you have *faith* in God?' The reporter thinks a second and says, 'Sure, I have faith in God.' The angel then tells the reporter, 'Then jump out this window, and I'll save you.' The reporter looks around, looks up at the angel, and doesn't seem to want to jump out the window. After a minute, the angel says, 'If you have faith in God, you must know I'm an angel and will have to save you from hurting yourself. I can't lie to you. Prove your faith and jump.' Well, that was enough for the reporter. He walked to the window and jumped out. He fell twelve stories to the concrete and splatted all over the parking lot like a pizza. The angel flew down to the reporter's body and hovered over it, flapping his wings. Then he looked up to the sky and said, 'I can't believe they let me into heaven, the way I fucking *hate* news reporters!' "

Jacobson's laugh exploded. Andy knew that he hated news reporters, too, knew that he would understand. Gabe smiled less enthusiastically, knowing this was only the first time she would be hearing it.

Andy and Gabe sat in the padded chairs in the captain's

office giving him another update on their work. Gabe poured out her notes, Andy interjecting with his feelings on the case, narrowing in on his meeting with Pisoli on the pier, what the mafioso had told him, and the man's subsequent contrived disappearance.

Andy told him that Pisoli was the key. It was his mission now to find the man, to make him talk, to force out of him the facts and the reasons for the killings and the mystery.

Jacobson thought it all over in silence. He reached forward, thrusting the pencil into an electric sharpener and pushing hard as the metal churned the wood and lead. He took it out and admired the new point.

"I know you're getting pressure," Andy started again. "That's understandable. Now the publicity will start, and the feds will be scrambling. But you have to leave us on."

"The FBI wants you off, and it's mostly their business, not ours."

"Right. But what about the marshals? Sunderland, what about him? What does he say?"

Jacobson thought for a moment. "You're right. He's asked his bosses to ask that you two be kept on the case."

"Right. And he's in charge. The way I see it, it's their case anyway, not the fucking Bureau's. Those are federal witnesses under marshal protection."

Jacobson appeared to be formulating what he was going to tell the deputy chief of operations.

"I have a lot more planned, Captain, besides finding Pisoli." Andy continued. "I have an important meeting set up for noon today with an organized-crime figure from New York. I expect some answers to some of these questions at that meeting."

Jacobson tilted his head and gave him a curious look.

"Gabe's gonna be following up some leads, trying to interview a few people. I have an important man to meet. A friend set up a favor—a *big* one. I expect an important answer to come out of it."

Jacobson exhaled, seeming relieved. "I can't block this heat for long, Andy. Let's have some concrete results, at least on our West Palm case. Give me something to show the higher-ups to justify all this flak from Washington. You know how sensitive the chief is about political headaches."

"Right. But I can't solve our one case without solving all of them. And now, I have to get some answers, and I have to find a missing federal witness who doesn't want to be found."

"You two have your hands full," Jacobson said.

"We do."

"I'm going to have mine full trying to justify this."

"You will," Gabe added. "But you know we get you results. And if we can solve this one, you know it'll be headlines, awards, and kudos to the boss that inspired us and pushed us ahead."

Jacobson responded as if he had bought the argument. Gabe had a way of putting into words what Andy could only hint at.

"One more week—and that's the max. No more than that. You're both overdue for your vacation. Seven days from now—next Tuesday—you have the final case folders on my desk, ready for approval. No extensions. Till then, you come and go as you please. If I don't see you, that's fine. In fact, I'd prefer *not* to see you. I can keep the heat off till then. After that, though, it's all over and you two are on your way to Key West."

Andy treated it like a deal he had to agree to. He thought a moment, then smiled and nodded at Captain Barney Miller.

"One week. Seven days. And no more talking to the newspapers. Especially not that jerk at the goddamned *Herald,* understand? Do we have a deal?"

"Deal," Andy bellowed. He rapped his knuckles on his boss's desk and walked out of the office.

"Deal," Gabe added. She winked at the captain and followed Andy out.

Andy parked the Saab at the airport short-term lot and waited. He listened to all his old favorite Miami stations on the fancy stereo, changing intermittently from one to another.

Carmine finally pulled up behind him in a red convertible El Dorado, about a half hour late. Andy got into Carmine's car, and they drove off toward their appointment.

They drove mostly in silence, except for some standard discourse about family and friends. Outside it was a typical, noontime August sun, beating down on Miami without a thought or care about the heat and restlessness it generated.

Andy showed surprise when Carmine turned off the causeway into the entrance of exclusive Star Island, a Miami Beach atoll of multimillion-dollar homes.

"A sheik, you believe that?" Carmine asked. "A fucking raghead sheik is who he bought this place from. Sand-niggers, I call 'em. The man went out of business or somethin'. The feds were after him for taxes, I think. You got to see this place, fountains everywhere, statues, a bowling alley, indoor pool, all that shit. Like the fucking Arab had nothing better to do with his goddamned oil money but spend it on every gimmick he could think of."

Andy nodded, smiling. Carmine was waved on by the island's gate guard and drove into the exclusive neighborhood.

"And this is only his fucking *summer* home; the place he's got for the winter is somewhere down in the islands."

Less than a block later Andy saw two unmarked police cars, each with two plainclothes officers. They were watching to see who pulled into the house, Andy knew. He guessed them to be from the Miami Beach police and Metro-Dade. The men looked curiously as he and Carmine drove past them in the Caddy to the end of the cul-de-sac and turned into the driveway of the multistory white marble and concrete estate.

Andy looked back. One of the officers snapped a picture of the El Dorado's license plate. He was sure none of the cops recognized him.

The double doors to the massive garage went up, Carmine quickly pulled in, and the doors reversed and closed behind them. The lights in the garage went on. Andy saw a tall, stocky guard in his late twenties or early thirties, standing by the door leading from the garage to the main part of the house.

From inside the house Andy heard a transmission from a walkie-talkie, then some squelch. He could also hear a radio, maybe the television, and a man laughing.

Carmine walked past the man without acknowledgment, toward the door. Andy followed. The guard reached out, grabbing the 9-millimeter Andy had in a shoulder holster under his jacket.

With a swift movement Andy had the larger man off balance. He followed up with a grab and a push, and the guard's upper torso slammed hard against the hood of Carmine's Cadillac. Andy had the man by the thick part of the wrist and pushed upward, toward his neck. One more inch or a little more pressure and the arm would break.

"Easy, Andy! The man has a job to do," Carmine said.

"I keep the gun. Unless you want to give me yours," Andy said to the man, whose face was pushed against the still-warm hood. He reached with his other hand under the guard's jacket, patting the .45 in the shoulder holster. The man only grunted.

"Don't do this, Andy. This isn't right. This is a meeting, nothing else. You don't need your gun. This man's only tryin' to do his job."

"I'm a cop. We carry guns—everyone knows that."

"Andy, this is Guardinaro's *house!* You wanted to meet him, this wasn't his idea. He allowed you to come here. Please, Andy, put the gun in my car."

Andy twisted the arm and the wrist as the man squirmed,

trying to get free. Reaching under his own jacket, Andy took out the Smith & Wesson auto and handed it to Carmine.

"I've got to check him for a wire," the man mumbled by moving his lips against the hood. Andy pushed his arm up.

"He don't have no fuckin' wire!" Carmine screamed. "He's with me, you asshole! Check with your boss, he's with me! You don't gotta check him for no fuckin' wire!"

Carmine opened the car door and tossed Andy's pistol onto the seat. Andy stepped back, giving the bodyguard room to come off the hood. The man straightened, glaring at Amato with contempt. He wanted to fight, and would have, Andy knew, if it weren't for Carmine being an old and close friend of his boss. He and Carmine went through the door; the bodyguard did not try to stop them.

The inside was like the outside. Gaudy statuary, stark white marble with some streaks of gray and pink. Lots of throw rugs, fountains, lots of windows. The far wall of the three-story living room was massive sliding doors that opened onto a bright and breezy Biscayne Bay. Andy took note of the fake classical pictures hanging on the marble walls, and the expensive clocks and bric-a-brac carefully placed by some interior designer according to the tastes of the powerful owner. There was a fireplace, flower vases filled with expensive blossoms, and small groups of expensive furniture pieces professionally arranged around the massive living room. Andy guessed that his whole town house had less square footage than this one room.

Freddy Guardinaro walked in with a bodyguard from a game room off to the side by the indoor pool. He wore swim trunks and a T-shirt. Both men carried pool cues.

Andy watched as Carmine shook hands with and hugged the youngest Mafia "boss of bosses" in history. Guardinaro was only in his late forties, but already he was said to be the most vicious boss of the Five Families in New York, some-

164

thing that qualified him for the highly prized and sought-after title. Physically, he wasn't that imposing. Andy judged him as five-eleven and of medium build. His face was just like the intelligence photos Andy had studied, but the hair was lighter and the body smaller than he expected. Andy knew that he came from an upper-class Sicilian family, was educated at an Ivy League business school, and had never been convicted of any crime.

"And this is a friend of mine, Lieutenant Andy Amato of the West Palm Beach police force. He is honored that you allowed him to come here, and he thanks you for your help in the matter which we discussed." Carmine sounded extremely formal.

"Amato. I heard a lot about you. I'll shake your hand only because I checked you out, and found out that you're a clean cop."

The man extended his hand and Andy shook it. No one paid any attention to or bothered to introduce the bodyguard.

They went back to the game room. Guardinaro, Carmine, and Andy were alone. The bodyguard left after being told to get some drinks. Andy stood near the pool table, admiring the quality of the bright blue felt and the workmanship in the designs carved into the wood.

"Carmine tells me you are a friend. You can be trusted to keep your word. You're Italian, so you have honor, even if you are a cop. He tells me I am safe to talk with you, that you understand it is for your information, nothing else."

Andy didn't hesitate. "That's right. I can't use anything against you or any of your associates. There is no recorder. As far as anyone is concerned, I was never here, and you never spoke with me. You have my word."

The man tapped the cue on the pink Mexican tile, leaned into the table, and completed an easy shot of the six ball into a corner. "Go ahead, ask your questions. I will give you the answers. Because you are the friend of a friend of mine, I will give you the truth."

They were interrupted by the bodyguard coming back into the room, bringing drinks. Andy waited for him to leave.

"There seems to be only one logical explanation for all the killings," Andy began. "The dead men are all stool pigeons in one way or another. Men that have put longtime, successful mobsters in jail. Men that have closed illegal businesses for the federal government. Men that the government has *paid* for their testimony. Men the Mafia would want to be dead. Now they are. We are assuming someone in the mob is killing them." He gulped the expensive Scotch.

Guardinaro nodded and shot at the eight ball, missing the pocket, sending it into a nest in the center of the table.

"It would have to be with my consent. If not my consent, even if it was something off on the fringes of our organization, it would still have to be with my *knowledge.* If anyone in the family knew anything, they would be committing a grievous sin by not telling me."

"I understand. I know how the organization works. I know who *you* are."

There was silence. Guardinaro appeared to accept Andy's statement as a sign of respect.

"Something like this, there would have to be a lot of planning. People bought off, others silenced."

"Exactly."

"It could not be done without the New York families approving of it, and that means not without my final go-ahead."

"That is what I'm asking. I'm a homicide detective, not an FBI agent. I have no quarrel with any of your people. I am not involved with investigating racketeering, gambling, loansharking, or drugs. I only have homicide cases to solve.

That is my line of work, my living. With these killings, I can go either way. I can believe the mob is behind it, or I can look somewhere else."

Guardinaro shot at another ball, this time hitting it, sending it against two cushions, landing it in a side pocket. Andy didn't think the shot was planned.

"I will tell you this, Lieutenant Amato. I will tell you what I think of the federal government and this whole witness protection thing. It's all been built up as a great defeat over the crime families. They've built it up as the only way these people can stay alive. They're wrong. Look who's in the program. Misfits. Malcontents. Mostly liars, thieves, scum-sucking lowlifes."

Andy nodded, gulping his Scotch. Carmine sat on a stool by the door, staring blankly at the billiard table.

"These people are not from us. With few exceptions, these are not people I would ever invite into my home. With few exceptions, they basically know nothing about the true nature of the organization. The way I see it, if you catch us, you catch us. It has happened before. As long as you are honest about it, that's your job. These so-called witnesses, many have lied and perjured themselves, all for the sake of protection. If you showed me a list of these people, I would recognize only a few names, and couldn't care less about any of them."

"Pisoli. Benny Pisoli."

Guardinaro nodded. "Benny is one. But he, too, is a liar and a fake. He's jerking the government off, just like most of them are. He's getting a free meal at taxpayer expense. He's getting a free face, free ID, and a free ride to do what the fuck he wants and get away with it. These people go on committing their petty, nuisance crimes. Benny is dirty, he will always be dirty. He's no good. He's unnecessarily violent. But when they get caught, they get out. The government cannot keep them in jail where they may be

167

recognized. I tell you, the FBI is wasting their time with people like Pisoli."

"Ferrigno, Veniziano, Portuno, Corrizi, Ripaldi, Aiello." Andy knew the names by heart.

"They mean nothing to me. A few I recognize, I've read about. One or two I've met on the way up. They are all mid-level or low-level mob people. None of them worth killing for. None of them worth putting together the kind of operation it would take to bribe the federal government and get their locations and have them killed. That would take *millions.* I could think of better ways to spend our money."

Carmine got up, went over to Guardinaro and whispered something.

"One of the names you said there was Portuno?" the boss asked after Carmine sat back down.

"Right."

He rapped another ball in, one that had been hanging over the ledge of the corner pocket. The cue ball followed it in but bounced back out.

"Carmine reminds me. Portuno, old Chuckie Portuno, was a hit from another New York family."

"That was the third one. On Palm Beach, the island. That was where the hit man got a bullet in the side of the head as he was about to leave."

Guardinaro stood and looked at Andy, then bit his lower lip. "We had nothing to do with the hit man getting that bullet. Only Portuno."

"Right. How did you find out? About Portuno? How did you find out where he was?"

Guardinaro looked at Carmine, who nodded his head, assuring the boss once again that Amato could be trusted. "We got a phone call. A tip on where he was. Someone dropped a dime to a friend of ours and said only, 'This is where you can find Charlie Portuno. Get there before they

168

move him.' So we did, and then that happened, what you just said."

Amato let it sink in. Here was a Mafia chieftain admitting to involvement in a homicide. He could bust the man, but that would be foolish. It would never get in evidence. Carmine indeed had powerful friends, and a lot of faith in Andy's word. *A tip,* he said to himself.

"I came here for your word, Mr. Guardinaro. I came here for your honorable declaration that the mob has nothing to do with these other killings. It's important to me. If you can't give it to me, that's okay. I'll understand. That will have meaning for me, and I'll know how to act. If you give me your word, I'll be guided by my belief that what you're telling me is the truth."

Guardinaro went after the remaining balls, finishing each one off with a clean shot from one end of the table. Andy saw that when the table was clear, not jumbled, he could plan shots and execute them with ease.

"You are a friend of a friend that I've invited into my home. You have my utmost assurances, Lieutenant. You have my word. I know nothing of any other killing, any conspiracy. And if someone in the mob was doing it, as our friend Carmine has told you, I would have to know about it and approve."

Andy nodded.

"This is the nineties. Things are much different. We run like a business, like a Fortune Five Hundred conglomerate. The last killing I authorized had a profit motive. The man was interfering, he was costing us money. This revenge stuff, sure, there's a little of that still around. Between members, not involving the organization per se. But not like the old days, not like when the Mustache Petes ran the organization. Killing for revenge, on the level you describe, would cost too much, bring little profit. I would never approve it. Better that Pisoli and the other misfits should spend their time in

169

hiding, being miserable, committing petty crimes, looking over their shoulders for shadows and silhouettes of things that are not really there."

"I understand. Thank you," Andy said.

The men nodded at each other. Guardinaro motioned for Andy to join him in a game. Andy walked over to the rack and picked off a cue stick. Carmine moved to the table, taking the balls from their pockets and placing them carefully into the rack. Andy lifted his cue to break.

He took the felt case from his pocket and unwrapped it in his palm, laying out thirteen long, thin strips of high-grade steel. Each was bent or curved just so; some had catlicks, some angled one way, then another. He took out and held up the one on the farthest end, then another from the middle, then removed a third. He rerolled the felt and dropped it back into his pocket, carefully placed the three steel picks together, and inserted them into the lock.

He hadn't rung the bell or knocked; he knew no one was home.

The lock was not the highest quality, but it wasn't cheap. It took his extra talent and finesse, and that additional little tweak of the precision instruments, to make the tumblers give way and the deadbolt turn. In less than a minute, he had it open. He dropped the picks back into his pocket, carefully stepped in, and closed the town house door behind him, locking it.

He felt their presence, Gabe's more so than Andy's. He heard their voices, saw their faces, even though they weren't there. But the town house exuded their vitality and he felt close to them. Very close.

You have something to look for.

He walked carefully, thinking of where he had to look. He would not waste time in the kitchen. It was obviously small and undersupplied, the kitchen of two people always out and

170

on the go. The living room had nice furniture, an expensive TV and stereo, and a grossly large glass bowl filled with matches from Florida restaurants. He decided not to look in that room, either. Too obvious. The Amatos were not that stupid.

He opened the door to the downstairs bathroom. It smelled of a woman, of ladylike powders and scents, of feminine things. He closed the door and went to the stairs.

In the den, their presence was strong. He imagined each at one of the desks, working hard on their cases. He walked to the computer, turning it on, watching the screen roll and blink, then the system load. He tried what he knew about computers, flipping through the disks in the box, running a directory on each; then he gave up, shutting down the unfamiliar machine.

They must not find out you were here.

He chose the desk he saw was Andy's and gently drew each drawer out to its full extension, squinting inside, carefully moving papers and envelopes, rubber bands and stamps. In one drawer he found a stack of papers, enough to make him curious. He went through each one, reading memos from Andy's homicides, case notes, and other items instantly too boring to matter. He shut the drawer, *knowing* that the desk did not hold the secret he wanted.

In fact, he *knew* that what he wanted would probably not even be in the town house. But maybe Andy Amato would be careless enough to leave a copy lying about someplace, ready to call out to him as he passed.

In the bedroom he felt welcomed, as if the essence of the Amatos had ushered him in and greeted him. He walked to one side of the waterbed and drew out the drawers. There were linens, stockings, jeans, and T-shirts. One drawer contained nothing but women's underwear, and looking at it was beginning to give him an erection when a noise behind him startled him.

171

A white flash ran out from the bathroom, through the bedroom and into the hall. His heart skipped a beat, his chest tightened, but then he realized it was just a cat, and he smiled in relief.

He held up the feminine underwear and felt its substance, twirling the silkiness in his fingers and imagining the woman wearing it, then slipping free of it. He sniffed the fabric, then rubbed the side of his face with it before dropping it back, unceremoniously, into the drawer.

The other side, the male side, held nothing interesting. Watches, rings, socks, magazines. Very few papers, and all meaningless.

He seemed to hear their voices again. The walls spoke. It was the muted voice of passion, the whispering of intentions and the moans of acquiescence, of mutual surrender. He stared at the blanket and sheets, reaching in and running his hand over them, laughing as he left his own mark on the privileged and private territory that was a man and woman's bedroom.

He was weary. The list was probably not there, not anywhere in the house. He could feel that. He had felt it at the front door, he had known, but he knew also that he had to try, to make an effort, and maybe learn something about his adversaries.

With renewed interest he riffled through the books and personal items on the headboard. The area was cluttered, so they were less likely to notice something unsettled. He looked through the pages of magazines, he shook open books, he looked everywhere it could be, in case he was wrong.

In case it's here.

Wrong. I can't be wrong. It's not here.

The erection was too much, the loneliness too deep. Exposing himself, he again ran his hand through the sheets. As he finished he stood and laughed. Better than the momentary physical pleasure was knowing that he had violated the one thing that the two lovers thought they had—their privacy. In his increasing irrationality, he thought he was now part of everything gone before and everything to come in that small, cozy bedroom shared by Mr. and Mrs. Andy Amato. His smile was one of double satisfaction as he put his manhood back in his pants.

The list. You want the list.

You have to finish. There is too much to do.

There is someone to find.

The cat was sitting at the open door to the room. It looked at him, then licked its paws, accepting him as an unwelcome guest, but one that was no threat to it.

11

Night on the Town

It was Andy's choice to take the night off. They had done all they could, and waiting around for the phone to ring was just too frustrating. If he couldn't be doing something constructive, he reasoned, he would just as soon spend the night out.

They left from the station and traveled down the interstate until they felt like getting off. They exited at Boynton Beach and drove toward the ocean. Andy was glancing around, taking in the sights of a city he'd been in only a few times before, and Gabe was on the lookout for a restaurant she thought they both would enjoy.

She found a large, colorful, and attractive diner set way back, off the street and on the intracoastal. It was still early, before six P.M., and there were no crowds, typical for a Tuesday night.

It had a bistro atmosphere—noisy, colorful, both quick finger food and full meals, standard and exotic drinks. The waiters and waitresses wore bright red outfits, smiles, and nametags. You had to be close to someone to hear what they were saying. Couples came and went down crowded aisles.

Off by the bar the sexual tension was evident as liaisons were enacted and newly formed couples paid their tabs and walked out of the restaurant.

Andy ordered a bisque of real crabmeat and pasta primavera. Gabe's choice was more conventional—a fried mushroom appetizer and a piled-high sandwich of corned beef and pastrami on rye.

They ate slowly, neither one talking about the killings, concentrating instead on the view of the intracoastal and some well-lit boats traveling well offshore in the encroaching dusk. Andy also watched the men and women at the crowded bar, amused by the touch-and-go, the opening lines, the turn-offs, and the connections.

When they left, it was dark, and Andy decided to travel back north, back to West Palm. They took A1A along the ocean, through the small oceanfront towns with their million-dollar mansions and small police forces. It was a narrow, two-lane road, with convex mirrors at every curve so the rich people pulling out of their opulent driveways could see what was coming at them. Andy kept the Saab below forty all the way, windows and sunroof open, both of them enjoying the sights and smells of Atlantic Ocean living. They passed a huge marina complex and pulled in for a few minutes as two large vessels, part of a commercial fishing fleet, maneuvered out of their slips and headed out the inlet toward the ocean.

Andy still didn't want to go home. He drove to his favorite after-dinner spot, the Carefree Theater in downtown West Palm. The old building, once a movie theater, had been closed for many years, having lost business to the highly lucrative suburban multiplex cinemas. Then it was reopened with stage performances and Andy's favorite, a Comedy Corner featuring stand-up routines.

He saw Gabe smile when he pulled into the lot. He was never sure if she was in the mood for the tiny smoke-

175

filled club with its sometimes off-color performers and randy humor.

The line of comedians started slow. The first one was a woman impressionist with some standard one-liners mixed with a routine of why she couldn't find any eligible men. Gabe laughed more than Andy did. The next one was a Rodney Dangerfield type with insults and short quips— nothing ever worked right and he couldn't get any respect. Then it was back to a woman, this one purely sexual in her complaining about men, lust, sex, penis size, and the like. Andy enjoyed it, and Gabe surprisingly let out a few laughs.

They stayed through a short break, had one mixed drink each, then left in the middle of a small, geeky, imitation– Woody Allen lament about why he couldn't hold a job or keep any serious relationships afloat. Andy was getting depressed; it was the right time to go.

They strolled onto the downtown street, and within just a few seconds Andy was a cop again, a detective lieutenant, a homicide investigator, not a comedian, and the cases flowed back into his consciousness.

He saw Charles Portuno in the bedroom of the Palm Beach mansion, saw him thrashing against his killer. He went back to the Lincoln and saw the New York killer's head smash against the right side of the dashboard, a bullet in its brain. He saw the jade green Porsche ignite and explode, disgorging the driver into the air and down near the pond. He saw the man in Jupiter, suspended from the ceiling, swaying with the rotation of the earth, a gaping wound in his chest. He saw Pisoli's car, the maroon Mercedes, the faked crime scene, and the fear in the man's eyes on the fishing pier when Andy had shoved the small revolver in his nostril. Finally, he saw the man on Executive Drive, castrated by bullets that exploded in his groin, forced to shoot himself in the head.

Andy became the killer. In each one of these Lieutenant Amato cast himself, thought of how *he* would do it, then nodded, *yes,* he could be that brutal, and that's just how he'd go about it.

It didn't bother him, thinking like that. That's what it took to catch a killer, he knew.

With three days of abstinence behind them, brought on by murder scenes, paperwork, and irksome, ugly details, they went into the bedroom of the town house and made love again. They stayed in the dark, undressing slowly and separately. When they hugged Andy reached out and took the initiative, massaging Gabe's breasts, rubbing her vagina, finding all the right spots. She reached out and stroked him, bringing him fully erect and fully alive, she knowing also what it truly took to cast off the deaths, dismiss the homicides, and become fully sensual, fully alive.

They made love tenderly, using their mouths on each other, leading each other to the brink of orgasm, then away, then back again and over the edge, the pleasure coming close to the first time they had done it, finding sexual bliss in the middle of death and gore.

They wasted not a moment on regaining strength—they melted together knowing that *that* would give them the strength. They moved rapidly and in unison, not exchanging words but only touches and brief glances. In the darkness each screamed when it was finally over, laughed, held on tight, not wanting it to end.

Gabe had long since turned over and was asleep. Andy stayed awake, still thinking about the cases. The words of Carmine D'Angelo and of Guardinaro, the Mafia boss of bosses, replayed over and over. Then, back at the pier, he could still hear Benny Pisoli:

"Do you know who's doing the killings?"

"Yes . . . I think so, I'm not sure. Let me say I've got a strong suspicion."

Andy reached up to the shelf on the waterbed's headboard. He needed his pad, he needed to write down exactly what he remembered Pisoli saying to him that night on the pier. He needed . . .

But the pad was not where he had left it. Always next to his clock, pen nearby.

He turned and sat up, then got out of the bed. Gabe moved with the motion of the waterbed but remained asleep.

The pad was on the shelf above. Andy looked through more of the papers on the shelf, becoming aware they had been disarranged.

He reached for the 9-millimeter, pulling it out of its holster. He ran from the room, unsure whether whoever it was was still there, had been there when they got home, had stayed when they went into the bedroom, undressing and making love.

He ran, quickly searching the second floor, then the downstairs. The town house seemed empty. He found Groucho on a kitchen counter, licking her paws, giving him the standard uninterested-feline look as he again searched the rooms, this time more carefully, gun pointing straight forward.

They had been invaded, he finally accepted. Someone had come in during the day, when they were at work, or maybe later when they were at dinner.

All the valuables were there. He kept thinking that he was missing something—something large and obvious was gone, something he was overlooking. He checked the drawers and all the hiding places. Everything was there.

The lock on the front door was intact. He remembered it being locked when they got home. He played with the deadbolt, making sure of its integrity.

Someone picked the lock. Then relocked it.

Back upstairs he went into the den, gun still out. He sensed it immediately. Not only were papers and file folders amiss and off kilter, but he had the strong sense of an invader. It was almost, but not quite, a *smell.*

178

He had been here. Not for valuables, nothing so simple. Looking for the list. The killer wants our list. But how would he even know?

Andy put the gun down to his side and went in to wake up Gabe.

She awoke with a start but she concentrated fully as he poured the story out to her. She got up, put on a nightgown, and looked around the bedroom. He could tell that she felt the same. Their things were amiss; she knew the killer had been there. All they had needed to do was come home and find him. He led her into the den. There was something he wanted her to do.

"Get back into your program," he asked. "Boot it up and get back to where you can input more material. I have some things I want to tell it, I want to see if it makes a difference."

She went to the computer, going through the boot-up ritual, entering the commands. She was in her A.I. program, the free-form data base she had built to help solve the killings.

"What do you need?" she asked.

"Three things. Tell it three things, then I want to see what it has to say."

She nodded, turning back to the keyboard. Andy looked at the desk clock. It was past midnight.

"Tell it that the killer is looking frantically for the list."

She typed and entered. Andy strained to arrange the second entry in his head before giving it to her.

"Tell it that Pisoli is *not* the killer, that the killer is *looking* for Pisoli."

She entered the information.

"Tell it the killer is someone we know."

Gabe looked up, then back at the keys, and typed in the line, then entered it in memory.

She hit a function key. The words scrolled up and Andy read:

```
CONFIRMING INFORMATION FOR INPUT-
-KILLER IS SOMEONE YOU KNOW
-KILLER IS NOT PISOLI; KILLER IS LOOKING FOR PISOLI
-KILLER IS LOOKING FOR LIST
OK TO ENTER INTO PROGRAM AND PROCEED? (Y/N)
```

Andy reached over his wife's shoulder and tapped in Y. The hard disk hummed, then returned to the program prompt.

"Ask it who the killer is," Andy said.

Gabe typed in the question and entered it. The processor took over as the words on the screen scrolled by again, Andy looking anxiously at the amber monitor, wondering if his mystery was about to be solved.

INSUFFICIENT INFORMATION.

He nodded his head, understanding. Gabe looked up.

"What next?" she asked.

"What does it need? You have everything in there, what does it require? What information is it missing?"

"There's no way to tell. Dealing with artificial intelligence means that the program can analyze things one way one time, then another way the next time. Theoretically, you can ask the same question twice and get a different answer. It has a threshold before it gives a positive response. It may *suspect* who the killer is at this point, or it may have more than one name in mind, just not enough information or mathematical certainty to point at one or another."

"Make it tell me who it suspects."

"It can't. That's not the way the program's built. It's founded on mathematical principles—all computers are. It deals only in absolutes. Blacks and whites, no grays."

He nodded.

"There's another way," Gabe said. "Something else we can do."

She paused long enough for him to give her a look urging her on. "I built this data to pinpoint not only the killer, but the victims. It's built to try and tell us where the next victim may be."

"Go ahead, ask it." Andy sounded anxious and knew it. It was something he only let happen in front of Gabe.

She entered a question. The computer took almost a full minute to respond:

-S. CHINICALLI, 708 BUNKER ROAD, WPB
-R. TROMPETTO, 7574 S. FEDERAL HWY, #11, WPB

Andy went to his jacket pocket, removing the copies of both Carmine's list and the U.S. marshal's. Both names were on each of them. They were mid-level people, each in the program at least a few years. Andy knew that they were probably not high enough to be getting direct protection.

"Call the PD. Call Sunderland. Have them protect both places," Gabe said.

"We can't. Something's wrong. We can't trust anyone but ourselves on this case. I can't put my finger on it. We can't trust anyone, not even Sunderland or the FBI. Not even our own department."

She shook her head, either not understanding or not wanting to believe in what her husband was insisting.

"Ask it when. Ask when the next most likely date and time will be."

Gabe typed in his request. Andy closed his eyes as the disk whirred around. He was tired, but he had to push on.

ANYTIME.

181

With that he felt close to the machine. It was what he had just said to himself.

Anytime.

Now.

Tonight; there would be another one tonight, he knew. He wanted to reach out and tap some compliments into the keyboard, tell the main processor that it was right, it was doing a good job, it was on the money.

He reached around the side and turned off the computer. Gabe swiveled in the high-back office chair to face him.

"You want to leave right now and cover both addresses?" she asked. She sounded confident that she knew what he was thinking.

He stayed silent.

"We'll have to split up, unless you're willing to call in some help."

"We can't. We're on our own."

"Then we'll split up. I'll take the one on Bunker, you go to the apartment house on Federal."

Andy shook his head.

"Too dangerous? Is that it again?" Her voice showed her emotion.

"For both of us."

"Or just me? Remember, Andy, I'm a police sergeant, not just your wife. It's *my* job, too, not just yours. I'm not just along for the ride, someone to keep you company."

They had had the conversation before. At least a dozen times, whenever they were facing danger, whenever for whatever reason he could not be there with her.

"I don't like to separate. It's not good for either one of us. There'll be no backup. Those places are at least six miles from each other—that's a good five minutes apart."

"We'll have radios. Patrol will be in the area if we need backup. We'll stay on the detective frequency—at this time of night there won't be any other detectives out there to hear us. If we see trouble the other can come over quickly; then we'll call patrol."

Andy didn't like it. His face showed her as much.

"It's the only way, Teddy. That or risk picking the wrong address and missing out on a capture. We're wasting time. You're the lieutenant—you decide."

He nodded. She was right. He would decide. The computer was starting to make him a believer. He sensed some truth in its mass of circuits and its mathematical exactitude and simplicity. It was right, he could sense it. It would be one of those two, and it would probably be tonight.

Which one, dammit? Tell me which one!

There was silence. The computer, and his own judgment—neither one could answer.

"You take Bunker. I'll take the apartment on Federal," he said finally.

She seemed relieved. He could tell by her look that she was happy that he was still showing faith in her, treating her like a cop, a detective, a sergeant, rather than a helpless woman, a Mrs. Andy Amato.

"Great. Let's go." She was full of energy. He looked at the clock; it was almost one A.M. She went into the bedroom and he could hear her pulling apart the Velcro on her holster to fit it around her ankle.

Then suddenly he wanted to stop her, to unplug the computer, forget it existed, and crawl back into bed, leaving whatever was going to happen to happen. He wanted to make love to his wife again and forget all about the lists and the killings.

Instead, just as he knew he would, he took the lists with him as he went back to the bedroom to dress.

Andy found the address without a problem. He felt extremely alone, the gray Motorola walkie on the seat next to him no consolation. He would much rather have had Gabe there.

It was an apartment-motel, two story, painted in Florida green with white trim. Floodlights lit up the front, and dull yellow box lights were set up along the ground by the pool and the edge of the apartments. He could plainly see number 11 on the end of the first floor. The place would be an easy target, much easier than a large house on Bunker Road, he figured. He hoped.

He drove the Saab around to the corner of the building, looking at the one side window to the apartment, seeing that it was closed and probably locked. He positioned himself in an empty parking lot across the street and a block north, able to see both sides of the building and anyone pulling into the lot from either side.

He picked up the walkie. "You there?"

"I'm here, ready to set up. All's quiet." Her voice was strong, without interference. It made him feel better about the whole thing.

"All's quiet here, also. All lights are out. No occupied vehicles in the area."

"Ten-four," she said, going back to standard codes.

He put down the radio. Federal Highway was deserted. He glanced up and down, seeing only a car pulling off a side street. He took binoculars off the backseat and fitted them to his eyes, then sat back, entrenching himself in the bucket seat. It was just past two on the dashboard clock.

Gabe had parked her Toyota a full block away from the house and on the opposite side. The neighborhood was old. There was a mix of wood-frame houses from the thirties and forties and some stucco and concrete-block structures from the fifties and sixties. Most houses were two story. The one she was watching was wood, plain white, a high porch and a circular drive leaving almost no front lawn. The neighbor-

184

hood looked to her to be a timeworn but respectable part of town. She had always imagined that the protected witnesses were more into condos, lakes, pools, and tennis courts.

She looked carefully for a U.S. marshal's car. Before stopping she had cruised the neighborhood, window down, engine barely idling. She saw and heard nothing. There was no other surveillance, she was sure of it. No one else was watching or seeming concerned with the house on Bunker Road.

He pulled up a block away, just as he had planned. The house would be around the corner, fourth from the end. White wood, two story, porch light burning. No marshals around. It would be just as he had seen it before. The man would be inside. He hoped, no, he *prayed,* that this would be it. This would be the end. He would succeed and be rid of him and all the problems he had developed because of it.

The killings were taking their toll. He was fearful of discovery—tired of looking over his shoulder, wondering if the next cop he saw was coming to arrest him. Wondering when someone would find the loose thread, pull it, and have his plan unravel, him along with it.

He fitted on the gloves and then opened the trunk. He reached in for the oversized Magnum revolver, grabbing also the flare gun. He held on to these with one hand and picked up the gas can with the other.

Pisoli had managed to escape. Up until now. This was it, he hoped. It had to be Pisoli. He grew weary of the pursuit. He wanted solace from the forces driving him. He would have it, he knew, when Pisoli was rotting in hell.

He took short, quick steps, staying close to the edge of the sidewalk. The night air was surprisingly cool. The sky was clear, with hundreds of summer stars surrounded by the dull ring of city lights from West Palm Beach, Ft. Lauderdale, and Miami. He turned the corner, studying the pathway down the sidewalk. A dog barked a few blocks to his

185

right. Other than this he detected only crickets, and traffic noise along Dixie Highway, far off to his left.

He stopped and listened even more carefully, also allowing his eyesight to adjust to the dull, yellowish vapor lights. He checked the darkened cars for silhouettes, looking 360 degrees around him, satisfied finally that he was alone. He checked houses for open drapes and curious neighbors. Just as he had found in his earlier surveillance, the neighborhood was asleep.

If the marshals are here with him, they're also inside. Too bad.

He walked forward, still staying on the far side of the sidewalk, almost on the grass, walking simply and steadily toward the house, holding the full gas can and the flare gun.

"Gabe?"

"Go ahead."

"All clear?"

"So far. Quiet. Can't see anything."

"Good. Check in every fifteen minutes."

"Okay, Teddy."

He put the walkie down and trained the glasses back on apartment 11. It was almost three A.M.

Instead of focusing on the house, she took the binoculars and looked up and down the street. At the far end of the block, at the corner, she thought she saw a figure. A male figure, medium height. Heavy. Standing near a tree, unmoving.

She focused. The figure was beyond two parked cars that partially blocked her view.

Then it moved. Swayed, and took a step forward, she thought.

She picked up the radio. "Teddy."

He moved slowly down the sidewalk, careful to listen for a passing auto that could be a patrol car. He looked inside each car he passed, checking for occupants, finding none. He looked up at each house, checking the curtains and windows, looking for signs of lights or someone awake. He looked at his watch, the face only slightly visible in the yellow glow. Three o'clock.

"Go ahead."

"Movement. A figure. A man, I'm sure. Walking slowly toward the house from the east. On the sidewalk."

"Get on the patrol channel and call for a marked unit to swing by."

"No, let's be sure it's not somebody out for a walk."

"I'm on my way over."

"Let's be sure."

"*I'm* sure."

His plan was simple and more direct than the others had been. He would burn the house to the ground. People would run out within the first few minutes. From the shadows, concealed behind the bushes, he would shoot whoever ran from the house. And whoever didn't run out would burn alive.

The walk became steady, she saw. The figure stayed far back on the sidewalk, against the grass, gait slow and plodding, but moving steadily forward.

He was carrying something. A bag. No, a can. A large can.

"Teddy."

Lieutenant Andy Amato knew it was time for the Saab's blue light and siren. With his free hand he took hold of the walkie, switched channels, identified himself to the patrol dispatcher, and requested available units to the Bunker Road address. Officers acknowledged. Andy could hear by their voices that they would hurry.

He was right, it would be tonight.

He was wrong, it would be on Bunker, not Federal.

He was one house away. He turned his slow, careful stride into a trot for the last few yards. He would have to act quickly to keep the element of surprise, he knew.

First he ran to the side of the house and splashed the wood siding with the first wave of gasoline. He followed with a line up and down the molding, then ran toward the front. He turned the corner, went up to the stairs, and sloshed at least a quart of the gasoline up onto the steps and the front door. In a moment enough of the wooden house would be covered. He would ignite it on the outside, then use the flare gun to shoot through the window. The inferno would be complete.

She saw him break into a trot. She threw down the binoculars. Her chest tightened. She grabbed the small revolver and yanked it forcefully out of the ankle holster.

She picked up the radio. "He's running toward the house! I'm going after him!"

Andy'll be mad. He'll tell me to wait. I'm a cop. I've got to do something.

She threw the walkie down on the seat. Andy would be coming, she knew. He would call patrol. Help would be there. Meanwhile, it was her against the killer. She didn't wait for him to answer.

He splashed the last of the strong-smelling high-octane gas over the hedges and wall on the far side of the house. Then he backed up, walking quickly, his revolver in his waistband, the flare gun loaded and now in his hand ready to fire. He raised his arm, ready to send the first blazing flare through the old, wooden front door, igniting the house.

A noise came from behind him and to the right.

"Freeze!" a female voice shouted out.

Everything had changed. He knew who it was. Nothing would be the same. His entire plan had to be rearranged.

The figure froze when she told it to. It was a male, shorter and heavier than average, dressed all in black. She saw a large gun in his hand and the now-empty gas can dangling at his side.

"Drop the gun and the can, real slow."

Her arm was extended, what she could see of her gun's sights centered directly on his upper torso.

Then he moved.

He did a somersault onto his right shoulder and at the same time aimed the flare gun in the direction of the voice and fired it. He sensed that she was hiding behind a large palm tree on the far side of the property. The explosion of his gun lit up the front yard, and he could see the trace of the projectile head right at the tree and the outline of the woman near it.

She squeezed the trigger when she saw him tumble. The small revolver kicked upward. It entered her mind, in a brief flash, a microsecond, that it was the first time she had fired her gun on duty, something that she hoped she would never do.

She pivoted right, along with his tumble, and fired again. Then she saw the arm and saw the whole night light up and heard the explosion when whatever it was hit the tree right next to her.

She fell to the ground, not knowing if she had dropped there all on her own for some reason or if something had happened to her. She tried to sit up and could do so, could feel her legs, and at first felt no pain beside the ache in her eardrum and eyes from the explosion.

189

Her shots had missed, she sensed it. By instinct she forced her gun hand up and toward the spot on the ground where his body must have fallen.

He was already up, on his feet. He had something again in his hand. He was aiming at her.

She fired.

He fired.

She saw his leg jerk and wobble like a cake of jelly but saw no sign he was going to drop down. She felt nothing, believing that she wasn't hit. She tried to steady the gun back toward his torso.

He turned and ran, more of a hobbling limp by a man who was hit in the leg but whose adrenaline level would not let him believe it, much less keep him from acting on it. She fired again, realizing too late that the gun was aiming slightly toward where he *had been,* not where he *was.*

Four. That's four. Two left. Got to be exact.

She heard sirens in the distance, heading toward her. She recognized the yelp of the siren in Andy's Saab, and could hear also the sirens of West Palm patrol units closing in on the old neighborhood.

She was on her feet. She was aware now of pain, but was unsure why. There was a burning on her right side. A searing hurt, something that felt as if it was traveling from her ankle up the side of her leg to her waist.

She ignored it. She started after him.

Andy would call her foolish. Andy would tell her it would be smarter to wait for backup. For other officers—bigger officers, faster officers, *male* officers. And the canines and the helicopter.

Stay back, let patrol surround the neighborhood, she could hear him say.

She ignored these feelings, as she had ignored them before, as she knew male officers ignored them and rushed toward danger.

190

Women are reckless. Men are heroes.

She turned toward the side of the house. He had run toward the back. There was a fence on one side, but not on the other, not by the yard of the house to the left. He couldn't climb, she reasoned. He had to go to the left.

She ran forward, gun with two bullets outstretched in front of her. It was dark—she had no flashlight. The yellow glow of the front vapor lights disappeared into the shadows.

She went around a hedge, past a small shed, toward the back, through the unfenced yard where he must have run. She crossed over into the next yard, the house behind, running more steadily now, running instinctively, ignoring the burning on her right side.

She could hear the sirens. They were close.

She turned the next corner of the house. Before she could react she saw and recognized the face, the body pressed against the house, the panting breath of a man hit in the leg by a hollowpoint bullet and running out of steam.

His hand reached out and the hard, flat metal part of the revolver slammed against the side of her face. She pulled the trigger, knowing as she blacked out that he had succeeded— he had made her misaim and fire the round into the side of the house, where it harmlessly lodged in the aged, rotten Florida wood.

Her last thought was of what he was doing there and why he was trying to set the house on fire and trying to kill her.

12

I Know Who You Are

Andy watched mindlessly as the evidence technicians turned off the quartz-halogen search lamps, dragged them away from the tree, and placed them in the van. It was almost daylight, and the men no longer needed the powerful lights in order to search for clues.

Jacobson had been there within fifteen or twenty minutes, it seemed. Andy was relieved when the senior commander arrived and took charge. Before that Andy was walking in a daze, not remembering what he said or what he did or what he ordered done, only acting out of instinct, telling himself over and over that everything would be okay, that Gabe . . .

He would think about her, about what he saw, about the empty car, the blood by the house, and he would close up. Shut down. The detective in him stopped working. He wandered from one point to another, staring at the policemen and -women, at the people asking questions. Officers and detectives had come up to him for information or advice. Some tried to comfort him. He had mumbled something, exactly what he couldn't be sure, and walked off.

But Captain Jacobson was a godsend. He wasted no time in taking charge, in doing all the things Andy wanted to but couldn't. He surrounded the house with crime scene tape, he set up a command post for the newspeople, he called in the evidence team. Andy finally gave up trying to look like he was working, like he was trying to help in the initial investigation of his wife's abduction—or murder. He walked away, back to the Saab.

Crying was something he never did.

Gabe was somewhere, he reasoned. Her car was still there, just down the block, just as she had left it, walkie-talkie thrown on top of the seat. When he first pulled up to the house, he ran frantically around the yard, then to each adjoining house, using his flashlight to follow some of the blood drippings. He expected to turn a corner, look under a bush, open the door to a shed, and find . . .

He hadn't been away from her in so long, he forgot what it was like. Whenever before he felt tightness and emptiness, he would turn to her. Now there were only the familiar faces of his fellow detectives and Jacobson. The emptiness of his loss felt so deep he would never be able to overcome it.

Captain Barney had called in the canine unit for a track, something else that had never even crossed Andy's mind.

"Look at this," Jacobson had said. Andy followed the men through bushes and yards, two streets farther south, through other dark backyards, led by a large German shepherd on a leash. The blood and fresh human odor ended by the side of the street.

"She's still alive. Someone took her. They drove her away," the captain had said. Andy wanted to believe it, but couldn't stop feeling helpless, emasculated.

Jacobson looked at him as though he were waiting for an explanation, but instead of asking for one, or ordering one, he would wait for Andy to get around to giving it.

But the captain was right. Gabe was still alive, of that much he was certain. Andy believed it not because of any blood trail or any other physical evidence, but because it was something he could feel. He *felt* Gabe thinking about him, or thought he did.

The German shepherd was back in the handler's car. The crime scene technicians withdrew. Jacobson was talking to another detective lieutenant, the one from the crime person division. A sergeant from the robbery division was next to them, listening in. Andy looked a block behind him, at two uniformed officers dealing with an anxious and raucous group of media people.

Andy saw an Insta-cam crew pointing at him, rolling footage of the bereaved cop-husband, probably for the "News at Noon."

Captain Jacobson came toward him. Andy leaned against the Saab, the sun all the way up now, and he knew that his boss would want an explanation, want a full story, and that he would have to give it to him. He knew that the man deserved it.

"We've re-created it all as best we could, Andy," Jacobson said when he walked up. "They were there in the front yard, the bad guy at the house, Gabe by the tree. He had just finished dousing the place with the gasoline. The guy fired one government G-nineteen flare, hitting the tree, probably scorching Gabe if she was nearby. Gabe shot probably three times with her revolver. From the blood, we think she hit him. Whoever it was also fired a round from a handgun, also a thirty-eight like Gabe's, hitting in the dirt, missing Gabe by inches. You can see where she fell; they have close-up pictures."

Andy nodded. "Thanks. I appreciate you taking over for me."

"No problem. You're not exactly up to it."

"I suppose you want to know everything?" Andy asked.

"In a minute. First let me finish."

Andy noticed that Jacobson was enjoying doing field detective work again, and that he was more than adept at it.

The captain continued. "We have the gas can he tried to use on the empty house. He must have dropped it when Gabe surprised him. We have the flare gun, a U.S. Navy model, the type they put in life rafts. I remember them from my Marine days. The techs are dusting both for prints right now."

"He wears gloves."

"Right," Jacobson said, nodding.

"He made a mistake. Gabe surprised him."

"Right."

"But he didn't kill her. Wonder why," Andy said.

Jacobson shook his head. "Don't know."

"Didn't kill her. If he did, he'd of left her here."

"Well, let's be thankful of that. We have an all-county bulletin out now—it will go statewide in just a few minutes. Attempted murder and abduction of a cop, it'll get plenty of attention.

"We've got calls in to all hospitals in the county to notify us if a gunshot wound or burn comes in, or anyone fitting Gabe's description." The captain continued. "The sheriff's office is watching all the main western roadways, checking cars for her. The Highway Patrol has got the interstate and the turnpike covered. People from our own department and others have volunteered to come in on their own time to help search. I want you to believe that we're doing all we can do."

"I know you are," Andy said. He wasn't listening closely, he was thinking. "Gabe and I were staking out two different places. I was over on Federal Highway, she was here. We knew that the killer would hit one of these two places. Actually, I *thought* he would, I wasn't sure. To tell you the truth, I believed we'd come up empty. If I'd known . . ."

Andy waited for the "Why didn't you have backup? Why didn't you call me?" but Jacobson stayed silent.

Andy continued. "It all happened so quick. We watched both places for about an hour. Then she sees someone walking down the sidewalk, next thing I know she yells on the radio that she's getting out and going after him. By the time we could get here she was already gone."

Andy was on the verge of a sob, but he held it back.

"Neighbors heard the gunshots," Jacobson said. "The woman who lives across the street saw one figure run to the side and in back of the house, and a second figure follow. Right after the gunshots. Some shots were fired into the side of a house, one block over. More blood. Signs of a struggle. They fought, up close. Gabe probably shot into the wall of the house, trying to hit him. Then he probably dragged her to his car."

"One or both of them are hit," Andy said flatly.

"There's enough blood. You're probably right."

A minute of silence followed. Both men looked over at the house.

"It was our killer. The one doing the mobsters. He was going to torch this place, barbecue whoever was inside. Gabe must've figured she had to stop him before he shot the flare gun and lit the place up like an inferno."

"The place is empty. Locked up tight. Looks like it hasn't been occupied in weeks."

Andy nodded. "We didn't know that. We had information that a protected witness was inside. We believed he might be the next target." Andy knew Jacobson would be curious but wouldn't ask where the information came from. Andy wasn't about to tell him about Gabe's crazy computer program.

"Who is your lead suspect? That Pisoli character? That who did this?"

"No. It's not. I'm sure of it. He's the target someone's trying to kill."

"Just him in particular, not all these protected witnesses?"

"That's right. Just him."

"Then why all the other killings?"

196

"To make us believe something. Make us believe the Mafia is involved, when they're not. Make us believe it's just a mob-related thing. And make us believe something else, something I haven't quite figured out yet."

"What?" Jacobson asked sternly.

"I'm not sure."

"But you suspect someone?"

Andy almost nodded. "I can't answer that. Don't make me answer that yet, Captain. There's too much I haven't gotten straight in my mind. There's too much." Andy trailed off. He felt like breaking down and crying.

"I can't keep you on this case now, you're too emotionally involved. You're too close. You're stunned, running at less than full capacity. Your judgment will show it."

Andy didn't say anything. He couldn't think of a response.

"I already set it up with Robbery and Crime Person. They're dropping all cases until further notice and working this exclusively. The first step is finding any possible fingerprints and putting out as much information as possible."

Andy nodded. He had no opinion, he wanted to make no statement. He knew that whatever Jacobson said, did, or ordered, it would have no effect on his plans.

"Tell me who it is. Who you suspect," Jacobson said.

Andy hesitated. "Someone from my past. Someone whose name I don't remember. Someone from Miami who has some mob scores to settle."

Jacobson looked as though he didn't understand. Andy was lying, and he sensed that the captain knew it.

"Get with the other divisions. Give them everything you can. I already set you up for a debriefing. Go over the entire case, word for word, from the beginning. Then it's theirs, not yours. I realize how much you hurt, how much you want to help and be involved, but you can't."

"Right. I understand. Do we have to do the debriefing now?"

"You've been up for twenty-four hours. In your condition,

197

you'll be up at least a few more. Go home, try to get some sleep. You've done all you could here. We'll take it and finish up. When you wake up, go into the station."

"Right."

There was silence. Andy looked over, sensing the arriving vehicle before seeing it. The marshal's car pulled in on the opposite side of the block from the media. Andy watched as Tom Sunderland flashed his ID card at the patrolman on the perimeter, then ducked his tall frame under the tape and walked toward him.

Sunderland shook hands with Jacobson and Andy. His face was blank. "I came over as soon as I heard, Andy. Everybody's with you on this. My whole office is out checking leads and harassing snitches. So are the FBI people. We want to help any way we can."

Andy nodded. "This house was on your list. It was supposed to be occupied. Gabe was here because we had information that this and a place on Federal Highway were the next targets."

"This is one of the houses Pisoli used. Briefly, up till a few weeks ago, when the killings started. Then we moved him and brought a few others in and out."

"But the list we have shows—"

"Too many things have changed. Probably a third of the list has been moved around. Security. We're trying to stay one step ahead. In this case, it worked."

You didn't tell me that, you big jackass. "Pisoli was here?" Andy asked.

"Right. We'd been keeping him here on and off. But no one knew that."

Andy was silent. *Pisoli. Always back to him.*

Jacobson excused himself and went over to confer with the crime scene people. Andy took Sunderland by the elbow and they walked away from the Saab, away from the media, toward the marshal's car.

Everything snapped into place. It had happened to Andy hundreds of times before. Sometimes it came in a dream, and might last through the fog of wakefulness. Sometimes it was in the shower, as he sang to himself. Sometimes it was during unrelated conversations with uninvolved people. Always, though, it came as a revelation.

But the problem here was that he wasn't sure. He didn't know if he *could* be sure. And he knew he couldn't say or do anything unless he was.

"I have a big favor to ask of you, Tom," Andy said as they walked on toward the car.

"Anything."

"Tell me where the government put Benny Pisoli."

Sunderland stopped. Andy studied his eyes for signs of a reaction. Andy knew he had just asked the most important question of the investigation.

"I don't know." The answer came quickly, with only slight surprise, and the eyes showing no reaction. He was telling the truth, Andy decided.

"He's not missing. He's not dead. The FBI or you people put him somewhere out of reach."

"I don't understand. I swear."

"Gabe's life is at stake. Every minute I'm delayed puts her more and more in jeopardy."

"It's not us. I thought he was dead, till you and Gabe showed me he was just missing."

"Okay. I believe you. I hope you're telling me the truth."

"I am. Why would I lie? What would I lie for? Can you tell me what's going on? I want to help. Tell me what you're thinking. Why would the FBI be hiding Benny Pisoli?"

"That's the final piece of the puzzle."

She came to with the burning sensation enveloping her right leg. It caused her to twitch, to move her leg toward her hand, but she realized then that part of the discomfort came from being tied up, hog-tied in a fetal position, lying on her side.

She was lying on something soft and musty, probably an old couch. Blindfolded. Her hands were behind her, tied at the wrists. Her knees were bent, her ankles also bound tightly together behind her. She tried to move, but couldn't. The only sensation she had was of the malodorous, tainted cushion under her, of the circulation cut off at her wrists and ankles, and the painful burning going up her right leg and thigh.

And her head. She could feel the moistness of her head wound, but could feel also that the bleeding had stopped, the blood had congealed. Her head ached, but it was only a dull throb. She was much more concerned about her leg.

There were voices from the other side of the house. More than one. *No, it's television.* She heard the metallic quality of the speaker. She thought *house,* but blindfolded, she could be anywhere. But it felt like a house. She was able to find a sense of surroundings. She concluded that she was alone in a room, a room rarely used, with the door closed. From the noise of the television she felt that she was in a big house, many rooms, probably a Florida ranch-style. No windows were open. No traffic on nearby roadways. No outside voices, no children passing by, no . . .

Her mind had avoided it, but now it was time to face it. She turned her thoughts to the man with the gas can at the house. The flare. The shots, the brief chase, being smashed on the skull with the man's gun.

He was there, in the house. She could feel him. He was out there, probably in the farthest room, watching the television, watching to see exactly what the news crews could capture; and he wanted to learn what the police knew about him.

She heard a noise like a chair pushing back on a tile or wood floor. Then footsteps. A door opened and closed in the interior of the house.

He was coming for her.

The news showed excellent footage of the exterior of the house from about a half block away. He could make out the evidence technicians, hard at work, taking photos and picking up and bagging evidence. He laughed when he spotted someone picking up the flare gun. He saw Jacobson. And Andy Amato. *That fucking cop-whore.* That asshole they had called in to torment him.

He was amused when the blond newscaster said in her delicate and sexy monotone, "Police are not saying what exactly they were investigating here at this empty house on Bunker Road, only that one of their own is missing, Sergeant Gabrielle Amato of the homicide division, who was on stakeout here. She is presumed at least injured, and according to one source, was probably abducted from the scene."

Of course she was, you stupid bitch.

He could not believe they had sent her. Alone. It had been easy. But he, also, had been surprised. It caused him to act quickly, impulsively, almost irrationally. She had scored points also. He looked down at his left leg, where he had stuffed the towels and handkerchief, and wrapped a belt to stop the bleeding. He was not concerned. It had missed the bone. The bullet had exited. It was only a painful and bloody flesh wound.

He was lucky they'd sent a woman. He thought she didn't have the stamina, lacked the experience. When she turned the corner of the house she was vulnerable and helpless. Smashing the gun into the side of her face was easy. He replayed pushing away her gun, laughing while she fired into the side of the house, smashing her again, watching her fall like a bag of sand at his feet.

He had picked her up, and even with his wounded leg he still was able to drag her the block and a half to his car. He had pushed her in the passenger side and driven away before the police cars started arriving.

The fucking house was empty. They lied to you again.

201

Time was running out. These new developments ruined everything for him. But now he had his final chance, he had stumbled upon his trump card—a wounded and helpless police detective. The wife of his tormenter.

He would have Benny Pisoli, he knew.

She pretended to be unconscious. She let her hands relax, then her arms, then her feet and legs. She took some deep breaths and let her breathing become shallow and rhythmic. She concentrated on hearing everything she could, and remembering everything she heard. As an investigator, she always used every sense available to her. She would *listen* for clues.

The footsteps were coming toward her. Heavy, short strides. He wasn't stopping at any of the other rooms, he was coming directly for her.

She looked deep into her consciousness and demanded of herself the courage to replay the face. It lasted less than a second, and was followed with the memory of the blow to her head and so much pain. But it was there—she had not erased it. She had turned the corner of the house, realized her mistake, pivoted on the balls of her feet to face the wall. There he was.

It was him. Just as she first thought. She put the thought fully in her consciousness. She felt the blow to her head again, then the dribbling of her strength and her loss of consciousness.

The door to the room opened. She twitched slightly. Fright. She wondered if he had seen it—if it had betrayed her.

"Are you awake yet?" he asked. The voice was obviously disguised.

She did not answer.

"I saw you move. You've been out for some time. It's late in the afternoon. You must be awake."

202

He moved closer. She tried to stop herself from taking a deep breath, or pulling away in fright.

"You are awake. I can see it."

"I'm awake," she finally said.

"How do you feel?" Still the artificial elocution.

"My head. My leg. They both hurt."

"Pity."

"How's *your* leg?"

"You mean, don't you, how is your aim? Your aim is fine. My leg, I'm afraid, has been better."

"Did you stop the bleeding?" she asked. Her voice showed concern, *real* concern. He was amused.

"Yes. Not a problem. And I stopped yours, too. The wound on your head is shallow, nothing too damaging."

"Are you going to kill me?" Gabe asked.

He snickered. "Why should I do that?"

She didn't answer.

"You're my ticket to Mr. Pisoli. With you here, your husband will deliver him to me."

"I don't know what you mean."

"Don't you? Did you believe that story they tried to pull? About Benny disappearing, trying to look dead? They thought I'd stop looking. They thought I was that stupid."

Gabe shook her head under the blindfold. She was positive now. As if the face in the night wasn't enough.

"Are you going to kill me?" she asked again. She tried to control her voice, but she could not cover the pleading.

Another chortle. "My dear, pretty lady. Why should I kill you?"

"Because I know who you are."

13

Clues and Whispers

Andy exorcised the most disturbing thoughts from his mind, and managed to drift off to a shallow and almost-gentle sleep.

Gabe was alive, he knew. And she was all right. That much he believed. Her captor wouldn't hurt her—he probably never intended to. It was *him,* not Gabe, he wanted out of the way.

So, for a moment, he let her face and voice slip away. Then Wesley, Pisoli, Gruen, Sunderland, Jacobson, the blown-to-bits Porsche, the dickless mobster, all the rest. They traipsed through his consciousness and then out, like unwanted and almost-unknown relatives at a reunion that he didn't want to attend. When his body collapsed, and his spirit finally accepted the sleep, only Gabe was left with him, and only as a smiling face and a warm body that could just as easily have been there next to him.

Andy drifted back to playing eight-ball with Guardinaro, with Carmine looking on. It was afternoon again; they were inside the Miami Beach island mansion. Andy sipped at his Scotch.

The Mafia boss of bosses hit in three striped balls, then missed. Andy stepped up to the cushion.

"The mob would never do something like this, do you believe me when I say this to you?" Guardinaro had said emphatically.

Andy took almost a minute to think. *"I believe you."*

Guardinaro nodded. Andy bent down, stroked, and missed his shot. *Respect.*

"Then who? Do you know who?" Andy asked when he looked up from the table.

Guardinaro shook his head. *"It's got to be something you're not looking at."*

The mobster cleared the striped balls off the rest of the table.

Gabe's face hovered just beyond his reach. She wanted to say something to him. He could sense it. But his wife couldn't speak, for some reason was unable to call out to him or let him know . . .

He went back to Boca. He watched from a distance, sitting in his car, watching the mobster approach the green Porsche, the U.S. marshal not far behind, watched him start the Porsche with his own remote starter. Andy waited, letting him get courageous, letting him sit in the driver's seat, put the car in gear, then back out, then go forward . . .

Andy was the killer now. He pushed the button. He looked down, no reaction, no remorse, no feeling at all, and he pushed the button. He looked down and shut his eyes and ears to the tremendous explosion.

Gabe called out to him. This time he thought he heard it—"Andy, I was almost there. I almost had it," he heard his wife's voice say in the dream. He turned over in bed, covering his eyes with his arm.

He was rereading Gabe's report about the Executive Center Drive killing, the one where the killer blew off Thomas Ripaldi's balls, then forced him to kill himself. "According to the neighbor, there were voices, a discussion, in the hallway. No force or shouting. Apparently normal conversation, and then there was quiet, making her believe they had gone inside the apartment."

Andy turned back onto his stomach. He thought of the loaded .25 auto that the man had kept hidden.

Why not get the gun?

He was on the Lake Worth pier. Pisoli was standing there, arms crossed. The night was darker than he remembered. All was quiet—there were no sea gulls. Pisoli's face was hazy, as if a fog had rolled in and settled over the old wooden jetty.

"Do you know who's doing the killings?" Andy had asked. He heard his voice resound at him. It was a ghostly metallic, an echo.

"I think so, I'm not sure. Let me say I've got a strong suspicion."

"Is it you? You behind it?"

"No way. What the fuck for? I've got too much to lose."

Andy had believed him. He still did, he decided.

I've got too much to lose.

There was eight or nine minutes of quiet solitude. The images and voices stopped. Only the dull hum of the ceiling fan registered. He was almost, but not quite, fully asleep.

"Teddy?"

He thought it was her voice. He thought it was real, as if she were standing in the doorway of the bedroom, as if she had managed to get away and come home. He didn't open his eyes, only waited. It did not repeat. He had imagined it. He snuggled closer to dreamlessness and actual sleep, then let his mind wander just a little further.

When the next image came it was jolting, as though he had been standing in a pitch-black room, fully awake, and someone had abruptly and unexpectedly thrown on the lights.

Everyone was standing there.

It was the small oceanside condo in Jupiter. They were there, in that little room, standing around the man with the

206

mask, his sperm on the carpet, and a gaping bullet wound in his chest.

Gabe, Sunderland, Gruen. The sheriff's detectives. The fat crime scene lady.

"What about Pisoli?" Andy had asked. *"He do this? After he took off, you search his place good? You find anything out?"*

"We did," Sunderland answered. The tall Swede nodded slowly in the dream. *"We found nothing. No notes, no letters, not a clue."*

Gruen spoke up. *"Do your homework, Amato. Pisoli doesn't have a gun. He's a knife man. A knife, always a knife."*

Andy sat straight up in bed, frightened.

Gabe spoke to him again.

The television had been on for hours. She wondered if he had kept it on while he was busy doing something else, or if he actually sat and watched the thing for hours.

Hours. The thought amused her. It was still Wednesday, she was sure, but she didn't know what time it was, or how much time had elapsed. She couldn't drift off to sleep; she was too uncomfortable. It was about midafternoon, maybe a little later, she guessed.

She listened to the TV. She couldn't make out any words. She decided to listen for a clue; she decided that for some reason it would be important to know the time. Soaps? Game shows? Some other show she remembered? Maybe she would hear the start of the 5:30 P.M. newscasts. Maybe even news about her disappearance.

That must be it, she decided. He was watching and waiting for news about her. About him. That's why the TV was on.

At times she thought she heard his voice, a single voice, like one side of a telephone conversation. It was too far away, the house was too long. She wasn't sure.

She worked again at freeing her wrists. The cord was rammed in hard behind each of her thumbs, wrapped two or three times around each wrist, then tying her hands together. She tried to bend her fingers far enough forward to begin loosening the twine and maybe slipping free. She couldn't quite reach; she expended too much energy, and she felt her circulation cut off as she struggled against the bindings. She let up, left them alone, content to try again later.

The blindfold was still on. She had tried to talk him into taking it off. He wouldn't.

In the middle of the silence he opened the door of the room and came in.

She was startled, but didn't gasp or twitch. She would make him believe she was asleep again, if she could.

"You're awake. Don't try to trick me."

She let a few seconds go by. "I'm awake."

"There's still nothing. They know nothing. Your husband may not be as smart as you think."

"He is. He'll find you."

"Won't matter. Not unless he brings someone with him."

"Who were you talking to?" Gabe asked. Maybe he would answer. She didn't know why she needed to know.

"None of your business," he replied, then chuckled.

A minute of silence. "If all you want is Pisoli, then call. I'll give you the number. Call Andy, tell him everything you've told me. He'll find Pisoli for you. He'll bring him here. Give him this address."

"Not that simple. You think you have it all figured out, but it's not so elementary as all that. This all has to end a certain way."

"Yeah? And how's that?"

"Pisoli has to die. Then maybe you'll live. Then both you and your husband and everyone else will have to leave me alone. None of this can come out in public."

"You have my word," Gabe said quickly.

208

"Not enough. Much more, I'll have to have much more."

The phone rang in the distance, from the other side of the house.

Just before he closed the door she heard a brief bit of television. The 5:00 "M*A*S*H" rerun was starting.

Good. She had a sense of time. And she thought she knew who had made the phone call.

Groucho purred loudly. She was nagging for dinner. Andy got dressed, then reached down and stroked her back end as she hunched up for him. The purring just became louder and more insistent.

"Later, baby. Later," he said and walked out of the bedroom.

He walked quickly into the den and sat at the computer. He reached back behind it and switched it on. The screen lit up. The red drive-lights on the front panel began to flash. In another ten seconds the hard-drive was going through its boot-up routine. Andy saw the date and time flash by him, fed in by the machine's clock-calendar card.

He had watched Gabe do it dozens of times, but hadn't paid much attention. It was a one-word command, he knew. He just couldn't think of what it was. He sat there looking at the blinking cursor and the empty screen.

He would do a directory. That much he remembered. He saw Gabe do it when she wasn't sure of the command.

The screen showed all the computer's contents. He found what he was looking for.

Mindscapes. That must be it, he said to himself.

He tapped in the word, then held his breath as he pressed down the ENTER key.

First he thought he had done something wrong because the screen just blanked and the drive stayed silent. Then there was a churning noise, followed by an introductory screen:

209

He was stuck. What file name did she use? He stared at the blinking cursor, trying to will it to give him a clue.

"If you ever have to use the computer, just speak English to it," he remembered Gabe saying to him.

He typed in HELP, then pressed the ENTER key.

The screen blanked again; then he was presented with a file listing, with instructions to use the cursor keys to move around the directory.

He took a minute to read and explore. She had almost a hundred files, some with names he recognized from past cases. Some names appeared to be coded, making no sense to him at all.

Then it reached out and found him, just as he was about to scroll down some more: SEABREEZE, it read. The street name in Palm Beach. Charles Portuno and the dead assassin in the Lincoln.

He moved the cursor under the name and pressed ENTER again, just as the screen said to do. The screen went blank, the hard disk turned, and the red LED glowed. He had found what he needed, he realized.

He tried to understand the program, to get his bearings. He experimented with different commands. He found he was most successful with simple English: LIST, SHOW, TELL, SORT. When the program didn't understand, it would say so. He would try something else or go back to the HELP screen.

The mass of data that Gabe had compiled told him nothing. She had left off with some entries from the day before. It was a jumble of facts, some actual insights, and some wisdom about the case that he knew only someone with Gabe's keen eye could have seen. Still, it all gave him nothing. Facts alone, he always knew, rarely solved homicides.

And he needed confirmation. Before he set off to do what he knew he had to do, he wanted Gabe's machine to give him the confidence that he needed.

"I need strength," he said out loud.

He went back to the HELP screen. He typed and entered a command on the lower half that sounded promising:

INQUIRE.

The screen flashed, went blank, then came up with:

READY >.

He typed in:

WHO IS DOING THE KILLING?

The machine took a second, then:

INSUFFICIENT INFORMATION.

He felt frustrated, but knew that he was on the verge. He realized his mistake. Gabe had stuck with the facts; she put in only what she *knew,* or could reasonably deduce or presume. She made no real assumptions; everything that he browsed through contained nothing close to speculation. Gabe was *reasonable.* Everything she asserted would have a reason behind it.

If he left it at that, he knew, Gabe was as good as dead.

He would make the computer think like *him,* not Gabe.

He typed in everything, line by line. He included the remote starter and the remote detonator. The .25 auto. He typed in every last thing that he remembered Pisoli, Wesley, Gruen, and Sunderland ever saying to him. He typed in everything from his dreams. Everything from Guardinaro. Everything from Carmine. Finally, he typed in all his suspicions, and everything that he thought. Even the sheer speculation. *Everything.*

He entered each thought, line by line. Finally, he felt exhausted. Nothing was left. The mass of wires and chips knew everything he did. He went back to the HELP SCREEN. Then he typed in:

SOLVE.

He felt foolish. He laughed to himself. A machine, a home computer, and he was asking it to solve a capital crime. Multiple homicides. More important, he was asking it to help bring back the only person really important to him.

The screen went blank. The disk hummed and he braced himself for INSUFFICIENT INFORMATION. But the processor continued.

Groucho jumped up onto the desk next to him, frightening him. With his left hand he reached out, scratched her neck, making sure she didn't step on the keyboard. Finally, the screen said:

READY FOR SOLVABILITY LISTING. 95% PROBABILITY OF SOLUTION. PRESS ENTER.

He hesitated. Groucho became more insistent. He picked her up, scratched her head, kissed her behind the ear, then put her on the carpet. His heart pounded.

He pressed the ENTER key.

The processor hummed. Then the machine's solution scrolled by. It was three short sentences.

He printed them out, then quickly ripped out the paper and held it tightly in his hand.

He nudged Groucho away, turned off the computer, quickly put on his guns, and headed out the door. In another two minutes Andy had the Saab well above seventy, heading onto the interstate, flying south toward Miami.

14

Wiseguy

It was not the same guard—Andy noticed that immediately. Cuban obviously, but much, much younger, with longer hair. The guard paid attention to him as soon as he walked in the door and kept eye contact. Andy hesitated, wondering if he was expected.

"Lieutenant Amato, West Palm Beach Police," Andy said as he held up his shield and ID.

There was no response. Andy watched the guard's eyes.

"I need to see Agent Wesley. He's expecting me." Andy lied. He didn't want the guard calling up to check. The man's eyes betrayed no emotion, no recognition.

The guard inspected Andy's badge, then unceremoniously reached under the counter for a visitor's pass. He handed it to Andy without comment and turned his attention back to the small closed-circuit monitors.

Andy clipped the badge to his breast pocket and headed for the elevator, not giving the guard another look or any reason at all to be suspicious.

It was well past five and most workers had departed, Andy

knew. He rode the elevator up alone. He knew also that Wesley was still there; he had spotted the agent's assigned car in its parking space.

He stopped outside the main office door and listened for voices. There were none that he could hear. No phones ringing. He opened the door.

The receptionist he knew was not behind the sliding window. He walked quickly past the empty waiting chairs to the interior door. It also opened. He looked inside, seeing no one. There were muffled voices far off, down a hallway, but it was down the opposite hallway from Phil Wesley's office. Andy had been to the office a year before, and still remembered the layout.

He walked quietly down the hall and up to Wesley's door. He listened. No noises. He felt expected, like a man about to walk in on his surprise birthday party, only it really wasn't a surprise at all, and everyone knew it.

When he opened the door Wesley was sitting at his desk, a file folder clutched in his hand.

The men locked stares, both looking surprised, both feeling awkward.

"Didn't think you'd see me so soon?" Andy said, somewhat nervously.

Wesley put the folder down. He moved cautiously, drawing his chair in toward the desk and putting his hands on the burnished oak. Andy moved a step closer, standing at the outer edge of the desk.

"Well, I'm here. I want some answers. And I want my wife back."

Wesley made a quick movement toward a drawer. Andy snapped forward like a rattler, grabbing his wrist, clamping it until he grimaced. Andy let go, and his friend pulled away, rubbing his wrist. Andy pulled the drawer open and removed Wesley's .38, placing the revolver in his own waistband.

Wesley hesitated, then moved toward the phone. With a tensing of muscles Andy stood rigidly erect and swung his right leg and foot over the desk, catching the phone with his heel and sending it crashing to the floor. Wesley looked astonished and disturbed.

A minute went by. Wesley composed himself. He leaned back in his chair and intertwined his hands as if he were about to engage an old friend in a genial discussion.

"Actually, I figured you'd call first. After figuring it out. Ask to meet me somewhere, maybe back down at the range. You'd tell me your suspicions, and I'd deny it. I didn't expect to see you so soon, no."

"No time for dillydallying. Things happened too quickly. I had a hell of a time figuring it out, but once I did, I felt it best to take the direct approach."

Wesley made a slight, almost-inconspicuous movement toward the other side of the desk. Within a second Andy had his automatic out of his shoulder holster and pointing at his old friend. Both men were still. Andy saw the heaving motions in Wesley's chest. He knew that the agent was only slightly more frightened than he was.

"Felonious assault on a federal officer is pretty serious, Andy." The hand moved a little closer to the other side of the desk. Toward what, Andy wasn't sure.

Andy pulled the hammer back on the 9-millimeter and aimed it at Wesley's face. "True, but accessory to murder, attempted murder, and kidnapping of a police officer are more serious, Phil."

"You don't know all the facts."

"I thought you were conveniently absent from the crime scene yesterday. Sunderland showed up, but there was no parade of FBI officials like I was used to. Palm Beach, West Palm Beach, Boca Raton, Jupiter. You were at every one of them. I didn't think anything of it at first, then later I fitted it in with the rest of the facts."

"I don't have Gabe. I don't know what you're talking about."

"Don't you? You may not *have* her, but you know where she is. Where's he hiding her, Phil?"

"Where's *who* hiding her?"

Andy paused a moment. He kept eye contact, and kept the Smith & Wesson squarely aimed at the FBI agent.

"The remote control starter was what first got me thinking. But you know what the police psychologists say about repressing bad thoughts, don't you? If you come to a conclusion that's really horrible, one that you just can't face, you sublimate it, you push it away, you deny it."

Wesley sat perfectly still, perfectly silent.

"There was a man, a mobster in the witness protection program, and the marshals give him a remote starter for his Porsche. Then he gets blown up by someone with a remote *detonator.* Now, how does that figure? Who the fuck would know that the marshals gave the guy a remote starter to begin with?".

"A professional has his sources, Andy. You know that."

"Not that fucking good. Nobody has a source that god-damned good."

Wesley continued gazing at the zealous police lieutenant standing in front of him.

"And before that, what fit in was the first killing, over on the island. The Mafia got an anonymous tip on that one. Where the guy is, exactly what date he's getting there. Even how to get plans to the house. And to top it off, they get an alarm key. But then the killer gets whacked out. Unbeliev-able. Fuckin' crazy, right? Until you think about it. What's the reason? Somebody wants us to find a Mafia hitter there. Someone wants us to know, to believe, that the Mafia is doing all the killing. Sort of a half-assed attempt to throw us off the track."

"Put the gun away. We can talk about this."

Andy kept the gun up. "Then my man on Executive Cen-

216

ter Drive, the one in West Palm Beach, the one that makes this whole mess my case, my headache. A mobster gets whacked out. Gets his balls blown off by someone who has a key to his apartment. But that's okay. I see the reason for that. He wanted us to believe that someone was selling information to the Mafia to do the hits, and then the killer just gets careless and drops a key. Who would believe that someone in the government, someone in the fucking FBI, for Christ's sake, is doing the killing?"

"You're crazy, Andy. You can't prove any of this."

"But something about that case nagged at me. Something more subtle. I almost didn't realize what it was. The guy's gun. The guy has a loaded gun, but he doesn't bring it to the door. A neighbor hears conversation, then nothing. The guy goes to the door, a guy under marshal protection and mob death threats, and he lets whoever it is inside without even going for a gun. You know why? Because it's someone he's *expecting,* someone he has to hide the gun from, someone from the fucking government."

"Sit down. Put the gun away. I can explain all of this."

"Not so fast, I'm not finished." Andy saw from Wesley's face he was doing a good job convincing the agent that he was a man on the edge, a man about to be pushed over.

"My connections in the Mafia tell me that it isn't them. Not that they wouldn't lie to me. They would, for the right reasons, under the right circumstances. They're ruthless, bloodthirsty savages. That's how I expect them to act. But when they've done something despicable and debasing, and they know I can't prove they did it, I've always known them to admit to it. That's their *power,* that's how they draw their strength, their *pride.* They always admit it to me, when they know I can never use their admissions against them. Yet in these cases, they're silent. On the biggest scam the mob could ever possibly pull, cracking the hated witness protection program, there's not a fuckin' peep."

"Gabe's not in any danger. I can explain it all to you."

"And then the final thing, the thing I had nightmares over. Gruen. Gruen tells me that Pisoli *always uses a knife,* never a gun. Well, Phil, Pisoli was never convicted of murder, just some chicken-shit extortion and racketeering. So, can you tell me just how it is that Gruen would know that unless he knew Benny killed his daughter?"

"We can still make this right. We can still end this with no one else getting hurt."

"That's when it all adds up. Almost. There's a few threads missing. Like Pisoli. He's missing. Rather, the FBI is hiding him, and the marshals don't know about it. If it wasn't for me and Gabe, you woulda had Sunderland believing that Pisoli was dead. That was a turning point. If Pisoli could somehow be believed to be dead, this whole thing could've ended." Andy took the computer paper out of his jacket pocket, opened it, and read the three lines again.

SOMEONE WITH INSIDE KNOWLEDGE.
SOMEONE CLOSE TO ANDY AMATO.
AN FBI AGENT. DONALD·GRUEN.

He put the paper away. "The gun is a thirty-eight, without a silencer. Mobsters hit people with twenty-twos almost exclusively. Someone with inside knowledge. Someone from the government."

"Could be lots of people."

"Only a few. Not Sunderland, not the marshals. There's no way you could make me believe that. Not for a minute."

"No, I guess I couldn't."

"The one thing I was missing was the motive. What on earth for? *Why?* All cops have these fantasies, to blow these assholes away, but who the hell can do it? Risk everything, career, pension, jail. For what?"

"It's not like that."

"Right. I believe you. It's not something as simple as

218

revenge or a sort of professional blowing off of steam, just with it getting a little out of hand. There's got to be more, more of a motive. Something that would want to make a senior FBI agent become a savage, multiple homicidal maniac."

"Shut up and I'll tell you."

"Then it hit me. It all added up. Pisoli was the real target, I always figured that. But the marshals always moved him. The FBI was always in on the game, but they never were the central players. The U.S. marshals ran the show, not the FBI. So an FBI agent could easily get to know where a specific house or apartment was that was being used, but never really know where a specific *person* in the program was. Not without asking a lot of very suspicious-sounding questions. That's why Gruen was so upset over Sunderland giving me the witness list. That's why Gruen broke into my town house, to look for the list."

Wesley nodded. If he was surprised by the revelation, he didn't show it, Andy noticed.

"To kill a specific person, namely Pisoli, he would have to just start hunting the mobsters down at random. You see, on Seabreeze Avenue in Palm Beach, what I didn't realize till later was that before killing the guy in the Lincoln, Gruen checked out the mansion to see if the guy inside was Pisoli, like he hoped. That's what he did, I'm sure of it. When it wasn't Pisoli, but old Charlie Portuno, he went into a frenzy. After that, he did everything he could to find and kill Benny Pisoli."

Wesley continued nodding. He ever so slightly moved his hand back closer to the drawer.

"And you knew. You knew all along. And FBI people in Washington knew. That's why they were down here, not because of any great concern over a few dead, mid-level mafiosos, but because one of their own had gone on a rampage and started killing people."

Wesley moved closer. Andy saw it. He let him inch nearer.

"Gruen's daughter was killed. Sunderland mentioned it to me, but it went right by me at the time. His daughter was attacked, raped, knifed, and left to die in the woods. I called the North Palm Beach Police Department records division on my car phone on my way down here. They read me most of the report. That's what started all this."

"That's right, Andy. It did. But you have to stop now and listen to me. You have to let me speak to you, one old friend to another."

"Gruen's daughter was killed. By Pisoli. Somehow Gruen found out who it was. He's been hunting the man ever since. And you and the rest of the FBI knew about it all the time."

"No. We found out well after it started. At the Palm Beach scene I only suspected. It all came together later."

"Whatever. I'll never prove any of this anyway. There'll be a huge FBI conspiracy of silence. You'll manipulate the facts, the faces, the names, everything. You'll get me out of the way, keep me silent, play up my sense of brotherhood, or somehow just shut me up. Maybe kill me. And you'll keep Gruen under wraps until it all blows over, then he'll get a nice, fat federal pension. He'll probably head up to the fuckin' Carolinas to fish, just like the rest of you."

"I know where he is, I've talked to him. Gabe's alive. I'm trying to get him to surrender her to us."

Wesley's hand crept again toward the edge of the desk.

Andy moved in and placed the muzzle of the gun close to the agent's face. "Don't do it, Phil."

Wesley pressed the button.

Andy grimaced and leaned closer. He put almost enough pressure on the trigger to set the gun off.

"You won't kill me," Wesley said. "Put the gun down and let me explain. There's something you have to know. There are things you have to try and understand. We're old friends, just let me explain."

"Back away," Andy said. Wesley moved the chair back.

Andy reached around the desk, feeling the button, realizing that it was too late, that his friend had already pressed it.

Andy let his anger show. "Whoever it is may find a dead agent, Phil. What about that? Don't think I'd do it? Don't think I have it in me? Remember something. She's a cop, she's my partner, and she's my *wife.*"

"Put the gun down and listen."

Andy reached forward. The Smith & Wesson 9-millimeter was on single-action, cocked back, within a pound of pressure of going off.

"I'm done listening. Tell me where my wife is. Tell me where Gruen's holding her. Then come with me and we'll bring her back. Then we'll talk."

The door cracked open.

Andy moved around behind Wesley, using the agent to shield his body, turning him around and positioning the gun to point over the top of his head.

The door opened. Pisoli stood there. The contradiction didn't register with Andy right away. Then he looked closer. Pisoli looked different. He held himself differently—not like a mobster. Then Andy realized what it was, something so innocuous and banal that it was often overlooked. On his shirt pocket he had clipped on an FBI ID tag. Andy pointed the gun at his midsection.

"Pisoli" was all Andy could manage to say.

The man smiled. He came in and closed the door behind him. Andy gave him a thorough frisking with his eyes, deciding for now that he was probably unarmed. Then Pisoli came closer, close enough so Andy could read the man's ID tag.

"Meet FBI agent Albert LaRocca," Wesley said.

15

Detours and Distractions

Surprise didn't show on his face, Andy was sure of it. "You're full of shit," he said before he could stop himself.

Pisoli's smile left his face when he first saw the 9-millimeter pistol aimed square at his chest. He moved to his left, and Andy followed with the muzzle. Wesley sat straight in the executive chair.

"Agent LaRocca has been in the FBI for the last eighteen years. The last fifteen have been as a deep-cover mob operative," Wesley said.

"You're full of shit," Andy mumbled again, letting the surprise show through. He was disappointed in himself.

"No, we're not," Wesley said simply.

"He's a well-known crook. He was prosecuted and found guilty. Extortion, racketeering. He was supposed to have been involved in murders, drugs, beatings, all sorts of crap. Now you tell me he's an agent?"

"That's right. He did his job well. Too well, actually. He got carried away. Things got out of hand. Before we could recall him he was tied in to so many people and so much trouble that we got him out the only way we could."

"The only way you could?" Andy asked incredulously.

"That's right. The marshal's program. We set him up in it as a way to get him away from the mob without . . . without—"

"Without embarrassing the Bureau?" Andy finished.

Wesley looked up at him. Andy motioned with his gun for LaRocca to sit in one of the guest chairs. He sat, an unpretentious smile on his face.

"Hundreds of people were put away with his testimony. Fucking *hundreds,* Andy. Do you hear me?"

"And what? And you couldn't reveal who he really was?"

"That's right. He committed crimes. It would all be revealed. It would be an embarrassment. Not only all those cases being lost. That wasn't the half of it. If the federal prosecutors got it, they'd rip us apart. Washington would come apart at the seams. They'd have the J. Edgar Hoover Building turned into a shelter for the fucking homeless. Christ, they'd bury us."

Andy thought quickly and believed what he was hearing. He could tell that his old friend was finally telling him the truth.

"Who knows about this?"

"Just the higher-ups. A few supervisors. Now you. You're a team player, Andy. We've counted on you before. You have to help us through this. You understand the importance of this?"

"Gruen's got my wife, Phil. There's not a hell of a lot I understand about all this shit right now." He backed up a few steps. Wesley turned the chair around to face him.

"We can't just let it out. We can't just confess this to the whole country. It went too far. He lost control, he lost his identity. He got into things and did things he shouldn't've done."

"That's not my worry. Gabe's my worry, and the homicide in West Palm is my worry."

"Right. Right. And we're gonna take care of that. I swear it. Gabe's not gonna be hurt."

"Gruen killed all those men. Murder. One of your FBI agents is killing people, Phil. All because of Pisoli—uh, LaRocca here."

Wesley acted for a moment like a skipper who's just had the wind taken out of his sails. He leaned back in the chair, giving Andy a helpless stare.

"Does Sunderland know about this?" Andy asked.

Wesley shook his head wearily. "No. That wasn't part of the plan. LaRocca would just go under the witness protection program. In a few years, everybody would forget about him. Then he'd take off, sort of just escape, or maybe—"

"Die." Andy finished the sentence for him. "Like he was supposed to have done in his Mercedes, out in the Everglades?"

"Right. Then everything would fade away. We'd be home free."

"As long as he didn't talk," Andy added, motioning to the man sitting before him. It was Pisoli, with a different look on his face, with a different way of carrying himself, and with a fucking FBI ID card on his shirt, Andy thought. He remembered back to the pier and shoving the barrel of his small revolver up his nose.

"He wouldn't talk. He still won't talk. He has just as much to lose as we do, probably more."

Andy looked at LaRocca and wondered why the man had so meekly walked into the room, and was now just sitting there, smiling at him, in the middle of all this.

"Gabe. We're going to get her back. Gruen's got her, and what he really wants is Pisoli, or LaRocca here. That's what he's gonna get," Andy said.

"We'll get Gabe back for you. I've talked to Gruen. He'll

release her. It won't be necessary to give him Agent LaRocca."

"Then what does he want in return? Why else would he release her?"

"Leave that to us, Andy. This is still mostly a federal matter."

Andy Amato laughed, probably for the first time since running desperately around Bunker Road in West Palm Beach, looking for his wife.

Federal matter. No shit.

Wesley continued. "We'll deal with Gruen. LaRocca here will remain a secret. And Gabe will be released unharmed."

"Is she shot?" Andy asked. He had suppressed it, but he found himself now having to know.

"No. Hurt. Her leg, her head, from the blast of the flare gun, but not badly. Not shot. Gruen's the one that got shot. Gabe hit him with one in the leg."

Andy was inwardly proud. He wished only that she had killed him dead right on the spot, hit him square in the chest, and maybe Andy wouldn't be in the middle of such a mess right now. The FBI would face its well-deserved humiliation.

"Where are they at?" Andy asked.

"My winter place. In West Palm, the North End, just off the water. Gruen used to share it with me. He has the key. He called me from there just a little while ago."

"Why didn't you stop him? Why'd you let him go on killing?"

"I told you, we didn't know right away that it was him. It wasn't till later things came together. Just the other day, really. That's when I arranged LaRocca's disappearance. But you guys showed up, and Sunderland and Gruen didn't buy it. We were gonna put a stop to it all, he was just moving too fast for us."

"You'll deal with Gruen by hushing the whole thing up, a giant cover-up, going right up the ladder to Washington.

225

He'll walk out with a pension. LaRocca, too. And I guess you figure Gabe and me will just forget all this."

"I trust you, Andy. That's why I'm telling you the whole truth. I feared that you'd get too deep into it. I hoped that you wouldn't come this close. I wish you hadn't gotten this far involved."

"This is *big,* Phil. This is too big for me, bigger than anything I've ever been involved in. I don't know how you plan on making it work. But for right now, just start planning on getting Gabe away from that no-good little cocksucker."

LaRocca laughed. Andy moved the gun to aim at his face and gave him an ominous scowl.

"You killed Gruen's daughter?" Lieutenant Amato asked.

"I did no such thing," LaRocca replied, then quickly stopped laughing. Andy saw that the Brooklyn accent had not been faked. And that the man was lying.

"He thinks you did. That's what started all this. He must have had his reasons." Andy continued to stare.

"I think you picked up his daughter. Raped and murdered her. Is that what you learned in the mob? You forget some things, like who's a good guy and who's a bad guy? You forget you were a good guy, is that it?"

"Look, whether he did or didn't kill her is not important at this moment," Wesley interrupted. "I've got some calls in to people all over, I'm trying to work a strategy to get Gabe back for you with the least amount of problem. I'm gonna have Gruen's Washington supervisor and some other people talk to him, assure him that everything can be worked out. He'll listen to them."

Andy had been saving the big question. Now he saw his opening for it.

"Does Gruen know about LaRocca?"

"No. He's never been told. There was never a need. The fewer the better, as I'm sure you understand."

"So he thinks he's been hunting down a mob killer, and

all this time it's been another FBI agent? And all these mobsters had to die because of it."

"You sound like you feel sorry for them," Agent LaRocca said.

"I have a sense of justice."

It was LaRocca's turn to laugh. He chortled and carefully reached into his shirt pocket for a cigar.

"Lieutenant Andy Amato, Miami PD, West Palm PD. 'A sense of justice'? I know all about you, Amato. One, you're a guinea, just like me. This shit's in your blood. You think just because you don't take money that you're one hundred percent clean?" The agent unhurriedly lit the cigar.

"No one is. But this is all too far out. You all know the rules, this stuff isn't even in the same ballpark. Murder, cover-up, all this stuff could end a lot of careers—"

"That's right Andy," Wesley broke in. "But we won't let it. We can't. It won't touch you, it won't hurt Gabe, it won't hurt the Bureau."

"The Bureau? Is that all you guys ever think about?"

"Put the gun away. We'll wait here for more people. People from Washington. People Gruen will listen to and believe. It'll all fall together, I promise you. Gabe won't be hurt, and we'll all get out of this without embarrassment."

The gun felt heavy. Andy thought of putting it back in his shoulder holster. He thought of trusting his old friend. After all, Wesley had come through for him before. He had seen and believed in the power of the federal government and the FBI. Maybe they could pull it off this time, too.

Without embarrassment. He thought over the words carefully. Andy hesitated a few more seconds, trying to decide.

LaRocca smiled at him. "Put the gun away, Amato. You can trust us. We'll take care of everything. Gruen'll get straightened out, and you'll have your wife back."

It was Pisoli talking. The man was talking like mobster Benny Pisoli, not any FBI agent, not any Albert LaRocca,

Andy knew. He saw it in the face, in the voice, in the words.

"Wrong. We're going up to West Palm. Us three. We're going to confront Gruen and get Gabe back. That much I'll make sure of myself. Then I'll leave you federal boys to do whatever the fuck you want to with this mess."

Andy led them out of the office at gunpoint, then made a hard right, pointing at the private stairwell that he knew led to the parking garage. He didn't know if any other agents were in the building, and didn't want to take a chance at being spotted.

He frisked LaRocca; the man wasn't carrying. He ignored an annoyed look from Wesley and frisked him also. Nothing—the gun in the desk had been it, and Andy now had that in his waistband.

They went down the barren, concrete-lined staircase, first LaRocca, then Wesley, followed by Andy, his 9-millimeter still out, cocked and ready.

The stairwell ended at a large black door with PARKING LEVEL stenciled in blood red letters. LaRocca dropped his cigar, crushing it with his heel. He opened the door and stepped through, holding it open.

LaRocca threw a wall switch, turning on a quartz lamp. Andy was startled by the bright light, was first off guard, then stood firm—tried to get his balance and anticipate what he knew would be coming at him. LaRocca's punch missed its mark when Andy instinctively turned, grazing his chin and landing harmlessly against his shoulder. Andy saw only a silhouette that was blocking out part of the light. The man reached forward, toward the gun in Andy's waistband. Andy moved quickly, landing the sole of his shoe against a knee, then following through and landing the butt of his pistol firmly against LaRocca's temple. He saw the body twist, then capitulate, just after LaRocca threw another punch that landed benignly against Andy's chest.

Wesley had moved to the right, out of view. Andy spotted him. The FBI agent was about to run, not attack, he knew.

"I'll shoot!" Andy yelled. Both men were still. The echo reverberated through the mostly empty concrete garage.

LaRocca moaned. Andy knelt down, turned him on his stomach, and handcuffed him, all the while holding the gun and most of his gaze on his old FBI friend.

"She's my wife. I'm not gonna let her die. Gruen wants this asshole, he can have him." Andy allowed himself to sound out of breath, and desperate. It was how he felt.

"Fine. All right. Easy, Andy. I'm not going to try anything," Wesley said.

Andy picked up LaRocca by the shoulders. The wound from the butt of the pistol was pouring blood over his left ear. He wavered, then steadied himself, his eyes coming open.

Andy waved Wesley forward, toward the middle column where the black Saab stood out from the other cars. Wesley moved cautiously, his hands raised.

"Walk backwards. Keep looking at me."

Phil Wesley turned and began walking backward.

"Another funny move," Andy said, aiming his pistol, "and first *he* gets it. Then you. Understand?" Andy moved the gun to the handcuffed agent's head.

"Gotcha, good buddy. No more funny business."

Andy opened the passenger door of the Saab, motioning Wesley into the backseat. The agent, hands still raised, climbed in. With a quick, darting move Andy brought the gun back down, hard against LaRocca's skull. His eyes rolled and he started to go down to his knees. Andy pushed him forward into the front bucket seat, and stuffed in his legs and feet.

"This man's a piece of shit, Phil. This whole thing woulda been a lot smoother if you'd treated him that way."

Wesley looked out from the backseat, wide-eyed and agreeable.

Andy slammed and locked the passenger door, and got into the driver's seat. He started the Saab's turbo engine, holding the Smith & Wesson in his left hand, pointing it across his own chest at LaRocca and Wesley. In ten minutes he was out of downtown Miami traffic and on the interstate, barreling back to West Palm.

16

The Last Intentions

He watched carefully as his hand shivered, as if the steering wheel were cold steel instead of warm leather. His stomach was tight, but manageable. He was sweating. He was holding his old friend, an FBI agent, captive at gunpoint in the backseat of the Saab. Another FBI agent, one much less wholesome, was bloodied and beaten, handcuffed and slouching on the passenger seat. Andy's own doing. He held the gun tight against his stomach, glad at least that he was keeping that steady.

LaRocca moaned, regaining consciousness, and moved his head away from Amato, leaning against the window. Wesley sat motionless, avoiding eye contact.

The word "conundrum" came to Andy's mind, something he read in a recent *Time* article—"a vexing problem without a solution." He scoured his repertoire of jokes to come up with something suitable, something to cut through the thick atmosphere and make his old friend laugh, but nothing emerged. He pushed on to Forty-fifth Street, the last West Palm exit, then geared down and slowed enough to pull cleanly onto the curved exit ramp.

"Let me out of here, Andy. I can't be a part of this," Phil Wesley said gruffly from the backseat. They were the first words spoken since Miami.

"You're gonna talk to him. He may listen to you. He gets this pile of shit." Andy pointed toward LaRocca. "I get Gabe."

"He's too wound up. I already tried talking, remember? He's not going to listen to anyone."

"I'm getting Gabe back. Somehow. That's all I know."

Back to silence. They drove east. Andy passed the jai alai stadium, the Florida East Coast Railway tracks, St. Mary's Hospital, and then the Dixie Highway.

"Let me and LaRocca out. I swear we won't say a word about all this."

"Can't do it. He's my only leverage."

"Gruen wants to kill him, Andy. You ready for that?"

He didn't answer. He let Wesley turn his head and gaze back out the car's tinted glass.

FBI Agent Donald Gruen held the cup to her lips and tilted it as she took a drink. She was thankful. It was her first in the last twenty hours.

"You can take the blindfold off," she said after swallowing.

"I guess."

"Why don't you, then?"

"I'm afraid."

Gabe remained silent, trying to understand his answer.

"I know who you are. I know everything. There's nothing you're hiding, and there's nothing you have to be afraid of."

A minute went by. Then she heard him move in the chair. Then she felt his presence lean toward her. She smelled his stale clothing and foul breath, and could still detect the faint smell of gasoline. A chill went up her spine. She held her own breath and tried not to show her fear as his fingers came around her neck and gripped the knotted cloth. First tightly,

232

then more relaxed. The blindfold loosened with a yank and a tear, then slid over her head.

He sat there in front of her in the same dark clothing he had worn the night before. His left leg was crudely bandaged, a reddened dish towel marking the spot where her hollowpoint did a through-and-through.

"I didn't try to kill you," he told her, almost meekly. "I wasn't aiming when I shot at you. That's why I missed."

Gabe Amato replayed the dark scene in front of the old house—the tree, the flare gun lighting up and scorching her, her falling to the ground, her firing a shot, his firing one. For some reason she believed his explanation. She believed it enough to feel pity for his wounded leg. The side of her head throbbed and she thought back to the hard whack he had given her.

"I wouldn't have killed you. That's not what this is all about. You're a cop. I haven't forgotten all that."

"Please don't kill me now," Gabe said.

He extended his smile, then shook his head.

"Only Pisoli has to die. That's all I care about. Everything else has gone to hell. I don't give a fuck about all that. As long as that fat slob is dead."

She asked him why. He told her, confirming most of what she'd already deduced. She cringed at the details about his daughter. He told her how he had tracked down the suspect on his own, doing his own detective work. How he found out it was Pisoli, a protected witness. A free-and-easy Italian playboy, picking up the innocent junior-college coed at a bar. How he began tracking down the mobster, staying tactfully in the shadows of the witness protection program, hoping the next safe house contained the man he hated and had to find.

He went into every detail of every killing, talking to her like a sister or a wife—or better yet, she realized, like the daughter that Pisoli had stabbed and left to die. The anonymous call to the New York mob after surveilling the mansion on Seabreeze—after realizing that the man wasn't Pisoli. Lifting the alarm key code from the marshals, having one made, and mailing it to the New York mob. When the hit man finally showed up, he killed him to convince everyone that it was the Mafia doing the killing. More or less an afterthought, he said. He killed the rest, even after finding they weren't Benny, to lessen his frustration and make the police believe it was the Mafia finally catching up with the nation's stool pigeons. If Pisoli had to die, the rest of them might as well too, he reasoned.

He told her also that he had started to like killing just for the sake of killing.

Then they talked about many things other than murder. Gabe was aware of a frightening scenario: a man in Gruen's position, now confessing everything, was subconsciously or perhaps even consciously preparing to end his own life, and would likely take her along with him.

"Your husband will bring Pisoli to me, I'm sure of it. I cursed him when he first became involved. But now it's all for the best. He'll bring that scumbag to me in order to free you."

"Andy's not a killer. He knows what you'll do. Let me make a call. Let me talk to him. Let me at least tell him I'm all right."

Gruen stood up, hobbling away from her, toward the bedroom window. He had left the door open. The television was loud enough for her to hear. With the blindfold off she saw it was dark outside. Listening closely, she heard the start of Wednesday's 9:30 "Cheers" rerun.

Andy's got to be on his way, she thought.

Gruen turned away from the window. "No. Nothing short of Pisoli being dead will satisfy this. I'm sorry. I've come this far. I have to see it through. I only wanted to kill Pisoli, but now I *understand* him. I wound up just like him. That's the other reason he has to die."

He gave her a sorrowful smile, one that reminded her of her father telling her they couldn't go to Disney World for her birthday some twenty years ago. Then the man turned away, as her father had done, and stared out at the blackness of the Florida night.

Andy remembered Wesley's house from a visit almost three years before. After only brief hesitation he found his way to the block, then aimed the car toward the corner house. Wesley stayed silent. Andy could tell that his friend was hoping he wouldn't remember and become lost.

He turned off the headlights and the engine. LaRocca moved his head, opened his eyes, and slowly turned toward him. Andy smiled.

The car coasted silently to a stop one house south of where Andy knew Gruen—whom he was convinced was now a psycho—was holding his wife captive.

"When your husband comes I'm going to trade you even-up for Pisoli. Then it'll be me and him. I won't even shoot him. I'll kill him with my bare hands."

Gabe believed him. She tried one last time to pull her hands free while he was looking out the window. The nylon rope held.

When she saw him anxiously separate the blinds she knew that Andy had found her.

The house was classic fifties Florida architecture, typical of West Palm—a flat, wide ranch-style, with Mexican barrel-tile roofing. High hedges around the windows. Black, curved, wrought iron gates at the entrance. Saguaro, hedgehog, and prickly pear cacti were neatly arranged around the stone sidewalk leading to the wooden door. Andy could see only one inside light on and none on the outside. Without street-lights and with only half a moon and the wind whipping the palm trees, Andy felt coldly alone. No one was home, he sensed, but he knew his feeling of solitude and isolation was caused by the fear knotting in his stomach, being held back by his sheer will to rescue his woman. He realized that Gruen would have to be in there.

Andy was out the driver's side and around to the passenger door before either man could hope to get out. Especially Wesley, who was pinned in the back by the weight of the beaten Albert LaRocca in the front seat.

Andy opened the door, gripped LaRocca tightly by the right elbow, and yanked the man out of the car and onto his feet. After teetering briefly, the FBI agent steadied himself. Andy, clutching LaRocca, motioned with the gun for Wesley to step out.

All three men stood silently in the wash of the moonlight, staring toward the house. The wind subsided, as if marking their arrival. Andy checked for nosy neighbors and saw they were alone. He closed the car door cautiously and motioned Wesley to the front, to take the lead. Then he opened the handcuffs, freeing LaRocca.

"Walk to the house," Andy told Phil Wesley. He held on to LaRocca with his left hand, holding the auto in his right, pointing behind the agent's right ear.

"Put him back in the car," Wesley said. "You and I can handle this. Don't get him involved. Don't make this any worse."

"He goes. Now move."

Donald Gruen turned away from the window and ran back to Gabe. He produced a long knife and leaned over her. Her heart skipped a beat.

He cut the length of nylon rope that was binding her hands to her feet. Sweating and panting, he freed her ankles.

He picked her up but she couldn't feel it; there was no strength in her legs. She knew that if he released her she would crumple to the floor.

"Please don't hurt me."

"They're here. They just pulled up. No lights, no noise. No voices. Just like cops. It's them."

"Let me talk to Andy. He has friends all over. He can help you through this."

He moved toward the door, dragging her along. She was surprised that her legs actually could move. She stumbled behind him.

"I'll do all the talking," he said.

"Please don't kill me," she repeated, realizing that she was pleading, realizing that she had never been more frightened.

"Shut up and move," he said curtly, and dragged her toward the front door.

Andy didn't see the FBI car. At first that worried him, but he realized that Gruen could have easily parked it in the alleyway, or even the next block. He cocked the large auto, putting it in single-action, quick-fire mode.

"Gruen!" he shouted. He watched intently for movement from the inside.

"I've got Pisoli! Come out and talk to me!"

There was quiet.

"I'll let you have him. Bring out my wife!" Andy bellowed.

Wesley tried to walk to his left. Andy pointed the Smith & Wesson and the agent stood still. LaRocca, still dazed, swayed. Andy pulled him close.

"Gruen!" Andy shouted again.

The front door opened a crack. Andy instinctively brought his gun up and pointed at the opening. Both Wesley and LaRocca stood motionless.

Gabe appeared in the doorway, Gruen behind her. Her hands were behind her back. Her knees were bent and she was obviously in pain.

Andy spotted the glare of the large, stainless steel .357 revolver in Gruen's hand.

"Amato!" Gruen shouted.

"I'm here. Let her go."

"First Pisoli. I want you to shoot him. I want you to do it for me."

The words hung in the air.

"I can't do that. Kill him yourself. Let Gabe go, let her walk out here to me, then I'll give you Pisoli."

"I can't trust you. You'll trick me."

"Why? I hate the son of a bitch, too. You can have him, I just want to be sure my wife goes free."

"Seems to me I have the better hand here, Amato. Seems to me you need to listen carefully and do what you're told."

More silence.

"Let her go, Gruen," Andy said again.

"Kill Pisoli. Put one right in the back of his head, or that's what I'll do to her." He moved the gun and pointed it into Gabe's ear.

Andy could see the bull-barrel at Gabe's head.

"I can't kill him!" Andy shouted. "I want to, but I can't. You can't either, Gruen. Let Wesley tell you why."

Gruen's face contorted into a scowl. Andy thought he looked like he was about to cry. Perhaps he already suspected the truth.

Wesley hesitated. LaRocca started to pull away. Andy took him by the shoulder and rammed the auto into his back hard enough to break a rib.

"Donald, we have to talk," Wesley began.

"Talk. Quick," Gruen answered.

"Pisoli's the Bureau's problem. He's not what you think. There's more to it. He's an agent gone bad. He's an agent, just like you and me. Undercover. In the mob. Real name's Albert LaRocca. It went too far."

There was no hesitation. "Bullshit! Lies!" Gruen blurted.

"No. It's true," Wesley continued. "Like it or not. It's true. He's one of us—"

238

"Shut up!" Gruen screamed, pulling Gabe closer to him.

Andy caught Gabe's eye. He knew she'd know what he planned and would drop as he brought the 9-millimeter's sights up to his eyes.

But he saw her only move her head slowly from side to side.

"You kill him," Andy said harshly. "Shoot him yourself. We'll call it self-defense," he added. LaRocca squirmed.

"No!" Wesley shouted. "Let her go. Let her walk out now. We can find a way to work this all out."

Andy pushed him forward—Benny Pisoli, FBI agent Albert LaRocca. He hobbled a few steps, trying quickly to steady himself and hold onto his balance, but then he fell forward, dropping hard against the stone pathway.

"Kill him. Go ahead and do it. Let's see you shoot a fellow cop. Let's see if you mean it," Andy said.

LaRocca pulled himself up. The three men were a triangle in the eerie moonlight: LaRocca at the head, Wesley to the left, Andy Amato to the right.

"Kill him, Amato! Kill him or she dies!" Gruen cocked the hammer back on the Magnum.

She couldn't bring herself to believe the scene laid out before her. The three men, the crazed killer, and the darkness reinforced the eerie feeling of a bad dream that had gone on far too long.

The one thing she was sure of was the feeling of the cold barrel as Gruen held it tight behind her head.

Andy was waiting for her to drop so he had a shot at Gruen. She was too frightened to comply, she realized. It couldn't work. She would die. She slowly shook her head.

She saw Andy push the man forward, then watched as he stumbled, fell, stood back up.

Gruen's hot breath was quickening in her ear. He loosened his grip slightly. She knew that something was about to happen. She heard Andy yell something, but couldn't

239

make out the words. Then Wesley. Then Gruen yelled back.

She felt the gun barrel pull slightly back, away from her. She felt suddenly free and unencumbered. Light, like a bird. If it was a dream, she knew, she would float away, on to some other place. A peaceful place, away from what was happening.

The gun moved completely away from her head.

Drop, she said to herself. *Drop.*

Andy saw the motion and reacted before he really understood. Gruen's gun came from behind Gabe's head and angled forward.

Andy saw Wesley drop to his knees.

Andy aimed the 9-millimeter straight at the body mass that was both Donald Gruen and Gabe Amato. His chest tightened. He tried to focus the front sight on Gruen alone.

Gabe dropped to a sitting position at Gruen's feet.

Gruen fired. LaRocca jumped back, like a man getting out of the way of an oncoming train. Then he fell straight back, landing with a sickening thud.

Andy put pressure on the trigger just as he was sure Gruen was clear. But Gruen bent down, trying to pick Gabe back up. Andy's sight picture had two faces, one of the murderer he was hunting, one his wife's. Gabe's face would not let him pull the trigger.

Gruen's revolver pointed and erupted again.

Instinct told Andy to jump out of the way; but his jump was slow. The synapses carrying the electric/neural impulses from the brain to his legs were just slightly behind the hollowpoint that whacked into his right arm.

The large automatic dropped to the pavement with a clang. Andy's vision went black, then bright yellow as the pain found its way to his consciousness. The bullet spun him around, dropping him to his knees, then pushing him backward until he was lying on his back, wondering if he was alive or dead.

Donald Gruen fought to get Gabe back on her feet. He tugged at her arm, holding the gun behind her head with his other hand.

From Amato's waistband Wesley snatched the revolver that Andy had taken from the agent's desk drawer.

Wesley raised the revolver toward the house.

One, two, three, four, five, six.

Andy counted as the revolver spat, but he was unable to move as the bullets streaked toward Gruen, Gabe, and the old wood door.

17

Gunplay

The funeral service was like dozens of other cop funerals Andy had been to. The weather was always cloudy, it seemed—and there was always some rain. At the moment, though, the rain had moved off to the horizon and the West Palm Beach cemetery was warm and muggy in the Saturday late-morning sun.

It was a Catholic priest, a man Andy had seen a few times before, an old, tall Irish man from an inner-city church. His white hair complemented the white and purple robe with the embroidered golden cross of Saint Peter.

Andy stood silently and alone just in front of the tent and behind the four rows of family and friends. He wiggled his fingers, looking down at them. His shoulder was in a cast, along with his arm, and the whole mess was in a sling.

He recognized the readings from the familiar Gospel verses and even recited along when the priest read from the Book of Wisdom. Then the Twenty-third Psalm. After that, the old Irishman suddenly seemed to have no more to say; he closed his Bible and moved off, away from the tent.

Andy saw that the rain was moving in again from the horizon—a famous Florida second pass over people who thought they would finally be dry.

Andy flinched with the rest of the crowd when the uniformed officers in the color guard fired off three rounds from their shotguns. Taps followed. Two men carefully folded the flag and handed it to an older woman in the front row. A short man in a dark suit, the hired mortician, announced that the service was over.

Andy watched the family leave. Phil Wesley gave Andy a polite and knowing nod, then walked on. Andy watched the crowd of uniformed officers as they quietly made their way back to their patrol cars, the dozens of men in suits, their federal ID tags all identically clipped to their right breast pockets.

Fogarty finally walked up beside him.

"How's the arm? I wanted to ask you earlier, but you wouldn't return my phone calls."

Andy looked at him and smiled. "Thanks, Larry."

"How's Gabe?" Fogarty asked in a tone showing genuine concern. Andy knew that he practiced it to use at funerals and other somber occasions.

"She's fine, Larry."

"She won't talk to me."

They both looked over to where Gabe was standing with friends from the department and a group of U.S. marshals, including Tom Sunderland.

"She doesn't like you, Larry. Never has. Nothing I can do."

"Okay."

Two dungareed men moved in and began loosening the straps that were holding the casket at the top of the open grave.

There was a pause, then Fogarty said, "I have to ask you some questions."

"Fuck off."

"Can't. Too much pressure from the editors. They want answers."

"Not from me. Not my case. Talk to the Bureau."

"We tried. Their press release was short and to the point. Not enough. They're not taking follow-up questions."

"Shame."

"Tell me about Pisoli. Our sources are saying he was a deep-cover FBI informant. They don't even know his real name. We have a team of lawyers and reporters in Washington trying to uncover the story under the Freedom of Information act."

"Good. That should take just a few minutes."

"Why did he go around killing mobsters? Why'd he kidnap Gabe? How'd he get shot with his own gun?"

Andy took a deep breath and turned to the shorter man. He looked at Fogarty's coat pocket and could see the familiar bulge of his tape recorder.

"Fuck off," Andy repeated as he turned away.

"You owe me."

"For the rest of my life, Larry? Every goddamn time some shit happens somewhere I'm gonna have to put up with you? If that's the case, just blow the cover off anything you want—just leave me the fuck alone."

"I need official confirmation from somebody on what happened. Tell me what really happened, I don't believe the FBI version. If you'll confirm it for me, then maybe I'll believe it."

"I don't wanna be in the fucking *Herald.*"

"You won't be."

"Right. Just like last time. 'Deep cover.' The only thing you left out was my name, you asshole."

"Tell me what you know about Pisoli. Please, Andy. As a friend. Forget owing me. Just tell me who he was."

"A mobster stool pigeon that went bad. A psycho killer."

"How did he kill all those guys? How did he get to them?"

"He infiltrated the FBI and U.S. Marshals Service files. It wasn't hard to do."

The *Herald* reporter scribbled passionately. "Tell me what really happened at that house the other night," he continued.

Andy looked down at his cast again and wiggled his fingers. His upper arm throbbed.

"It was quite a scene, I don't remember much. There was a fight, I was shot, I hit the ground. It was crazy."

"What about the FBI version from Phil Wesley? Is that what happened?"

Andy thought. The ache in the arm subsided.

"Right, Larry. That's what happened. We went there to try and surprise Pisoli and get Gabe back. There was a fight. It all happened fast. Pisoli shot me. Wesley, Pisoli, and Gruen fought. Gruen got his gun away and shot him with it. Somehow, before he died, Pisoli managed to get hold of Wesley's gun and kill Gruen. Crazy, I know, but that's how these things happen."

"And the three-five-seven Magnum? What can you tell me?"

"Just like the Bureau said. Pisoli stole it from an FBI evidence room he somehow got access to. The man was a deep-cover informant, so anything's possible."

"And all those murders?"

"The gun matched up. The three-five-seven that Pisoli had did them all."

"And why'd he kidnap Gabe?"

"Because he knew we were on to him. We were moving in for an arrest. He thought he could bargain his way out of trouble."

Fogarty shook his head. "If you swear to all that I'll believe it and print it."

"I don't care either way."

"My editors want a confirmation, Andy. Please give it to me. Don't be difficult. I won't use your name."

"If I confirm will you leave me alone and drop off the face of the fucking earth?"

"You got it."

"I'll confirm."

"Thanks," Fogarty said. Disbelief showed in his face, but Andy didn't care. The reporter walked swiftly toward his car.

Lieutenant Andy Amato stood by himself as the cemetery cleared. The two workmen slipped Gruen's casket off its railings, panting and heaving as they lowered the heavy box by the straps. Andy turned and saw Gabe standing silently by the Saab.

Andy walked toward her, leaving FBI hero Donald Gruen behind for the gravediggers.

Epilogue

Key West, Florida

As they always did, they took the Conch Tour train, getting off near Hemingway's house. They paid their six dollars at the gate to the old gay guy with the wig, and went in to see the six-toed cats, eccentric furnishings, and remnants of Papa's life on the famous island.

Nobody noticed or cared about Andy's arm. But then, he thought, just as Hemingway had written, nobody cared about much of *anything* in Key West. Nobody stared at anybody because they'd have to stare at everybody. And nobody had the time for that.

Andy had his first Rumrunner at Sloppy Joe's—Hemingway's hangout. As usual, the tourists took up the north side of the bucolic, dirty but charming beer parlor, and the bikers, writers, and artists filled up the south end. Gabe had lemonade.

They walked to Jimmy Buffet's Margaritaville and Andy

had two of the place's namesakes at the nearby raw bar. Then they visited some gift shops, thankful to be out of the heat and into the air conditioning. Andy bought a Margarita-ville bumper sticker for the Saab.

They stopped at a small news and smoke shop. Gabe had already pulled him past the place once. This time she just leaned against a post, resigned to what she knew he was going to do.

Andy threw the old man a dollar for the Sunday *Herald*, then tossed most of the paper in the garbage. He went back to Gabe, and found the article he was looking for. It was a half-page story:

DEAD MOBSTER WAS FBI INFORMANT, POLICE STATE

Lawrence Fogarty
Herald Staff Writer

West Palm Beach—In what an FBI spokesman called an "all-out fight for survival," one FBI informant and fugitive is dead, a police lieuten-ant was wounded, and a kidnapped police ser-geant has been rescued unharmed, *Herald* sources have learned.

Federal officials have been releasing only sketchy details concerning the remarkable facts of the FBI and police shootout last Wednesday in the otherwise quiet W. Palm Beach neighbor-hood. The scene as described in official FBI and police reports just made public indicates a dar-ing attempt to rescue West Palm police sergeant Gabrielle Amato, who was being held captive by suspected murderer Benny "Beans" Pisoli. Her husband, Lieutenant Andy Amato, accompanied two FBI agents to the residence, where a fight ensued.

The reports state that Pisoli shot and wounded Lieutenant Amato before being disarmed in a fight. FBI agent Phillip Wesley of the Miami FBI office wrestled with Pisoli, removing the man's gun and seriously wounding him with it. Pisoli was able to disarm Wesley in the scuffle and shoot West Palm Beach FBI agent Donald Gruen, hitting him six times in the head and upper chest. He was killed instantly. At the scene Pisoli died later of the single gunshot wound. Sergeant Gabe Amato was unhurt during the incident.

The gun used by Pisoli to shoot Lieutenant Amato was found to have been taken from an FBI evidence bin. The gun has also been tied into at least four other murders of protected federal witnesses, all around South Florida. In an exclusive interview with Lieutenant Amato, the *Herald* has confirmed that Pisoli was a longtime associate of the FBI, and was an informant for the Bureau while operating deep inside illegal Mafia activities. His motive and involvement in the murders of the federal witnesses remain unclear, and FBI and police spokesmen refuse any comment other than "The investigation is continuing."

Fucking Fogarty, Andy thought.

He threw the remainder of the paper into the garbage. Gabe leaned against the post and looked off, uninterested in the news.

* * *

At the south-end Mallory dock Andy started his fifth Rum-runner, carrying the plastic cup from a nearby bar. They sat on the rough concrete, looking west at the Gulf of Mexico and the start of the sunset. A man in a T-shirt and a Scottish kilt walked the dock, playing "I Wanna Get Back with Ol' Sweet Mary." A Rastafarian was alternating between walking a tightrope and rolling down the dock in a large, human ball to the applause and laughter of the tourists. A Jamaican Calypso band played their loud, hard steel on the opposite side of the docks. Jugglers, dancers, and magicians worked the crowd, also drawing applause and laughter.

Dozens of boats passed, everything from raucous, mostly naked college students to old men wearing beards and boots, refusing to wave at the crowd as they set off for the nighttime's fishing.

Gabe was quiet.

The sun hit the water just to the left of the small mangrove island, just as it always did. People in the crowd hissed, giving the Conch Republic sign of approval to the sunset, starting a ripple of laughter. Everyone was happy.

Gabe turned to him. "This is our vacation, isn't it?" she said.

He put down the almost empty plastic cup. The bagpipe player finished a fast-paced march on a high B-flat.

"It's our vacation. All week," he replied and nodded wearily. He was feeling the drinks.

"Then don't forget what you promised," she added.

He hesitated. "What?"

She leaned close to his ear, even though she could have stood up and shouted it out and no one in the Key West sundown crowd would have blinked.

"We have to go make a baby," she whispered.

Andy finished off the last of his Rumrunner and joyfully watched as the sun finally sank below the water.